# Seducing Adam

## LizAnn Carson

**Seducing Adam**

Second edition © 2015 Elizabeth Carson

ISBN: 978-0-9949036-4-8

## Thank You

To Margo, Sarah, and Jen, my beta readers, and always, to Michael, my husband, who was my first reader and has supported me all the way.

Needless to say, any mistakes are my own.

## Dedication

This one's for Jacquie, who kick started it all.

# Chapter 1

"I'll have two eggs, scrambled, on whole wheat toast, dry. Sliced tomatoes. Coffee. I don't have much time, so be quick."

*Jackass.* Stacie Halloran, owner and mildly ticked off operator of Halloran House Bed and Breakfast, allowed herself a split second to glare at the woman staying in room Three, now seated in the breakfast room. Three was big city all the way – fashionably thin, perfectly dyed red hair, couture vacation wear. Look-down-the-nose-at-the-country-bumpkin expression.

Stacie had read that you couldn't feel high blood pressure. *Lie.* Hers spiked. Ignoring it, she pasted on her sweet face. "I'm so sorry, we don't have any whole wheat bread at the moment. I'm sure you'd enjoy one of the meals we have on this morning's menu, puffed omelet with sautéed vegetables or blueberry stuffed pancakes. I made extra since you didn't pre-order."

*As I ask you to, as you might possibly have noticed on the card on your pillow.*

Her voice professionally pleasant, she continued, "The egg dish is closest to what you requested —"

"I didn't request, girl, I placed an order. Your job is to bring my order to me." Three's voice dripped with derision.

*Girl?*

*Yes, ma'am. Anything you say, ma'am.*

1

*Professional, Stacie.*

Well, sometimes a guest did wake up with a headache or have a fight with a spouse or something. Stacie had learned to roll with these punches and accept that she was collateral damage, not the real target. Halloran House was worth the occasional irritation. Her internal rant simply helped her defuse her equally internal desire to boot the woman down the front steps on her skinny fanny.

"And you, sir?" she turned to Three's companion.

The man in Two was at least more polite, even though he hadn't pre-ordered either. Businessman all the way, with sandy hair in that kind of spiky short cut that looked like someone had been running fingers through it, dress slacks and business shirt with a burgundy tie. Slender, although Two definitely could do with some exercise. She guessed that Two had maid service and ate out and hadn't seen a jogging trail or the inside of a gym in ten years or so. *Overall, not half bad, though.*

Stacie herself was fit. Running the B&B was seriously physical work, for one thing. But at least it saved her from doing less fun things, like pumping iron or watching what she ate. Not that she got to show off the resulting assets when she was on the job. Her morning uniform was plain and businesslike, light gray shirt tucked into dark gray slacks, dark hair confined by an elastic into a low ponytail.

Still, she figured she looked pretty darn good. Even if the almost-hunk in Two – alone in Two – hadn't looked at her twice.

Not that it mattered. Getting cozy with the paying clients was a big no-no, as far as Stacie was concerned. But still …

He'd followed her dialogue with Three with something approaching amusement. It didn't last. Two's voice was formal and vaguely bored. "The pancakes sound good, thank you. And coffee."

The couple in One left the table under the window. "Fantastic," the husband called out to her. The wife giggled. Just married, Stacie knew. She'd provided a basket with bubbly and some local gourmet nibbles to keep them happy, not that they seemed to need her help. Over half her business was honeymooners, so she *knew* honeymooners. Surely there was no worse company on the planet than a newly wed couple.

*Careful, Stacie, you're risking a slide into a little bitterness there.* Couldn't be denied, though, this Friday morning had taken a turn that was enough to make her question her career choice.

She waved back to the couple in One, turning on her big smile. She poured coffee for the pair in Two and Three, delivered a carafe of freshly squeezed orange juice to their table, then headed for the kitchen and those scrambled eggs. The customer is always right, even when they're totally, obnoxiously, wrong.

She hadn't figured this brittle couple out. They had checked in the previous evening, looking grim and never once looking at each other. A less likely pair to turn up on Malaspina Island would be hard to imagine. Not outdoor types, not unwinding – so far, at least – and for sure not looking for the romantic ambience Stacie's B&B offered. Not anything that made sense.

Given the jet lag thing, anyone coming from Toronto to an island off the coast of British Columbia should be first in the breakfast room, shouldn't they? Instead of turning up ten minutes before time to shut the kitchen down.

At the moment, the pair in question were frozen in silence, the woman looking discontented and the man looking like he'd kill for the morning paper.

*Sorry, the first ferry's only just in. Paper available about 10:30, just like it says in all the helpful information in your room. Deal with it.*

The teenager who helped out with the yard work came in the back door to her private apartment, kicked off his shoes in the mudroom, and hovered at the entrance to the kitchen. "Morning, Stacie."

"Hi, Mike. Coffee?"

*Eggs beaten, toast toasting, pancakes cooking, please God let me have a tomato.*

"Sure." Mike ventured into the small commercial kitchen that served the B&B and helped himself from the back-up carafe. "I've got something to tell you."

She looked up from the pan where she'd just poured the eggs. "Any odds it's not anything good."

"Afraid not. The waterfall won't start. I think the pump's broken. There's this sort of humming noise."

"Damn." *Double damn with sauce on it.* "Could you get the pump out of the fishpond? One of us can run it into Sam's. Maybe it needs cleaning or something."

"I'll take it in later. Lawn doesn't need cutting yet so it's just some weeding this morning."

"Thanks, Mike. You're a real asset." A garden care company would take over the heavy maintenance once they got into full-on summer. In the meantime, Mike saw to basic weeding and raking, so things looked good out there, for May.

Eggs and pancakes plated, she made her way back into the breakfast room. The couple appeared not to have changed position. They just sat there, united in disdain. Stacie ignored the serious antagonism vibes they put out, set the plates in front of them, said sweetly that she hoped they'd enjoy their breakfast, and moved to the window to bus the table that One had vacated. Stacks of crockery balanced expertly on her arms, she returned to the kitchen, loaded the dirty dishes in the dishwasher, then went back to the door.

Good. Two and Three were eating. Without any visible enthusiasm, but at least it didn't look like they'd be calling her over to complain.

It was the point in the day when she loved the breakfast room best. Light flooded the room, turning the pale yellow walls into a form of interior sunshine. The décor tended to sophisticated rather than kitschy – no white geese here. The giant paper flowers decorating the walls, carefully positioned so they never faded under direct sun, glowed in the filtered morning light.

*No time for wool gathering.*

She let the door swing closed behind her and tackled kitchen clean-up. The morning settled into routine, other than whatever was wrong with the damn pump. She'd deal with the kitchen first. Then the breakfast room, the washroom, the downstairs vacuuming, dusting and tidying. Later, when hopefully the guests had taken themselves off somewhere for the day, she'd tackle the bedrooms.

Halloran House had only four guest rooms. Even at that, she accepted that her morning hours would be spent cooking and cleaning. No matter how efficient she got to be, realistically, it took her that long to bring Halloran House to the gleaming perfection she expected of it.

Sometimes it really did feel like a slog.

*Well, it's a living. And you're where you want to be. And there's work to do.*

Where she wanted to be was Malaspina Island. She'd tested the waters on the mainland, sure, but Malaspina had drawn her back. For Stacie, this was home.

The morning blitz on the B&B was an excellent time for musing, and there was plenty to muse about this morning. Two and Three, for instance.

Two's real name was Adam Fraser, and he was city through and through. He'd arrived off the ferry the previous afternoon in a business suit and leather shoes, for heaven's sake. Stacie idly imagined a teachable moment, such as his slippery soles landing him flat on his butt on the dock.

*Might not happen, but a girl could hope.*

*Not a bad butt.*

She shook that thought right out of her head, since it was going nowhere. Stacie didn't mix business with pleasure. She, or rather Halloran House B&B, had a reputation to maintain, after all.

*No penalty for noticing, though.*

Besides, the man seemed prepared to look down his nose at her, Halloran House, and probably the whole island.

*No, thanks.* Two could take his attitude right back to Toronto.

It looked like he and his attitude were going to be underfoot for a while, though. Stacie was in the middle of vacuuming the breakfast room when Two next turned up.

She switched off the vacuum. "Can I help you?" The public, pleasant persona fastened itself to her face.

"I'll have another cup of coffee. It's good."

"It's locally roasted. Most of what we serve is local, either to the island or to Vancouver Island. Please help yourself." She kept the coffee fresh all morning, as well as providing hot water and an assortment of teas.

He did help himself. Then – she knew it was coming, given the way the morning had gone so far – he sat down. Stacie sighed as her schedule went to hell. "I'll finish up in here later."

Two didn't seem in the least aware that he was disrupting her work. She got the vibe that he was settling in for a chat, even though so far this morning he hadn't cracked a smile. Did a man like that even know how to chat? He settled in sideways to the table, his long legs stretched out and crossed at the ankle. "So, I wonder what people do on this island. What sort of recreational activities there are."

*Polite, Stacie. Make nice with the paying customers.*

"I've put brochures in your room."

"I've read them. But what I want to know is, what do the locals do? I can't see everyone here rushing down to the dock to pay for a kayak tour or a guided hike through the forest."

He said 'the locals' as if she and her friends were some mutant form of life. Being nice to this guy could give her an ulcer.

*In the movies, mutants clawed people, made them bleed.* Stacie found herself flexing her fingers.

She clamped down on her thoughts and leaned on her vacuum. "Mostly we just get on with our lives, I guess. We take care of our homes and run our businesses and buy groceries. Back yard barbecues in the summer. Hang out with friends – there's a coffee shop on the Square."

She carefully didn't mention the other coffee shop, the one tucked down a side street a couple of blocks from the Square. She felt slightly guilty about depriving Dick and Doreen, the owners of The Brew Place, of business, but would they want the business of this particular snarly couple, or whatever they were? She sincerely hoped not.

"Just an ordinary life, one might say."

*Except that no one on Malaspina would ever use 'one' in that royal way.*

"Exactly."

"Nothing romantic about it." He had his gaze fixed on her, a puzzled frown pulling his eyebrows together. What did he see, for heaven's sake? Scrambled egg in her hair?

"Nope."

"And yet you run arguably one of the most romantic establishments on the west coast. Rate-Your-B-and-B-dot-com says so."

She shrugged. "You mix sea and gardens and decor and you've got romantic. It's no mystery. My own apartment features a second hand sofa. I live like everyone else."

"And can't afford a decent sofa?"

The front door opened. Her pal Jessica Thomas stuck her head into the breakfast room. "Hi, Stacie. Just wanted to alert you that the shop's running low on soap and lavender wands. Any chance of getting some more?" Jess owned the Ocean Thyme Gift Shop, down by the harbor.

"Morning, Jess. I've got the soap, but I'll have to make the wands, so it won't be till after harvest."

"Great. I'm way late, see you." Jessica was gone in her usual flurry of long blond curls and even longer blue jeaned legs.

Stacie straightened, glad to have her cozy chat with Two interrupted. "Is there anything else I can help you with? I have a number of things I have to see to."

"No. No, that's all. Thanks for the coffee." He unfolded from the table and left, taking his mug with him. Stacie watched him go, then turned the vacuum on and went back to her work.

He was right. Halloran House was romantic. The house had been her grandmother's, and retained the charm of yesteryear. Now, of course, the charm was bolstered by all modern conveniences, such as marble bathrooms with jet tubs, double glazed windows, and WiFi. Gardens rolled down to a little cove where the Pacific could crash if it got mad enough, but generally was sheltered and tranquil. Other than the garden, she cared for it all herself, which made life challenging, and sometimes confining. But it was the life she'd chosen, and overall she was proud of what she'd accomplished in the three years Halloran House had been open.

A restful morning was too much to hope for. By 11:30 Three, whose name was Katherine Sorenson, was on her case. Demanding a remedy for indigestion, undoubtedly caused by the white bread she'd been forced to eat with the scrambled eggs.

*Gee, Ms. Sorenson. Must be contagious.*

Stacie commanded her stomach to unclench and pointed her guest to the drug store in town. She went back to dusting the guest lounge, across the entry from the breakfast room.

With Two and Three's late breakfast, it was a given that she wasn't going to finish the cleaning by noon.

The couple in Four had left at 8:00, heading out for an all-day hike. Stacie had given them an early breakfast and arranged bagged lunches in town. One had disappeared for a hand-holding wander around central Windon Harbor. Those couples, at least, looked like they'd enjoy their stay on Malaspina Island.

Dusting finished, she headed upstairs. Now, if she could just get Two and Three out of there.

With the morning cleaning done – except for Three, where the Do Not Disturb sign was displayed – and the morning long gone, Stacie made her usual cruise through Halloran House, looking everything over one more time and checking to see who was there, if anyone. Usually by late morning all her guests had left to take advantage of the island's activities. Today, however, she heard the voices from the guest lounge well before she got to the door. Which, she noticed with disapproval, they had pulled almost closed, as if claiming it as their private office space.

"I'm well aware of that," Two was saying. He sounded bored. "We both agree that this is ridiculous. But here we are. Live with it."

"I am living with it. Every damned minute." Three virtually hissed her words out.

"Do you have a hookup yet?"

"No. Do you remember if the password had a capital letter?"

"Bucolic. Capital-B-u-c-o—"

"Shut up, Adam. There. WiFi established." For a minute there was only the quiet tap of computer keys. Stacie hovered at the door, debating whether to go in. Investigating the mystery of these unlikely guests was tempting. She wanted to know what they were up to.

"Get a note off to Ralph, would you? We're here, lovely place, blah blah. And send a note to Janet, so she'll know her job's on the line when we get out of here. Booking us into this kind of place ... her idea of a joke, I suppose."

"I'm not laughing. And send your own notes. I'm not your secretary." More typing.

"Okay, fine. I will."

Since One and Four were away, Stacie decided to leave the charming couple to their emailing the outside world from the guest lounge, and headed for her apartment. At least part of the mystery was solved. This was a business trip, and a secretary named Janet who didn't value her job had booked them into romantic instead of businesslike. She wondered how their workplace saw them, what the connection was. For that matter, who they worked for. The trouble-making Janet had entered only home addresses and phone numbers in Toronto when she made the reservations.

Safely in her apartment, she put her little stovetop espresso maker on to do its thing. Then she collapsed, anticipating a few minutes of peace.

Stacie's apartment was her retreat and hideaway. She'd used most of the back half of the ground floor to create it. It wasn't elegant and the layout was a little wonky, with the bedroom off the living room and the windowless bathroom sort of squished in between, because that's where it was easiest to reach the plumbing. Her living room had a door, with lock, into the B&B's entry, and her kitchen had a door, also with lock, into the B&B's kitchen. Her outside door opened into a little mud room. And no one got in unless she wanted them to.

The espresso maker gurgled. She made an Americano, then sat down at her kitchen table and thought. *What business would a couple of people like these have here? What business interests from off the island would care about us?*

*Business interests …*

Abruptly she was on her feet and heading for the phone. The rumors had been all over the island for weeks. Maybe, just maybe, she had the point people in her sights.

The Forest. Nathan's Forest. Owned by some mega corporation back east. The rumor said it was going to be logged. She had to talk to Abby Fox, the town manager. And also her mother.

About equidistant from Vancouver and Victoria, Malaspina Island retained a small town, once-upon-a-time feeling. Windon Harbor, the only urban center on the island – 'urban' in this case meaning 'really small town' – hosted an assortment of social activities and festivals.

The romance of Malaspina Island relied on illusion, of course. The magical effect the island had on visitors could only be maintained with a sophisticated infrastructure. Both the island and the town of Windon Harbor had everything needed for road maintenance, financial management, publicity, and so forth. And that's where Abby came in. She'd been town manager of Windon Harbor for fifteen years now, and it looked like she'd be there forever.

"Mom?"

"Hi, honey. How're things?"

"Busy as always. We're full."

"What's up?"

In a rush Stacie told her about the strange couple, the separate rooms, the obvious business trip, the tension.

"They're totally nasty, Mom. And they're booked in for a week. I'm going to try to get them out of here before I lose my mind. Or my other customers. I could be completely off base with what they're about, but I thought you might want a heads up."

"Thanks for letting me know." Her mom swatted crises aside like gnats. She'd figure something out, Stacie was sure. "We'll kick some corporate ass if we can. In the meantime, want to come over for dinner?"

"Need you even ask?" Dinner plans made, Stacie made one more phone call, this one to the hotel on the waterfront.

The rest of Stacie's day was uneventful, for which she thanked whatever gods happened to be listening. Early evening found her flopped on the sofa in her mother's country kitchen, blue-jeaned legs tucked under her. "I'm wiped, Mom. Feed me."

Her mother aimed a smile in her direction and went on basting salmon fillets. Not the frilly sort, Abby Fox presented a no-nonsense image with her straight, well behaved graying hair and modest denim dress. After a successful career and a bad marriage back east in Calgary, Abby had found a home on Malaspina Island, and the love of her life, her husband Bill.

Everyone knew Abby, and nothing on the island escaped her. Including Stacie's awkward couple. "I think I saw your guests in town, late this afternoon. Checking out the dinner options, maybe? I can't say they looked comfortable."

"They're not. But for some reason they want to fit in." Stacie made quotation marks with her right hand only, since her left was wrapped around a beer bottle. "Not that they said so in so many words, but he was pestering me this morning about what the natives do with their spare time. Why would he care?" Stacie took a swig of her beer and burrowed deeper into the corner of the old sofa.

"If they are who you think they are, they may want to know what we think about the forest, and how much resistance they're likely to get if they decide to cut it down."

"Don't say that. You give me shivers."

Abby raised her glass of cider in her daughter's direction. "To their ultimate failure."

"I'll drink to that." Stacie drank, then frowned. "But they're not likely to fail, are they? They own the land, dammit. They have the timber rights. I don't guess there's much we can do about it."

Abby plated the salmon. "With any luck we can snatch partial victory from the jaws of certain defeat," she said. Then she stuck her head out the back door and bellowed, "Bill!" in a voice that could possibly be heard over on the mainland. "In the garage practicing," she explained to Stacie in a more normal voice. "They're playing tomorrow night." 'They' being the Windon Fiddlers, a local band of variable composition, depending on who was available and who felt like playing.

She put the plates on the table. "Come eat, and I'll tell you what I'm thinking."

Bill ambled in. His weathered jeans suited his weathered face and gray hair. He gave Stacie a hug. "Hey, girl."

"Hey, Bill. Taking good care of her?"

"I reckon I'd better. She feeds me." Bill hugged Stacie's mother, a bear hug rather than the polite, shoulder-to-shoulder version she'd received, then swung into his seat.

"So, what do we do?" Stacie asked around a bite of salmon glazed with something that involved orange marmalade, soy sauce, and garlic. "If the evil is upon us, how do we fight it?"

"Hexes," Bill said promptly. Stacie wasn't sure but she thought her mother might have given Bill a gentle kick under the table.

"We could consider that," Abby said. "The local coven would be thrilled, I'm sure. I was actually thinking sugar."

"Mom, are you saying I have to be *nice* to these people? Seriously, I don't know if I can."

"I raised you to have a steel backbone. As an example, if they should turn up at the barn dance tomorrow night, then let's make sure they have a chance to dance, if they want to. And have people to talk to. We can put out the word about that."

"Seduce them," Bill put in. "Make them see the wonder of Malaspina."

Abby nodded. "I agree, that might be a tall order, but it'll improve our odds. Stacie, your main job at the moment is to confirm they are who we think they are. If they're an advance party from Callaway Forest Products, we need to know it."

"I'll give you a call as soon as I know." Stacie's focus was on the salmon, and there wasn't much room in her head at the moment for anything else. "Mmm. Good," she added, waving her fork.

"Glad you think so. Roger and I spoke this afternoon." Roger was the Island Administrator, Abby's equivalent for that part of the island that wasn't actually in the town limits of Windon Harbor. "No worry about cooperation there, obviously. But this corporation, they do have the logging rights, so there's nothing we can do about that. We can work with regulations, water quality, for instance. Maybe something about fish, it's steep on the south side of the forest so runoff could be an issue."

Abby was on a roll. "Probably our best bet is going to be the effect on the tourist industry. We can see the slopes of Nathan's Forest from most of the island. Publicity of course. Incite the province, the nation, the environmentalists, whoever'll listen. And play on their nobler side —"

"If they have one," Stacie put in grumpily.

"Good citizens of the island and all that. Getting to know your people will give us a clue whether there's anything to be won in that direction."

Abby mused a moment, then added, "I'll probably invite them over one evening, once we're sure who they are. Start the schmoozing."

"Take a bite, dear," Bill put in. "Your soapbox is showing."

Stacie grinned. She got along great with Bill, and he brought out this massive happiness in her mother. Now, if she could find a way to make the same thing happen for herself. Her mom had been well into her forties when her luck came along, so there was still hope.

Abby shot a smile at her husband. "Sorry. Critical importance."

"We're thinking about doing a little gig on the Square tomorrow afternoon. Kinda warm everyone up for the dance," Bill said. "Any way we can use the band?"

"I'll think about it. I don't see it yet. Thanks, sweetie." Abby reached over and patted Bill's weathered cheek. "You're a peach. Speaking of which, have you been to the garden center? They've got a selection of heritage apple trees in. I'm wondering—"

"Your wondering usually means digging ahead for me. Look at the garden, Abigail. Where'd you put another tree?"

Her mother laughed. "Fair point. Just dreaming."

The conversation wandered off to local people and events. Stacie ate her salmon with gusto and worried about the logging and thought life didn't get much better than this.

Well, having a good-looking guy along to share this dinner with her mother and Bill might qualify as improvement. But over the three years she'd run Halloran House Bed and Breakfast she'd learned not to have pie-in-the-sky dreams. *So,* she thought, *Yeah. As good as it gets.*

# Chapter 2

Adam and Katherine had spent most of Friday in the guest lounge, catching up on their respective workloads. Now, on Saturday, they walked around the harbor and the Square at the heart of Windon Harbor, looking politely interested in the craft shops, browsing the wares in the General Store. They'd had a lunch that even Katherine had to admit was perfectly adequate, clam chowder with a half club sandwich, in a cubbyhole of a restaurant. They wondered what to do next.

"Something tells me this isn't the best way to meet the locals," Adam muttered.

"My heart's broken."

"Oh, grow up, Katherine. We've got a job to do. We make some friends and an overall good impression, and get a feel for what the locals think about the forested part of the island. Then we arrange for a town hall type meeting. Invite all the lovely people. We give the illusion there's an option and we'll consider all points of view. Then we pull out and the company pulls in, and the forest goes. For you and me, a week max, if we play it right. It's all optics and politics."

"Well, I don't see how we're going to schmooze with the locals. They peg us as tourists and walk the other way."

"No, they don't. They peg us as tourists and fall all over themselves to be helpful." He broke off when laughter poured from the coffee shop. Locals, no doubt.

"I tried to chat with the woman in that General Store place. She was polite at best."

"You led off your 'chat' with a comment about how the clothes seemed to be geared to rustics, hikers and such. The implication was written all over you. You couldn't dress like the people here if your life depended on it. Which reminds me, the heels might not have been the best plan."

Katherine had on sandals with two inch heels, no doubt modest in her view. Most of the people they saw wore either runners or sports sandals.

"Why on earth would I want to? This place is—"

"Hicksville?" Adam's voice was amused, but with a strong undercurrent of irritation. No one watching or listening to them could possibly think he and Katherine Sorenson were friends, or that they were in any way happy to be in Windon Harbor on a Saturday afternoon. "Still, there is a certain quaint charm, if you're into that kind of thing."

"I'm not." Katherine's voice was flat. She wasn't going to make this trip easy, he could see. Adam frowned. Not that they ever really got along, not in years, but the thought of another five days of Katherine was decidedly unappealing.

A band had set itself up in a corner of the square. Now it burst into music. Fiddles or something, Adam thought sourly. People drifted over, a few actually started dancing. He suspected a headache was in his future, if this kept up.

He and Katherine sauntered over to a large notice board in the middle of the Square and browsed it idly. Someone had a tractor for sale, someone had fresh fish on the dock at 5:00 pm sharp. There were ads for child minding and yoga lessons.

And right in the middle of it all … "There." Adam stabbed his finger at an orange photocopied sheet. "There's a dance." He glanced at his watch, a complicated machine with multiple dials. He didn't know how to use most of them. "Tonight. We're going."

Katherine read the poster. "A barn dance? Don't they do square dancing at those things?" Her face registered her distaste. "What if there's hay? This is a new low, even for Ralph."

*Ralph, their boss, the Callaway vice president who held the strings controlling both of their corporate fates.*

"You should know." He let the innuendo hang. She didn't pick it up. And that was enough to make him a little nervous. What if she really *was* sleeping with Ralph? What did that do to the balance of power? Having failed to get a rise from Katherine, Adam carried on. "Don't think the idea of this dance thing thrills me. It is why we're here, though. Dear."

*Given the right emphasis, 'dear' could be turned into a four-letter word.*

Icicles from Katherine. He carried on. "We'll have some preparations to make if we're going to blend in. I suggest we go back to the B&B. That woman who runs it might be able to give us some clues about what would be appropriate to wear."

"Better than hanging around here. I feel conspicuous."

"You are, darling." Adam struck off across the Square, heading for their rental car, and leaving Katherine, with her heels, in his wake.

Stacie watched their car pull up. She assumed they'd been in town, a ten minute walk. But you couldn't expect folks like that to walk, now could you? *Not in those sandals,* she thought cattily. Then had a momentary twinge of pure jealousy, because the sandals would be perfect for the dance tonight, and with her height challenge she was always open to something with a little heel.

Whatever. It wasn't five minutes before there was a tap on the swinging door between the breakfast room and the commercial kitchen.

*Surprise, surprise.* She glanced up from her cookie dough to find Two looking at her. Hadn't even waited for her to answer, just pushed the door open. At least he didn't walk in. "I'd like to ask you a question or two."

She sighed and shoved into the breakfast room, forcing him to step back. "How can I help you?" she said in her professionally pleasant voice. The breakfast room was closed for business at this time in the afternoon. Maybe she should invest in a lock.

"Sit down." He pulled out a chair for himself and sank into it.

*And there went my well-set table for tomorrow morning.* Two seemed determined to claim the table as his personal property or something.

With no polite way to escape, she gave her watch a pointed scrutiny, then sat across from him.

"Tell me about this dance tonight," he said. Or commanded. "I didn't see a notice around here. Is it only open to locals?"

"No, it's open to anyone who wants to attend. I can't imagine it would be your type of thing, though."

"Is it square dancing? Katherine thought it might be."

"Oh, there could be one or two country dances," Stacie said airily. "More to the point, it'll be entirely family oriented, lots of little kids underfoot. Somehow I can't imagine that would be your scene."

"I can assure you that we both love children," he stated.

*Probably loved them best as a menu item.* God, she wished that just once he'd crack a smile.

"You know, somehow that's totally unbelievable." Stacie's hostess persona slipped right off and fell to the floor, where it waited to be trammeled underfoot. She felt herself moving into something more suited to a boundary dispute, and commanded herself to behave. For all the good that did.

"No, truly, I think we might go. How should we dress?"

*Dress? Now she was supposed to dress them?*

*Get a grip, Stacie.*

"It's only May, so the weather's variable. Casual, not sloppy, and layers. For you, khakis or new jeans. For Ms. Sorenson, well, it's one time we do sometimes wear casual skirts. Not the kind of clothes I suspect you have with you." Did this guy even own casual clothes? And from what she'd seen, Three's wardrobe was about ten notches above the barn dance. "The General Store on the Square's a good bet."

*And maybe that would put them off. This charming couple at the barn dance? God help them all.*

"Thanks, we'll give it a try. Something smells good." He looked hopefully in the direction of her apartment.

"Something's going to be good, in about two minutes. You'll find a plate in the guest lounge later this afternoon. In the meantime, there's something I've wanted to discuss with the two of you." She took a deep breath, then plowed on. "I've checked with the hotel, and they have two rooms free. I can't help but think you'd be more comfortable there than here. You don't seem very happy with Halloran House. Of course we'd transfer your luggage, and apply any balance on your deposit to your hotel rooms." She smiled at him, sweetly, a smile that said, "Please go now," as strongly as she could make it.

The timer on the stove rang. "Sorry, gotta go. Just let me know about the rooms. No trouble at all if you decide to move. And it's closer to the action." Having said her bit, she rose, gave him a totally fake smile, and took herself off into the kitchen, letting the door swing decisively behind her.

A few minutes later, her second batch of chocolate chip cookies in the oven, Stacie noted the dour couple's departure and breathed a sigh of relief.

*Move? And not be around this little dynamo of a woman?* Talking to her had left Adam in a strange mood. Was it the way she'd leaned on the shaft of the vacuum cleaner when he'd interrupted her routine yesterday? The way she clearly wanted him out of her hair, but did her best not to show it? And the hair itself, so dark, straight except for the crimp from the band she'd used to tie it back into a ponytail. The way her eyes squinted at him when she was trying to make up her mind what to do with him. Or maybe it wasn't the squint at all, but the eyes themselves, which he'd seen close up when she sat down across from him. She was direct, he'd give her that, she looked straight at him. And her eyes were the darkest brown imaginable. Like looking into pools of melted dark chocolate.

He was intrigued. He hadn't been intrigued in a long time.

*Move? Not a chance.*

He went to find Katherine. The thought of the dance didn't do anything for him at all, but the thought of Katherine's discomfort gave his spirits a much needed boost.

He found her in her room, frowning at something on her laptop. "Come on, gal," he called out jovially. "Let's go find us some country duds."

She threw a balled-up piece of paper at him, but otherwise ignored him.

"You'll be so adorable in a cute little cotton sundress. If we're really lucky we'll find something with ducks or roses or something on it. I can hardly wait."

"Adam, shut up or you'll be sorry."

He dropped the routine. "Fail to turn up at this barn dance and you'll be sorry. I'm taking the car. Come on if you're coming."

Katherine clicked to save or send or something and folded up her laptop.

"Well." Adam didn't have anything more to say.

They stood at the door to the Barn – it looked like it might have been a real, honest-to-God barn at one time – and watched the bedlam in front of them. Most of the population of Malaspina Island must be there, and they all had things to say. Loudly. The band was on a little raised platform at the other end and at least it wasn't all fiddles and squeeze boxes. He'd been worried, since the concert on the Square that afternoon. But there was an electric guitar and a bass and someone might play the piano.

*Which didn't rule out 'Good Night, Irene'*, he thought mournfully. What a winner of a way to spend a Saturday night.

Katherine had pulled herself together well, he thought. The skirt she'd found at the general store paired nicely with a short jacket she had with her, and the sandals actually seemed to work. She'd kept the makeup under control. Overall, she just might fit in.

As for himself, well, the new jeans were comfortable and he liked the way they emphasized the length of his legs. And de-emphasized the slight thickening around his waist. The shirt, a purplish plaid with snaps, he was less sure about, but at least it seemed to be similar in style to what other men were wearing. He planned to charge the thing as a business expense.

There were tables set up around the sides of the room, so he and Katherine, by mutual unspoken consent, found two chairs facing the center of the room at a table no one had claimed so far. They watched and waited. Resigned to his short-term fate, Adam let himself be a little curious, rather like an anthropologist running headlong into a strange culture. He relaxed a little and watched the goings-on, paying no attention to Katherine.

A striking older woman, her graying hair loose around her shoulders and wearing a long, flowered skirt with a tailored white blouse, slipped into the seat between them. "My dear," she said to Katherine, "what a lovely jacket. I've seen the skirt at the store, but I'd never have thought to pair it with something like this. It really works. You have a fine sense of style. I'm Abby Fox. That's my husband Bill over there with the band, the guy on the fiddle. He's been playing so long he's going deaf, but nothing's going to stop him." Abby shook her head in fond despair, communicating an age-old message that even Adam could interpret. *Men. What are we going to do with them?*

Katherine, Adam noted with pleasure, was caught flat-footed and tongue-tied. Finally she got out, "Thank you. I was fortunate to have the jacket with me. This is quite different from—"

"From Toronto. Of course. Best thing's to relax into it and have fun. It's a party, not a challenge, right?"

*And wasn't* that *a weird thing for her to say. Do we look so out of place? And how the hell did she know about Toronto?*

"You're the folks from Halloran House," Abby Fox chatted on. "We certainly hope you'll find your stay on Malaspina Island enjoyable. We do love our visitors. What made you choose this place? I don't see any immediate draw here."

Adam stepped into the conversation. "In other words, who are we?" He switched on his most engaging smile, the one that could sweep even late middle aged women right off their feet. "You're right about our being unlikely visitors. But we're both interested in learning about island life, and the company we work for does have connections here, so we thought we'd give it a look-see."

"We'll do all we can to ensure you enjoy yourselves. And you couldn't have picked a better place to stay, although it is more geared to honeymooners than business colleagues. It's possible you'd be more comfortable in the hotel. I hear there are a few vacant rooms right now. Save me a dance," she said as something of a parting shot at Adam. Then she rose gracefully and disappeared into the milling crowd.

Katherine was ready with the commentary. "Look-see? You have got to be kidding me. And aren't you skating a little close to the real reason we're here? God, Adam. You're acting like an idiot."

"Dear Katherine," he said with feigned patience for her ignorance, "of course we can't lie totally about why we're here. Because they're going to know sooner or later, and then where would that leave us? Future planning, darling. Required management skill, one you may need to brush up on. Now, would you like something to drink? It looks like there's a bar thing set up over there."

"I'm sure it's too much to hope they'd have martinis."

Adam didn't comment but took himself over to the bar thing, where he waited in line and finally was asked, "How many?"

"Oh, er, two."

The man behind the bar poured two glasses from a pitcher and placed them in front of him.

"Thanks. How much? And, well, what is it?" The people on this island had pulled some sleight of hand. He didn't get it. He felt like a bumbling yokel, when *they* were supposed to be the yokels.

The man grinned. "Lemonade. Sandy McMillan over the other side of the island made this batch. If you come back later you'll get someone else's, as long as it lasts. Depending on who made it, they never taste quite the same. And no charge. Comes with the admission."

*The admission of five dollars each. A bargain? Maybe. Time would tell.* He carried the glasses back to the table and set them down. "It doesn't get much further from a martini than this." He lowered himself back into his chair.

A hush fell over the crowd, as if they all knew by osmosis that something was about to happen. A man got on the microphone and started talking about kicking off the season, decorating the town, community spirit and such. Adam suppressed a yawn. Then the man said, "So let's get started, shall we? With one we know no one can resist."

Instead of the band playing, the loudspeakers pounded out the first notes of a song that grabbed Adam by the scruff of his neck and demanded his attention. His muscles went into temporary revolt, wanting a piece of the action. His whole body responded to driving rhythm of "Take a Chance on Me". He'd die before he let it show. He caught Katherine's eye, not that he'd wanted to, it just happened.

Katherine was ready for him. He must have twitched before he caught himself. "Reverting to your childhood now?"

"Could be." Abruptly, and for reasons he couldn't explain, Adam was happy. It seemed that everyone in the building except the two of them was out on the floor. And then a young woman, a teenager most likely, approached him with her hand held out, and he was out there, too, self-conscious as hell, trying to maintain some hint of dignity when everyone else was bouncing up and down as if the Barn were a gigantic trampoline. He was aware, in some dusty corner of his mind, that bouncing up and down might be fun, but he'd never let Katherine see *that*.

When the song was over his young partner disappeared, seeming to forget all about him, so he went back to the table. The lemonade looked good, so he took a long drink.

"Let me know when you start chewing on sticks of hay and eating corn pone, whatever that is," Katherine said.

"Don't be a spoilsport. And don't forget the point of why we're here, to win over the locals. Gather information.

Participation, girlie, that's the name of the game." He grinned when she winced at "girlie".

The dance went on with a mix of music from the 1950s up to present day, and a few children's songs thrown in. As Eustacia Halloran – he'd read the business license in the entry – had warned him, there was a swarm of children there. After a while the recorded music wound down and the band started, fielding requests from the crowd. They weren't bad, he reflected. Not polished, but they played with enthusiasm and, seemingly, played everything under the sun.

No one had joined them at their table. No one had sat down at all, anywhere. So after a while Adam got up and cruised the room, leaving Katherine behind to figure out her own strategy. He schooled his face to look open and friendly, and several times he even got to say good evening to someone, or comment on the music, the weather, whatever. Brief, but always pleasant.

The band swung into a waltz, just as he came face to face with his hostess, in a below-the-knee denim skirt and without the ponytail. A chance heaven-sent, because Eustacia Halloran had definitely caught his notice.

"Ms. Halloran," he opened.

"Mr. Fraser. Enjoying yourself?"

"I haven't had a chance to waltz in years. Do you?" He didn't mention that waltzing, dating from the embarrassment of dance lessons when he was about thirteen, was something he'd hoped never to do again in his life.

"Waltz? Sure."

"Good. Let's try, shall we?" The dance floor took up most of the available space, even weaving around the tables, so it was easy enough to pull her a couple of steps toward the center of the room, put his hand on her back, and nudge her into the first steps.

He looked at her again, from close up. Yes, the effect was still there, she had an attraction about her that caught at him in ways that could make him wish for more. Time to turn on a little charm. "According to the license for the B&B, your name's Eustacia."

She wrinkled her nose. She followed his lead well, but kept a little distance between them, dancing formally rather than provocatively. "And that really suits me, right? It's after a grandmother, but I don't know what my parents were thinking. I use Stacie now, except on legal documents."

"Stacie. Cute."

"Thanks for the put-down. Have you considered my offer to shift you to the hotel? We could handle it first thing tomorrow."

"I've considered. I think I'm happy where I am. For several reasons. Sorry."

"Sorry that you're happy where you are? Shouldn't I be flattered? What does 'several reasons' mean?"

"Your place is comfortable. The breakfasts are good. And you're a good looking woman, and I like good looking women. Several reasons."

He'd tweaked her pride, or something. Not the smoothest compliment he'd ever landed. Still the flash of anger on her face intrigued him. Her ire was up. She said, "Well, how very shallow of you. Do you prefer them intelligent or stupid, or does that enter into your equation of 'like'?"

"I'm an unattached man. Where an attractive woman in my arms is concerned, smart or dumb isn't necessarily something I think about. There's no way you're in the dumb category, though."

"Gee, thanks. I think."

Adam was quiet for a few steps. Then he said, "You're not exactly a fan of mine, I take it."

She looked up at him – he must have six inches on her, even with her heels – and stated, "You're a guest at Halloran House. I can't say I have any opinion about you beyond that fact. And the sense that you're not the usual type of person who books into my B&B, so I worry whether it suits you."

"It suits me fine. You could have a word with Katherine. She might be interested in moving."

"Tweedledum and Tweedledee go their separate ways?"

"We're colleagues." More and less than colleagues – once more, now decidedly less. They were roughly equal in terms of power and influence at Callaway Forest Products, and they both knew the next promotion was the crucial one, the one that would put one or the other of them in the president's inner circle. They both intended to win that promotion, and if that meant trampling the other one underfoot, well, good riddance. One less complication down the road.

*Hard to even imagine that they'd been together once.* But that was years ago, and didn't amount to anything more than a nasty little complication.

"Maybe, since we're dancing so nicely together, you could tell me why you're here. Colleagues from Toronto doesn't sound like a vacation to me." Her voice had an edge to it.

"Does it matter?"

"Not really. I was just a little curious."

He pulled her to a stop. "You're irritated by me and you can't figure me out, right? You think I'm up to something —"

"Both of you," she interrupted. "Whatever you're up to, she is, too. I have a feeling you're busy distancing yourself from her to get something out of me. Although I can't imagine what."

He smiled a little grimly, and wished he could coax an answering smile out of her. Distancing himself from Katherine would indeed be a goal. He'd have to work on it.

They began to move again. She followed well, even his rusty moves. "At the moment I'm dancing with you. As I pointed out before, you're an attractive woman, and I'm a single man. That's a place a business relationship doesn't go."

Then the waltz was over, and she smoothly twisted herself out of his arms. "And ours is a business relationship. Thanks for the dance. See you tomorrow morning." She slipped into the crowd.

Had he won any points there? He didn't think so. But on the other hand, she had lasted the entire dance in his arms. She hadn't slapped him or stormed off or anything. Stacie Halloran triggered thoughts that weren't businesslike at all.

*Thoughts that under no circumstances would Katherine ever find out about.*

Back at the table, a group of four or five people had joined Katherine and they were all doing their best to make conversation. The culture gap was a veritable Grand Canyon as the new group chatted away about events at the elementary school and the work bee the following weekend to spruce up the town for the summer season. Katherine, with no kids and no clue about the work bee, and of course planning to be back in Toronto well before the event happened, had put on her polite face and looked alert and interested. He expected she was seething inside, which didn't bother him at all.

Then suddenly it was 10:00 and the whole thing was over. Just when he might have expected the evening to get going, the town went home, rolling up the sidewalk behind them. He overheard some shouted plans about getting together first thing in the morning to clean the Barn, the band played "Auld Lang Syne", Katherine groaned, "They've got to be kidding" in his ear, and that was that.

Back in the car, he let his hand rest on her thigh and said, "Frustrated?"

"Take your hand away, Adam." He grinned at her but moved his hand. "You seemed to be doing pretty well chatting up our little hostess. But short of turning on the sexual wiles, how exactly are we supposed to find common ground here?"

He stared out the windshield and drummed his fingers on the steering wheel. "I'm wondering if volunteering is the answer. It sounds like half the island's going to be at this spruce-up-the-town thing, but I don't know what the options are when we've only got a few more days." He turned to face her. This was business, after all. "My instinct is to stay low-key. Do the tourist thing – pleasantly, if you can manage it. Chat with people when we get a chance. Perhaps arrange to meet with some of the local administration, so we know our contacts before we head home."

Then he grinned, a little nastily. "As for my wiles, you have to admit they're good."

"Used to be. I'd be willing to bet you couldn't seduce that little waitress you were fawning over."

"It's called dancing, not fawning. She liked it. And don't forget, I got you, didn't I?"

"You're older and paunchier now." Her contempt was withering.

"Experience. Women love it." Once again he reached over to put his hand on her thigh, this time squeezing.

"Wager?"

"Two fifty."

"Don't rate yourself very highly, do you?"

"Just trying to save you some pennies. Five hundred."

"It's a tight schedule, Adam. But I'll be charitable. I'll give you until whenever the mass meeting happens. Maybe you can lure her down your garden path by email."

If he was concerned about the timeframe – and he was – he wasn't going to let Katherine know. "And assuming she's single, but that seems likely. No sign of a man around other than the kid in the garden. But I'm not messing with a married woman."

"Scruples suddenly?"

"Some, believe it or not. I'm surprised you've even heard of them. But more to the point, an enraged husband with a shotgun wouldn't do me or my job here any good. Clear enough? And by the way, she's offered to move us to the hotel. She said she thought we'd be more comfortable there. You might consider it. At least then you can get what you want for breakfast."

"And miss having a ringside seat for the great seduction? Forget it." She offered him her hand and he removed his from her leg to shake, sealing the deal, competition and distrust on both of their faces. Then Adam started the car and they headed back to the B&B.

For him at least, the next few days suddenly looked like a lot more fun. As for her, she could go to the devil, for all he cared.

# Chapter 3

Sunday morning, for Stacie, was just another morning. Guests to feed, rooms to clean and polish. She noted that few of the cookies she'd left in the guest lounge had been eaten, but took that to mean that no one had been around to eat them. She didn't stay in to monitor who was there and who wasn't, not when there was a dance in town. The guests' room keys all worked on the front door as well, so she left them to take care of themselves. She knew that Two and Three had been at the dance, and thought she'd caught a glimpse of Four as well. As for One – *honeymooners,* she sighed. *Bet I know where they were.*

This morning's menu featured French toast with blackberry syrup or an English style breakfast of eggs, sausage, fried tomatoes, and toast. Predictably, Two and Three hadn't bothered to pre-order, and still hadn't shown up by the time One and Four were finished and off to make plans for the day. Stacie liked chatting with her guests about what to expect on the kayak or horseback excursions, where the best beaches were. They'd gone off happy and now, with twenty minutes before she'd close the kitchen, the breakfast room was quiet.

Suited her just fine. She allowed herself a grin that tried to be wicked, even if she knew that on her it would look cute. If Two and Three never showed up it would still be too soon.

She began dusting in the guest lounge, thinking back on the dance.

*Danger zone, Stacie.*

Danger or no, she had to admit there'd been something about that waltz. Two wasn't a half bad dancer, and he had great hazel eyes.

On the other hand, there'd been an edge of threat to his talk. There was something a little too slick, a little too polished. Something too practiced about the smile. As if he was thinking about putting moves on her – but not because of her. As if, if he chose to flirt with the good looking woman who served his breakfast, it was to get something out of her.

*And for that I should be flattered?*

*I don't have time to be flattered. He gets points for the eyes, though.*

A throat clearing at the door. Three, of course. "I don't suppose I could get breakfast?" the woman said in a voice that could be patented as a lethal weapon.

"Certainly, Ms. Sorenson." Stacie really wanted to say, "Certainly, Madame," with a curtsy, but caught herself in time. "You didn't pre-order. Have you chosen what you want?"

"Pancakes. Made with whole wheat flour. With maple syrup, and don't try to fob some of that fake stuff off on me."

But three days of this was really the limit. Stacie's voice dripped cool. "I'm sorry, that's impossible. I can use whole wheat sourdough for the French toast, if that's your preference, or there's the English breakfast. That's what's on the menu today. You could get pancakes at the hotel."

Their eyes locked. It became a battle of wills. Stacie figured she was in some kind of winning position, since it was her kitchen, so she waited it out. Finally, "Very well," Three said. "French toast. With maple syrup."

"I'll see if we have any." Stacie made for the door.

"And I do expect you to wash your hands thoroughly before you prepare my breakfast. You could be reported."

"I'll make a point of it, since you insist," she replied tartly. She dropped her duster in the downstairs storage closet, made a big show of stopping in the washroom to scrub her hands – with the door wide open to be as visible as possible – then disappeared through her private apartment door.

*No sign of Two,* she noted. *I wonder if he's been murdered in his bed.*

When she went into the breakfast room to pour coffee and place the carafe of orange juice on Three's table, she asked. "Is your companion planning on breakfast this morning? It's almost time for the kitchen to close."

Three laughed, the kind of laugh women use when they want you to know something. "Oh, I expect not. He was worn out from last night."

Stacie nodded. *I hear your message. And I think you're faking. I'll find out for sure, lucky me, because I get to clean your rooms. Whoopee.* She retreated to the kitchen to make the French toast, deciding on the spot that no, she didn't have any maple syrup.

"Hi, Mom." Stacie settled down on her sofa with the telephone.

"Hi, Sweetie. I didn't get a chance to talk to you last night. Have fun?"

"Sure. Can't beat a barn dance. You?"

"Oh, yes, apart from hardly seeing Bill. He was playing or twiddling microphones or something all evening. Did you get any of the lavender lemonade? I think she used old lavender, personally. The flavor didn't exactly sing."

"Ooh, catty. No, it was gone by time I got there. My timing sucks."

"Not entirely. I did notice you enjoying a dance with our mystery man."

"'Enjoy' isn't quite the word I'd choose. He dances nicely, though. And he does have really nice eyes and a hint of a chin cleft. What more can a girl ask for?"

Her mother laughed. "Glad there's something going for him. Any more information?"

"Mostly he dodged questions and asked me stuff, like about my name. I think he thinks he can play me. He's got the looks, but the attitude – jeez." Stacie shook her head on her end of the line, suspecting that her mother would pick up on it even though they couldn't see each other.

"Keep digging, when you get a chance. Anything at all could work to our benefit, you know. But especially whether they're just going to descend and do whatever the heck they want to the forest, or if there's something else going on. We can hope for something else. Keep me posted, will you?"

"Sure, Mom. Except that you always know everything anyway."

"Later, daughter." Her mother hung up on a laugh.

# Chapter 4

"Latte."

"Skinny Latte."

"You two are so predictable. There's something to be said for variety, you know." Doreen took their money. Dick and Doreen, the sixty-something couple who owned the Brew Place, knew everyone on the island and almost as much about what was going on as Stacie's mom. "Go sit. I'll bring them over."

"Something's gone wrong, Jess. We're predictable. We were going to be wild and crazy and no one would ever be able to figure us out."

It was Monday, ostensibly Stacie's morning off, although so far she'd spent it cleaning and baking, throwing muffins and scones into her freezer for the week ahead. Still, not having to cook breakfasts one day a week was a treat. By providing her B&B guests with gift certificates for the hotel dining room, she bought herself some space to breathe.

The new people in One and Four were the kind of guests who turned up on Stacie's good days. One was an older couple who'd been there twice before. She enjoyed their traditional good manners and the way they seemed to appreciate any little thing she did to make their visit special. Four was another pair of honeymooners. It seemed that already there'd been mother-in-law trouble, just which mother Stacie wasn't entirely sure.

There had been tears, poor kids. Today the young couple was just hanging out in the garden holding hands.

*Weddings. So much fun.*

*Ahem. No cynicism allowed, Stacie.*

"Here you go." Doreen plunked the coffees down on their table and perched on a spare chair. "Stacie, I hear there're spies in your midst."

"They spent most of Sunday holed up in the guest lounge pecking away at their laptops. Who works on a Sunday? I haven't seen them today, thank goodness."

"That bad, eh?"

Stacie approached her latte with fervor, and surfaced with a mustache. She licked it off. "Probably not. Just big city and corporate and that makes them something I don't understand. And I could be wrong, you know. I can't guarantee they're from Callaway Forest Products. I just know it's odd. He told me that they're colleagues, and that has to mean they were sent here or why would they be here? If anyone has any other ideas, I'd like to hear them."

"I also hear he dances a mean waltz," Jessica chipped in.

"Yeah, I'll probably never live that one down," Stacie conceded. "He'd asked me and had me out on the floor before I knew what was happening. And since you're both staring at me, I'll report that he can actually waltz, and he has hazel eyes. Very nice. The rest you've seen as well as I have. Okay?"

"Seen, but you actually got to put hands on him. Personally, if you don't want him I'll have a go. He's got the looks, and he moves like he's got the moves. I did note that he was hot for you." Jessica rarely pulled punches in their conversations.

Doreen tended to mother hen the younger women on the island. They in turn loved Doreen to bits, so it all worked out. Doreen now gave Jess a light swat on the arm. "Just you watch out, young lady. Both of you. He's a man – single?"

"He says so."

"Oh, so the topic came up. In what context, I'd love to know?"

"Damn it, Jess." Stacie caught the avid look on Jess's face and capitulated. No way was she going to be able to fend this one off. "In the context of how I'm an attractive woman, so it's fine for him to look. Almost a requirement, in fact. Okay?"

"Very okay," Jess said. "No roommate, no ring, and ogling you."

Doreen added, "Well, watch out. Even single, he's still the Enemy."

It was the first time Stacie noted the capital letter in the way people said 'enemy'. She expected it wouldn't be the last. "I'm watching," Stacie said. "Frankly, Doreen, most of the time I'm too worn out to be seducible. Anyway, he is so not my type."

"I'll let you know the next time a burly woodsman or some such comes in." Doreen went back to the counter, leaving Stacie eye to eye with Jessica.

"And we've known each other exactly how long?"

Stacie sighed. "Twenty years, give or take. And I know where you're going."

"Not your type. Smooth good looks. You were the one who drooled over Cary Grant, remember."

Stacie sipped the latte. "If looks did it I'd be practicing some moves myself, if I even remember any. Maybe I could use sex to get his secrets out of him? Pillow talk about Nathan's Forest, how romantic is that? But the fact is, he's inconsiderate and frequently rude. And sleeping with the Enemy is so twentieth century. I guess I'm just plain too old," Stacie grumped. "Thanks, but no thanks."

"I assume your Mom's on their case?"

"In the politest way imaginable she welcomed them and hoped they'd enjoy their stay. She figures we have to win them over. Make them love us. She's even planning on schmoozing them, backyard party or something, assuming they are who we think they are."

Jess nodded. "We can't win, so we salvage what we can. Which means kill them with kindness, seduce them to our way of life. Or maybe just seduce them, period?"

Stacie ignored the last bit. "Turn Mr. Fraser into an islander, if not a burly woodsman. Ms. Sorenson, too, his less than enchanting travel companion."

"Your mother's good." Jessica's eyes turned wicked. "I bet she's got it all laid out, how we approach them, what we hang onto, what we let go. The economic benefits, the good citizen stuff, the legalities."

"And to do this, we make them part of the community."

"We make them love us."

*Maybe not literally,* Stacie thought.

# Chapter 5

Two turned up at 9:55 Tuesday morning, five minutes from closing the kitchen.

*Probably does it just to spite you.* Stacie did not glower.

The sleeves on his dress shirt were rolled up a couple of turns and there was no tie in evidence.

*Nice arms.*

*Irrelevant.*

*Just stating the facts.*

No stony look this morning, either, merely something that she might define as innate superiority, me-up-here-to-you-down-there. The kind of attitude you got from guys who knew they were hot, or maybe powerful. Not that she'd met many of the powerful variety.

*Or the hot variety, not in a pathetically long time.*

*What is it about rolled sleeves?* She jerked her gaze away.

"Good morning, Stacie. Do you mind if I call you Stacie?"

*Should she mind? What the hell.* "No, I don't mind. I'll get your coffee."

"No rush. Katherine's not down yet?"

*No rush? At four minutes to ten?* Stacie was moving toward the coffee station. She stopped and turned to face him. "Oh, you didn't know? She left. You might as well go on and order. Today we have poached eggs with fried potatoes, or waffles, both options served with bacon and stewed tomatoes. I can do either one, although it *is* easier if you remember to pre-order."

He looked at her as if she didn't know what she was talking about. "That doesn't sound like her. Not much of a morning person. Did she go out for breakfast?" He frowned.

Stacie felt a little smug. She hadn't read anything into her brief business encounter that morning with Three, but maybe her good-morning news would wipe the superior look off his face. "No, she told me to say goodbye for her. She checked herself out, paid the balance on her room, and left to catch the 10:10 ferry. They'll be boarded by now. She said that her office had been in touch and needed her back urgently. That's all I know," Stacie concluded.

Two's face drained of color, and there was something panicky in his eyes, like a man with a guillotine in his immediate future. This time Stacie's switch into hostess mode was genuine. "Are you okay? You really didn't know?"

"No. I didn't." Abruptly he got up and left the room. She heard the front door slam, then open and slam again. He came back into the breakfast room, steaming. "The bitch," he muttered. "She took the car."

"Maybe she left it for you at the ferry dock?"

It was obvious that neither of them thought that was likely. He sank back into his chair and the two of them stared at each other for a moment. Stacie wasn't sure what was going on, but she was sure of one thing. This man had taken a serious blow, like he'd just watched a major business deal go south. Something juicier than the unexpected departure of an irritating colleague was unfolding here.

The ferry chose that moment to signal its departure. The horn could be heard all over the island. No one set their watches by it, that would be dumb, but it was a comfort to hear it all the same.

She grabbed the coffee carafe, then came back and poured him a cup. "Drink. I'll get you some breakfast." She couldn't and wouldn't get Katherine Sorenson back for him, but she could feed him. He didn't stop her and she was glad to make an escape. He had a fast recovery time, or maybe it was adrenaline. Whatever, he was coming around from the blow. Stacie saw a man plotting something unpleasant, a man out for revenge, something seriously nasty.

*Whew. And all of this in quiet little Halloran House Bed and Breakfast, where the most dramatic thing that ever happened was honeymooners in a snit.*

She chose the waffles, figuring she might as well use up the rest of the batter. She set the waffle iron baking, and five minutes later she was putting a plate in front of him. One last trip for orange juice and he was set – only he didn't look set at all. The anger had faded while she was in the kitchen. He looked rattled, a tightrope walker fighting an unexpected gust of wind. This man had more moods, and cycled through them more rapidly, than anyone she'd ever met. She could use a scorecard just to keep up.

"Mr. Fraser, is there anything I can do?" Stacie settled back into good hostess mode. "I've already asked this, but are you okay? I can get you to the clinic if you're not feeling well."

He seemed to wake up and notice her, then noticed the meal in front of him. "Thanks, Stacie. I'm fine. But this could be a disaster in the making. How the *hell* I'm going to deal with it from here …" He waved his fork at the breakfast room, the B&B, the island, Stacie wasn't sure which. He drowned the waffle in syrup, then used the fork in the way it was intended and speared a bite. He swallowed, nodded. Maybe he'd found something to like? "She must be planning to pay out the lost fee on my car key. Is there any way I could mail it in from here?"

"Sure, it's happened before. Give me the key and the information and I'll see to it. I'll give them your home address, you'll probably get a refund."

He looked at her as if he was really seeing her for the first time. He grinned. "I like the way your mind works."

*Well, what do you know. The man can smile. Even when he's not after something.*

But, why and how was it that he started pouring the whole thing out? And how was it that she found herself grabbing a mug of coffee and sitting across from him? She propped her chin on a palm and listened while he talked and ate. "We're both up for promotion, and the next step up's a big one – CFO. Do you even know what that is?"

She sighed. "Chief Financial Officer. Some people would say that falls into the common knowledge category."

"Right, sorry. The one who gets it gets the president's ear, it's the inner circle. If they've called her back, it could mean … but it might not. It'd be like her to make the whole thing up. Or get herself back to headquarters and stab me in the back. I suspect she's sleeping with Ralph, that's the VP we report to. She doesn't deny it anyway, but that could be messing with my mind. I mean, could he have such bad taste? Really? Tell me, Stacie, what did you think of us at that dance Saturday? Were we fools on display?"

*Huh?* "Why on earth would you think that?"

"We were out of our element. I was well aware of it." He grimaced, then stuffed another bite into his mouth. The waffles were clearly a hit. "I know we don't fit in here," he said around the bite of waffle. "Neither of us had a clue what we were being parachuted into. But I did try to, well, to be pleasant. To participate. And for the record, this is one bitch of an assignment."

"Well, that's intriguing. Maybe you were sent here to test your mettle or something. See how you cope in difficult situations. Maybe you'd like to tell me a little about your job?"

He ignored that. "Why would Katherine get called back?"

"By which you mean, why her and not you."

Two slowed his food intake long enough to look at her. "Yeah, I do. This could be my job on the line. If she has anything to do with it, I'll have my walking papers when I get back. There were no signals, nothing. I am so screwed." He drained his coffee, then instead of waiting for her to serve him he got up and strode across the room to the coffee machine, where he poured another cup.

Stacie watched him cross the room. She liked the visual – which didn't change anything one iota.

*The Enemy, Stacie. The nasty, ill-mannered Enemy.*

"In answer to your question, I don't think either of you disgraced yourselves at the dance. You waltz well. It would have been good manners to ask one of the older ladies to dance, the young guys often do and it thrills them. But maybe that's not how you do it in Toronto. I haven't heard anything negative about you around the town, other than your being from back east and probably clueless. But we expect that."

"Clueless?" Back in his chair, he was wielding his fork again. A bite of waffle got in the way of speech, so he did his best to glare at her instead.

*Go ahead. Try to pull off a successful glare with your face stuffed full of home cooking.* She'd pricked his pride for sure, there. He swallowed. "I might have a different skill set, but I can assure you I'm fully competent at what I do. Better than *she* is," he muttered, dripping contempt. "But try to tell Ralph that. Wiles, Stacie. She's got them and she uses them."

"Too bad there isn't a female vice president to report to?"

He missed the implication in her snarky comment. Two's mind must have migrated to some office tower in Ontario. He shoveled in another bite. The waffle might be Katherine, he ate with such ferocity.

She'd watched the entire display. He'd moved from furious, through stunned, into something like bewildered, and the disdainful attitude toward her and her island seemed to have been lost in the shuffle. Out of the blue, foreboding hit her with a healthy wallop.

*Not good, Stacie. Not good at all.*

Because she realized – speaking of the last thing she wanted – that she was intrigued by this angry, hapless man, who was a fish out of water on the island, and at the moment seemed to be outside the goldfish bowl in his own world, too.

Time for her to be a little nicer, a little sweeter? Time to wheedle some information out of him using her mother's sugar approach? After all, a big part of the future of her island could depend on winning him over, giving them an ally in the enemy camp.

Time for all that good stuff, yes. Sometimes, though, the imp took over. Looked like this might be one of those mornings.

"There's something flying around between you two besides business. I'd have to be blind to miss it." *Or to miss Two's bitchy implications Sunday morning.*

His laugh was bitter. "Not now. Years ago. The kind of thing, you realize you've walked into a disaster and you get out, even if it means a few broken plates. She's a barracuda."

Stacie settled in, again propping her chin on a hand. This wasn't the information they needed, but it sure was getting interesting. "Using you for corporate advancement?"

He sighed and traced patterns with his fork in the pool of syrup on his plate. He watched the fork, not her. "It made a kind of sense at the time. Two young executives on the fast track. Competent, committed. But what it worked out to be was a way to let off steam. Only it ended up keeping the pressure at boiling point, once we both started getting more competitive." He looked up. "And why the hell am I telling you this?"

"You're kidding. You'd sleep with someone just to shed some tension?"

"Like I believe you've never had sex because you happen to need sex?"

"Never. Maybe it's a guy thing." she didn't feel like admitting that her overall experience in that realm was limited, at best.

"Revenge? To get back at an enemy?"

"I don't have any of those."

"Not only am I trapped on an island that's barely on maps, I'm dealing with a goddamn virgin," he stated.

"Guess again."

"Okay. I'll guess. You're probably in your thirties, but not by much. You're not married. Possibly divorced. No kids. Am I close?"

"Real close. Thirty-four, never married. No kids."

His eyes narrowed. "You're the hottest woman I've met in a long time and every time I see you you're dressed in that gray outfit and vacuuming. Waltzing with you was enough to make me want more, in case you're interested. There's no way you'd be on your own in any place that actually had a countable population."

"Did I say I'm on my own?"

"Oh."

"Not having a resident male doesn't mean no male at all, you know."

"So there's a guy."

An outright lie might be going too far. "Well, no. But there might have been."

"And when you break up with someone, I suppose it's all very civilized." He sighed, shoved his empty plate away, and swallowed down the last of his coffee.

"Yes. We're big on civilized behavior. Maybe you don't practice civilization in Toronto, but here it's sort of a given." Now that *was* an outright lie, passions could get out of hand on Malaspina Island as easily as anywhere else, but Stacie was enjoying pushing this pompous man's buttons. Did he really think he could waltz in here – pun intended – and call her hot and get away with it? When he paid her to be nice to him and serve his breakfast?

*Foreboding*. Two wasn't the only one hanging on to an attitude.

Ah. She'd got to him. The anger was back. He slammed down the coffee cup. "Later."

"Much, much later." She gave him her sweetest smile.

They both stood and they both turned to the door. Where they collided. When they simultaneously turned to glower, their eyes met.

And locked.

She felt it all the way to her toes. But with a serious contraction about half way down.

"Oh, no."

"Bloody hell."

They'd spoken at the same time. And simultaneously broke the eye lock. He looked as startled as she felt. "That didn't happen," she said.

"Absolutely not." Then, "Why is it an insult if I say you're hot? It's true."

"It's the relationship thing. You pay me, so it's inappropriate. Even if you didn't pay me it would be inappropriate. You don't even know me."

"Maybe inappropriate. But not unheard of," he stated. The startled look had faded, replaced by his usual disapproval. But then he grabbed her upper arms, pulled her to him, and she had a brief moment for a thought – *hey, wait a minute* – before her mind seized up like misaligned gears, because he planted a fast, hard, and poorly executed kiss on most of her mouth. Then he said, succinctly, "Damn," and left, storming up the stairs.

*It's inappropriate,* she thought as she stood there, stunned, *because I say it is. Because you just made me realize that you're the one who's hot, and if Katherine Sorenson's really ever had her hands on your body, I could happily murder her in a jealous rage. If she hadn't conveniently left.*

*Stacie, you have a little problem here.*

Stacie next ran into Adam late that afternoon. He'd spent most of the day on his laptop or on his phone, sounding variously furious, commanding, wheedling, or brisk and businesslike whenever she picked up his voice as she went about her chores. He'd moved restlessly between his room and the guest lounge as if he couldn't settle in one place for more than half an hour. Now he was studying the tea service in the lounge, where every afternoon she offered an assortment of teas with home baked cookies. He looked puzzled. Good, but puzzled, with those sleeves rolled up to show the dust of sandy hair on his forearms. He also looked trim and neat and made her feel positively dowdy in her peasant skirt and oversized red T-shirt.

She made the opening move. "Before you say one other thing, I wonder if you'd care to explain that – incident – earlier?"

He flushed. *Could be fun having a sandy haired man around, they're so cute when they go red.* But his look suggested she might be a bug underfoot or something. "I apologize. My behavior was anomalous. I suppose you know what that means?"

"I'll go get my handy dictionary, why don't I?"

He seemed to have been holding his breath. Now he let it out. 'Okay, I'm sorry. I'm on edge."

"You should try more casual shirts. Free your neck up a little. Might help you relax into the ambience." She wanted to bite her tongue, goading him like that, but boundaries had to be set, didn't they?

"This is as casual as my wardrobe gets on workdays. Unlike yours, clearly." His voice was carefully neutral.

*Okay, she deserved that.*

"No coffee this afternoon?" he asked.

"Not after noon. Coffee's best brewed fresh, and I do like to take some time off occasionally. There's a coffee shop in town."

*Leave. Go.*

*Or maybe not?*

"Then can you advise me here? You've got too much selection."

"You aren't trying to please the mix of guests I get." She came over next to him, 'next to him' being defined as at least a foot of air space between them, and took the box he was waving around. "The one you're holding is lemon verbena and mint, as you can see. A local company, and organically grown. It's nice. Refreshing and well balanced." She took the box from him and set it down with a thump. "Not usually a guy selection."

He looked at her. "So people really drink stuff like that."

"Oh yes. It's considered a luxury. A delicacy, even. Perhaps Toronto hasn't caught up yet."

"Lay off about Toronto, will you? It's a sore point." He poked around some more. Stacie had at least ten different teas available to her guests, knowing from past experience how particular some tastes could be.

"Don't you have anything that's ordinary tea? Like you'd get at the grocery store?"

"Grocery stores might surprise you these days. Here." She picked up another box and put it in his hand. "This one tends to get shoved to the back. Lots of my guests are more adventurous, but it might appeal to you. Basic orange pekoe. Brews up nice and strong. Manly, if that's how you like it."

"God, Stacie. Give me a break, will you? We hardly know each other and you're on my case like we're – like you're Katherine or something."

*Well, that shut me up,* she thought. *Her, like Katherine? The shrew?* "Sorry. Long day."

He put a tea bag in the cup, added water from the insulated jug. "I've got to ask you about vacancies. I've been on to Head Office this whole damn day. And guess what I've got for my pains? Orders to stay put. You're going to be looking at me for another two or three weeks."

To be fair, she could see the news wasn't any more welcome to him than to her. This was a man who seriously needed a massage involving lavender, and maybe a healthy slug of scotch, given his visible agitation.

"Take out your tea bag. In one cup, that'll get undrinkably strong quickly unless you're a regular tea drinker, or you have a particular need to scour out your insides. And your news doesn't affect me. I'm booked up, so you're on your way on Thursday. You could try the hotel. Which, I seem to recall, I've already recommended to you."

He pinched the corner of the tea bag between his thumb and finger, pulled it out, and plopped it in the waste basket next to the old mahogany buffet she used for the tea service.

She watched, then narrowed her eyes at him. He looked down, noticed the small covered container. "Oh. Wrong basket?"

"We compost. That's where you collect your organic waste and —"

"Believe it or not, I know what compost is." He gingerly retrieved the tea bag and dropped it into the compost bin. He stared at his cup for a moment, then added a spoon of sugar and some milk. Sipped, grimaced. "I didn't drink tea growing up. I'm not sure it's my thing."

"Sorry, I don't serve martinis. Try a cookie. Some people like to dunk 'em. That's when we're not goin' off fishin' or settin' around whittlin'."

His turn to glare. "Words fail me. As they obviously do you. At least the English kind."

They stood there, Two looking as irritated as she felt.

"Well."

"Well."

Another silence. Stacie was in the mood for escalating hostilities, but since that wasn't acceptable hostess practice, she said, "Do we want to talk about it?"

Frosty look. "No. We don't. I've apologized. I'm not usually so —"

"Spontaneous? Willing to show your human side?" *So much for not goading,* she thought. *Accept the damn apology, Stacie.* "Consider it forgotten."

Another silence. "A pair of great conversationalists, aren't we?" he said. "Sit down. Join me."

*No, I won't. Not a chance.*

"I'll just make myself a cup." Because she absolutely had to show her independence of mind, Stacie chose the lemon verbena and mint tea, even though she really didn't like it all that much. She poured water over the bag and settled in a chair for one, sending signals with all her might that he'd better not repeat that kissing business.

"This has been one hell of a day." He put the tea cup on the coffee table and perched on the arm of the sofa. He'd grabbed an oatmeal cookie from the antique plate on the buffet. Instead of eating it, he played with it, back and forth in his fingers. His voice shifted from normal to formal. "I do want to thank you for your concern earlier. It was almost the only bright spot, other than getting rid of Katherine. That was a shock, but I can't say I'm sorry she's gone. She made life around here that much more difficult."

*More difficult?* She wasn't about to let that go. "It's my job. And I'm so sorry you find life around here difficult. Most people don't, you know. But then most people aren't here with an agenda."

His eyebrows went up at that. "You think I have an agenda?"

"Of course you do."

The stick-up-the-ass tone was back. "No doubt that assumption is why we keep having these tiffs. I can assure you I'm not trying to irritate you." He bit into the cookie.

She stared at him. "Did you really say 'tiff'?"

To her delight, he flushed. The snooty tone disappeared. Was it possible the man could laugh at himself? "I guess I did. Not a common word around here?"

"My grandmother used it sometimes, I think. I can't imagine anyone else even knows it."

"Probably not. It just slipped out. I guess my mind thought it sounded appropriate."

"Appropriate to what?"

"Well, the island. It's so quiet here. It feels like your grandmother's language would fit. Sort of old fashioned, slower."

She frowned. "I can't figure out if you're insulting me again."

"I'm not. I promise."

She sipped. "Do you like the big city?"

"Of course. At times I'm amazed anyone would want to live anywhere else. Restaurants, culture at your fingertips. Everything convenient."

"I expect you live on the twentieth floor of a downtown high rise."

"Fourteenth."

"No need to chop down a tree to heat the homestead, huh?"

He sighed. "Let up, okay? I get the picture. I thought we might try to be civil for a few minutes." He tried another sip of the tea and wrinkled his nose. "This is an acquired taste, I think."

Time to get the agenda out of him. Her earlier attempt to get information had failed, so this time she'd go for a frontal attack – er, approach. "Okay, let's talk about something neutral. Like business. Who do you work for?"

Silence hung in the air. Two looked like a fish on a hook. Then he shrugged and said, "Callaway Forest Products, Canadian Division."

"I was right, then. You're here to cut down Nathan's Forest."

"Nathan's Forest? What's that?"

"You've been on the island what, five full days? And you haven't figured out where your forest is yet? What have you been doing with your time?"

"Dealing with barn dances and you. And Katherine. And business that followed me from Toronto. Of course I know where our land is. It's the name I didn't recognize."

"The forest takes up most of the south end of the island. Here, look." She rose and led him across the room to a large, framed map of Malaspina Island. "Mostly all this green bit. No one's sure where the boundaries are anymore. These are hiking trails, here's a nature area where there are some exhibits and animals for the kids in the summer — "

"Wait a minute. Callaway didn't put in any nature parks or trails. That's meant to be wilderness. Trees and stuff."

"Not exactly a forester, are you?"

"I'm in finance. Procurements, disbursements, mergers, that kind of thing."

Stacie shook her head. "Whatever turns your crank."

"So tell me about these amenities. How they got there."

"We put them there, of course. The people who live on Malaspina consider Nathan's Forest one of our prime recreational areas. We're pretty sure the kids' area isn't actually on your land, but as I said, no one knows for certain, and there's never been any reason to get a survey done. On around here ..." she indicated the southern coast of the island, "there are picnic areas, some safe places to wade if you don't mind freezing your toes off. Campfire pits on the beach, away from the forest – we aren't dumb, contrary to what snotty easterners think." She caught the start of a sigh, but he had the good sense to swallow it. "And a few trails going up. Most of the gentler trails, the ones you might be interested in, for instance, are on the north side, though."

*If looks could kill.* "The trails I'd be interested in."

"Not the put-down you think it is. I simply don't believe you get out hiking a lot. The higher trails are really rugged. The kind you don't do on your own. The kind I don't do, ever. And I suspect my legs are stronger than yours."

Two stepped away from the map and looked her over, down, up, down again. With the flowing skirt and loose T-shirt she wasn't giving him any clues. "I'm trying to imagine," he said.

"Don't bother." She returned to the chair, grabbing one of her cookies on the way, leaving him standing.

"But people do hike. You all go into the forest, right? Nathan's Forest – why Nathan? Who's he?"

"Old guy who lived here in the early 1900s. Had a cabin up there. We used to go camping —"

"It's still there? The cabin?"

"No, pulled down years ago. But I got the last year or so of it when I was a teenager. We'd go up there and try to convince ourselves it was haunted. Never worked for me, but some people swore they heard bumps and things."

"So, hiking. I've even seen signs in the town for tours."

"Sure. Why is that so hard for you to get?"

"Because Callaway owns it."

"And your point?"

They ate cookies in silence for a minute.

"Well," he finally said, "it's trespassing, for one thing."

Stacie rolled her eyes, exasperated. "Here's the thing, Adam from the big city. This is an island. With a smallish resident population and a tourist industry. That forest has been sitting there for hundreds of years, and as far as we can tell, no one from Callaway has so much as laid eyes on it. Ownership ceases to have any meaning after a while, you know? We make use of it. And take care of it. If it catches fire, guess who gets to put out the fire? Not Callaway. It'll be crews from the island as first responders, and if it's too big we call in the province. We have a community that values and even loves Nathan's Forest."

She was getting heated, and she knew it, but she couldn't seem to stop. She managed to hold herself back from jumping up and jabbing a finger into his chest, but only barely. "We use it in ways that are respectful and ecologically sensitive. And you come in here with a deed in your pocket and wave it around and translate every one of those trees into dollar signs for your corporation and your juicy salary and don't give a damn about what you might cost us. Right?" Stacie stopped to catch her breath.

Two stared at her.

"Am I right? What's your answer to that, mister corporate big shot?"

"God, Stacie." He was across the room in three steps, pulling her up, and this time the kiss was just as firm but wasn't ending after a half second. And wasn't poorly executed at all.

And this time, after necessary token resistance, she hooked her arms around his waist and kissed him back. Things got … intense. Hands wandered. Knees shook.

Someone at the door said, "Excuse me?"

It was the woman from Four. Adam broke off and relaxed his grip, but they didn't exactly jump apart. It was more like they clung to each other's arms for stability. She noted in some faraway part of her brain that he looked shell shocked. She probably did, too.

Stacie gave herself a shake and stepped away. "Please come in. The cookies are fresh. Is there anything I can do for you?" It was a challenge, but she went from passionate-embrace to cool-hostess in a split second, ignoring the possible embarrassment of the situation. Adam followed her lead, returning to his perch on the arm of the sofa, casually positioning an arm across his lap as if he didn't have anything to hide, and retrieving the cookie from where he must have dropped it on his saucer before he launched that … that … *hell, Stacie. You've got some figuring out to do.*

Once she'd dealt with the woman at the door, she turned back to him. "And what was that in honor of?"

"Look, Stacie. Sit down again, will you?" When she did, without a hostile riposte, he said, "You are quite possibly the last thing I could want in my life at the moment. It'd sure as hell make things easier if whatever this is between us weren't happening, but it is. So I needed to kiss you. So I did. I couldn't care less that you're my landlady or whatever you call yourself. I wanted to kiss you. Okay? And it'll probably be best all around if I see as little as possible of you for the foreseeable future. I hope we're clear about that."

"Not exactly a hopeless romantic, are you?"

"Not romantic at all. You're in the way of my work."

"I expect you could move to the hotel early. I'll see if that room is still available."

"It's only two nights. I think I can bear it here."

"As long as you avoid me like the plague?"

"I am not having this conversation," he muttered. Then, "Yes, since you put it that way. You're a distraction I can't afford."

"Because I'm hot."

He shook his head. "Because we're hot. Think about it."

He watched her while she tried to figure out a suitable reply, so he also watched her fail. Then out of the blue he turned a real smile on her, the kind of smile a person smiles when he's happy, for instance – *God help us, he's got a gorgeous mouth!* – and headed for the door.

She followed, picking up his almost full teacup to take back to the kitchen.

# Chapter 6

"Hi, Jess." Stacie waved but left her friend alone while she dealt with a customer. No rush. There was always something fun to browse in the Ocean Thyme Gift Shop, and she enjoyed seeing how ably Jess handled the customer, gently guiding her to a purchase with no pressure whatsoever. Most people who came into Ocean Thyme did so because they weren't looking for a stuffed moose in the red uniform of the Royal Canadian Mounted Police. Jess's customers were the type to seek out the unexpected, something unique they just had to take home with them. Ocean Thyme dealt in quality, not souvenirs. Even locals could find something in Ocean Thyme.

Finally Jess rang in the sale and the customer left, looking happy. She joined Stacie. "Her husband's taking her to Roscoe's for dinner tonight. She'll feel like a queen. She swears that necklace and earrings set will be perfect with what she plans to wear."

"Heck, I'd feel like a queen if anyone took me to Roscoe's, even without your jewelry. Maybe we could talk them into doing an open house or a special for locals at 5:00 or something."

"Like it hasn't been tried." The people who owned Roscoe's were from off the island, and hadn't made many moves to integrate. Not every islander was a local, was the way Stacie thought about it.

"I brought you the soap. This is the last until I find time to make some more. But no promises, okay? I think I had more energy to be ambitious a year ago. Or maybe I was younger. Do you have time to take a break?"

"Sure. I've got pop. We'll hear the bell if anyone comes in." Jess led Stacie through the curtain that divided the store from the office and storage area in the back. "So what's the news?"

"Tons. Half of the evil pair has left. I get the feeling that she somehow shafted her partner in crime, he was really upset. So I made him waffles."

"Does this mean we only have one evil force to deal with? Here you go." Jess handed a diet cola to Stacie, then popped the lid on a regular cola for herself.

"Same evil force, but fewer prongs on their pitchfork. Now they can't divide and conquer, but I don't think that would've worked anyway. He says he's been told to stay around for another two or three weeks, so they're planning something. Mom's going to have to talk to him. Oh, he is from Callaway."

"Therefore, he is the Enemy. Are we having any luck getting him involved? Making him appreciate us?"

"Not so far. Not much, anyway, the dance is all. But I did give him a little lecture yesterday afternoon on how much good, wholesome use we make of Nathan's Forest."

Jess grinned. "Did you point out the make-out spot?"

"Darn, I forgot to mention that. So then I sort of went into a rant about how it's as much ours as theirs because we care for it and all, and then he kissed me until Four —"

"Whoa, girl." Jess's eyes were wide and laughing. "He kissed you? Because you love Nathan's Forest and he's going to cut it down? I love it. You may be our secret weapon."

"He kissed me because we're hot. That's what he said. Sort of. He also told me that anything would be better and he'd be avoiding me in the future. But he refused to move out." Stacie shook her head and swigged enough cola to make her choke. She coughed and added, "Between you and me, Jess, I am so in trouble."

"Room to be sensible?"

"Not much. But it's only for another couple of weeks, and he's out of the B&B on Thursday – like tomorrow. So there won't be as much pressure."

By now the two women were sitting on the stools Jess kept in the storage area. The bell in the front was mercifully silent. Stacie leaned with her elbows on her knees, her can of cola dangling in both hands between her jeans-covered legs. "The thing about him is, besides being certifiably good looking, he's so helpless. He must be here to pave the way or something, but he doesn't have a clue how to relate, or how to dress, or what to do. I mean he wears a dress shirt every day. It's kind of endearing."

"And mother hen Stacie is right there to show him how it's done, yes? You can't fool me, I know you too well. Just don't let him get to you too much, kid. You don't know what his expectations are or what he's after. Though now I think about it, I guess he's given you some clues, hmm? But bottom line is, he's from an alien planet."

"True. But he blushes. And he likes waffles."

"Obviously. Getting a wee bit pudgy around the middle, from what I saw at the dance."

"Not pudgy really, just a little handle – be fair. But not a six-pack, that's for sure." Stacie giggled. "Felt good."

"Oh, God. Don't go there, Stace." Jess drank some cola. "So what's next?"

"I don't know. Get him out of my hair, that'll be a relief. Watch and wait. Let Mom know what's going on … well, maybe not everything. And you don't tell her," she added, pointing a finger at Jess. "Some things she doesn't need to know, right?"

"Oh, yeah, like I'm going to go up to Abby and say, 'Hey, Mrs. Fox, your daughter's in serious lust for the hunk from Toronto.' Have more faith."

"Just threatening. There's your bell." Jess hopped up and slid smoothly through the drapes to greet the customer. Stacie stayed put.

*Is that what this is? In lust?*

Sure felt like it. But it felt like something else, too. She couldn't quite pinpoint what that something might be.

Wednesday afternoon, Adam was back in the General Store, trying on jeans. Again.

He had realized by now that virtually everything he'd brought with him was inappropriate for any but the most formal restaurants on Malaspina Island. And it didn't seem that the locals ever went to those. So he had to add to his wardrobe. Today's quest was for a pair of looser fitting jeans. The pair he'd bought for the dance looked good on him, he knew that, but might not be so well suited for exercise. And he planned on exercise.

He'd signed up for a guided hike into Nathan's Forest.

It was to be an all-day thing with lunch provided at one of the picnic areas on the beach. The man in the tour shop had shown him on a map where they'd be going and cautioned that there would be some difficult places. Looked at Adam's shoes and suggested the sporting goods store a few doors down.

Adam knew that the other people on the tour – there were two others signed up – would be tourists and not of interest to him, but the tour guide himself might be. He could let it be known that he didn't know the landscape but wanted to learn, ask lots of questions as they hiked, impress the guy with his enthusiasm. Maybe get some idea of how attached the locals really were to this weirdly named forest. He could use this hike to glean some useful information to send to the team in Toronto.

The plan had also been to contact the island administration from Toronto, but head office had let him know that as long as he was here he might as well be the front man.

*How lucky can a man get?*

This afternoon he'd be in touch – he'd located the contact information from their web site – and begin the negotiations for a forum, where Callaway would listen to the locals and look and sound reasonable, how much their opinions mattered and so forth.

After the forum thing he'd be gone. And just as well, because he was getting a strong sense that he wouldn't be very popular around town once Callaway moved in the heavy machinery. He sort of wished he could salvage something with Stacie, though.

He didn't like going into situations cold, so he was taking his time, talking to as many people as he could before arranging the meeting.

*And that certainly wasn't proving to be a problem.* All he had to do was drop into the coffee shop on the Square and he'd have a conversation, maybe several. Everyone glad to meet him, everyone polite and pleasant.

Based on his casual questioning, everyone was in love with Nathan's Forest.

From his notes he could plan his approach. But in the meantime he was a little at loose ends, discounting the ongoing flow of work arriving from Toronto. Hence the hike.

Satisfied with his session in the change rooms, he strode to the cashier with another pair of jeans, two more shirts, a cotton sweater, and an anorak. He suspected he was going to end up looking like the General Store display window, but that couldn't be helped. It was better than a jacket and tie.

Next stop, the sporting goods store for boots and socks. Even he knew his leather shoes wouldn't do for a walk in the woods.

Adam felt good as he walked back to the B&B. Walking being the only option. There was only one rental place on the island, and of course they didn't have a car available. His name was on a wait list. In the meantime, he was making the best of it. It was a pleasant walk along a winding, tree lined street that climbed gently, with occasional views over the ocean. He'd made the trek several times in the day and a half since Katherine had flown the coop with the car, and he was sure he was already better for it, fitter, his muscles happier. He used to go to a gym, but somehow that had fallen by the wayside.

As had all the things he'd boasted to Stacie about, come to think of it – the culture, the restaurants. He couldn't remember the last time he'd gone to a concert, and meals were usually takeaway, or a scrambled egg. Somehow, the city wasn't living up to billing. But he didn't need to tell her that.

His contact with Callaway had been minimal that morning and nothing at all this afternoon. Somehow that had resulted in fewer knotted muscles, less desire to lash out at something. He'd do their bidding – and he'd win the coveted CFO position, dammit – but if they wanted to leave him marooned in this outback, he'd damn well play it his own way.

A car drove by, tooted its horn, then pulled over to the side ahead of him. It was the going-gray woman from the dance. She got out of the car and walked back to him.

"Lovely walk, isn't it?" She turned and looked out over the ocean. "I never get tired of this view. I hope you'll be here when there's a storm. The ocean changes character completely. It becomes threatening. Personally, I like watching the violence from a distance. I know some people like to be closer to the waves when the weather's rough, but maybe I'm too old for that."

Adam stood beside her and dutifully looked out. "It is beautiful. Like a postcard."

She wrinkled her nose. "Postcards are usually too perfect. We have one for sale in town that shows the Square without a person on it. It's never like that, and we wouldn't want it to be. We're a dynamic community and the people matter. It's the same with the ocean. You can pretty it up with paintings and postcards or you can take it raw and natural. The same with the forest. It's living and dynamic, not a thing. It has a presence. You'll see. I hope you'll feel that tomorrow."

Adam looked at her, astonished, but before he could say anything she laughed companionably and said, "I know everything. I'm Abby Fox, we met at the dance. I'm the town manager. And you're Adam Fraser, of Callaway Forest Products. Surely you don't think we haven't been paying attention to you, do you? We take your presence here very seriously, believe me. And we want to make your experience of our island memorable." She held out her hand to him.

Adam shifted his packages to his left hand and shook hers. The setting might be a bit unusual, but this was clearly a business meeting and he understood the protocols there very well. "I'm happy to meet you, Ms. Fox. I'd planned to call in at the Town Hall ..."

"We usually say Admin Building, but Malaspina Island Administrative Center is the proper name. I'm manager for the town, but Windon Harbor has a mayor as well, and there's an island administrator. It's easiest if we all work in the same building."

"Yes, I see that." He released her hand, but kept his eyes fixed on her face. *Management 101. Let them know they have your full attention and admiration. If they're an attractive woman, even an older one, so much the better.* "Anyway, I did want to speak to you, so this is fortuitous. Thank you for stopping."

"My pleasure. And since I did stop, I'd like to invite you to a barbecue Friday night at my home. There will be several others there whom you might enjoy meeting, and my husband grills excellent chicken. Will you come?"

*Will I? Hell, yes.* "Thank you, I'd be delighted. My social calendar isn't exactly overflowing," he chuckled. He could do self-deprecating very well. "So I'm sure I'm free."

"Good. We'll look for you about six." She handed him a business card that already had an address written on the back, then turned an enormous smile on him. "Bye," she said, and walked to her car.

After she drove off Adam continued up the road to the B&B, thinking that this could be a heaven-sent opportunity to meet the people who mattered.

It looked like they were eager to meet him, too. Good. Casual seemed to be the order of the day on this island, so the more he could do his bridge-building in informal situations, the more smoothly it should all go.

As for how she knew so much about his movements and plans, well, better not think too much about that. Or her comment that they were watching him. It was creepy, this little place, the way people knew things.

*She looks vaguely familiar. I wonder if I've met her before somewhere.* He concluded that he was remembering her from the barn dance.

Back at the B&B he checked around for Stacie but didn't see her anywhere, so he went to his room and changed into the new jeans. Then he got out his laptop. Ignoring the button that would launch his email program, he began a new spreadsheet to keep track of billable expenses. Clothing, for instance. Necessary for winning over the locals.

# Chapter 7

Thursday afternoon found Stacie at the Windon Harbor Activity Center, staying in shape.

Well, sort of. Somehow the yoga version of staying in shape seemed to work in a whole different way from the housework version, or even the walk-into-town version. Stacie had a notion that this should be getting easier over time. Since it clearly wasn't, maybe she should cut her losses.

Still, enough of her friends were also here struggling to bend in ways the human body was never meant to bend that she figured she might as well stick with it. Every week it was, "Should I go? Do I want to go? Is it doing me any good?" And every week she found herself back here on her mat.

At least there was Savasana to look forward to. Corpse pose, when for ten blissful minutes she could lie there, knowing that no guests could find her, no housework could demand her attention, no errant thoughts of, for instance, Adam Fraser, would dare assail her.

Didn't stop errant thoughts while she was in downward dog, though.

Stacie was torn in different directions. The man was okay, in a big-city, corporate sort of way, sure.

*You're kidding whom?*

Okay, maybe he was sort of more than okay. Maybe he was sort of hot. But surely she'd had enough life experience by now to resist hot, especially when it came packaged with dangerous.

At her age she wasn't going for just-the-sex-please. Or rather, she could, and sometimes she thought that if the right male of the species came along and offered, she would. But she always seemed to end up considering the long term consequences. And besides, when was the last time the aforementioned right male had appeared in her sights? It had been a long, long time.

Plus, if she wanted anything at all – and a lot of the time she wasn't sure she did – it was the long-term-commitment thing, aka marriage, family. She and Jess were the only ones unattached in her circle of friends. She surveyed some of those friends through her legs, upside down. Were they any happier than she? Hard to tell. Most of the time Stacie was perfectly content with the life she had. She released downward dog and flowed – *now, that was a joke* – into the next position in the Sun Salutation.

Somehow the right guy hadn't come along. She'd been proposed to, once, back when she was still in university. Another relationship had blown up after five years and no proposal. Looking back she couldn't say she was sorry. But here she was at thirty-four, single, no prospects.

By the time her mother was thirty-four, Stacie herself was twelve. What did that say?

Of course, she *could* go for just-the-sex. She sighed.

After the class she met Jane and Donna at the Brew Place. She had known Donna, Jane, and Jess since high school. There weren't many secrets between them. The miracle, Stacie thought, was that they all still liked each other. Maybe even better than in high school. *Must come with maturity*, she mused.

As usual, Doreen was on duty. "Skinny latte, chai latte, small decaf?"

All three of them grinned at her. "You're good," Donna said.

"So surprise me. Order something different."

"Nope," Jane put in. "Consistency implies an examined life. That you've attained a certain level of maturity in your tastes. Anyway, it's nice that you always know. There has to be some compensation for living in a gossipy small town. Not the nicest day to sit outdoors, worse luck."

"I'd rather stay in. It's spitting," Donna added. The weather had turned and rain threatened. They'd all noticed the clouds building up to the southwest. Mid-May, not full-on summer yet.

The women paid and headed for a free table by the window. "So, Sweetie," Jane said, staring straight at Stacie. "I hear you've been getting some ... shall we say romancing?"

Stacie groaned. "What part of 'do not say anything' does Jess not get? The last thing I need is the reputation for putting out for the guests."

"If I can move my legs tomorrow it'll be a miracle. Cobbler pose kills me." Jane put on her inquisition face, the one she probably used when she had a recalcitrant witness in the box. You didn't cross Jane when she was in full-blown lawyer mode. "Come on, Stace, tell all. I've been married something like fifteen years. I need some excitement."

"And that really is getting close to TMI, you know."

Big grin from Jane. "Don't worry about Spencer and me, I'm just venting. You know, when you get married, somehow you never think that fifteen years down the road, then thirty, then fifty, this is still the only guy who's ever going to be in your bed. Sometime soon, other men won't even notice anymore. So when a friend has something on with a tall, dark, handsome stranger – well, maybe not dark – it's cause for celebration. Vicarious thrills, all that. Spill, girlfriend."

Doreen arrived with their drinks and sat down in the vacant chair. "We're all ears."

*No escape.* Stacie buried her head in her arms to add a little bit of drama, then looked up. "Okay. He grabbed me and landed a fast one Tuesday morning. Like split second. Followed by an equally fast swear word. Later that afternoon, same thing, only not fast. He's good," she reported. "If either of you'd like to queue up."

"Not me." Donna rubbed her tummy. Still flat, but they all knew she was expecting her third. "Not with Junior here. Does something to your fidelity genes." She sipped the decaf. "Good," she said to Doreen. "I could almost pretend it has octane in it."

"Face it," Jane added. "We're all the ultimate boring good girls. Love our men, no interest in running around on them. I think they put something in the island's water."

"Yeah, even Mom," Stacie added. "Since she met Bill she doesn't even *see* other men. Not that at her age she should —"

"Oh, come on," Doreen put in. "Your mom's not old. She's not even sixty yet."

"And who says it's all over because you're over fifty?" Donna added around a luxurious stretch. "Or sixty? Life's long. I plan to live it to the full, if you catch my meaning."

Doreen, who was well into her sixties, didn't say anything, but chuckled.

"Some of us could do with a marriage that gets started in the first place," Stacie grumbled. "Or maybe not. I'm usually content. I've got my lovely house and guests to mother and pamper, pals to hang out with. Savings slowly growing with no kids to feed. Why would I want a man?"

"You have to ask? It has been too long."

"Perhaps you'd like to tell us how you reacted to being the recipient of those kisses?"

"Yeah, like, are we talking tongue?"

"Skilled." Her friends had always seen more than Stacie wanted them to. She sighed. "Ever have a wonderful, perfect night's sleep, then when you wake up it's like all your senses have come alive? Sunshine and birds and stuff."

"Oh, boy." Doreen got up and headed for the counter to serve another group.

Donna and Jane both looked at her as if they'd been fed the best chocolate mousse ever. Donna especially seemed about to bounce in her seat. "He got to you! Oh, I'm so *glad*!" She reached across the table to give Stacie's hands a squeeze.

Jane had always been the most serious of them. "But what does it mean? First, he's the Enemy. Second, he's gone in a few days. Is he worth a fling?" She shrugged. "Maybe so. There haven't been many opportunities for flings on the island, not since we were teenagers and every guy we knew was potential fling material. No new breeding stock, so to speak – and I don't mean that literally, okay? So, what are you going to do about it?"

Stacie grinned. "Part of me thinks I could do a Mata Hari on him. You know, seduce him into my bed and get all his secrets out of him. But straightforward seems to work just as well, with less wear and tear on my sheets. I asked him straight out who he works for, and he told me. He was incensed that we'd dare improve 'their' forest – called it trespassing."

"The only thing they have is legal title. We're the ones who take care of the forest."

"And use it. It's just board feet of timber to them."

"I bet they haven't even looked into how economical it would be to log. The upper slopes are almost vertical."

"And the trees aren't all *that* big."

"Trust me," Stacie said. "Mom has all these facts at her fingertips. Anyway, the latest is that he's been ordered to stay here for another couple of weeks, which tells me that something's happening at the end of that time. I didn't ask because the kissing thing kind of got in the way. But Mom's invited him to a social evening Friday, and she'll get it all out of him."

"Your mom's an irresistible force when she's on a campaign, that's for sure. Remember when she decided we ought to wear those God-awful black gowns for grad?"

"We were devastated. All our lovely prom dresses hidden by those hideous things. Like bats."

"We fought with everything we had. But she won the parents."

"You're right. We never had a chance."

"And Jess flashed the audience, opened up the grad gown and showed her dress. So fast no one could stop her."

"No one wanted to. Mom was way wrong about that one."

"At least in a year or two she'd retreated. My kid brother got to wear his tux. Purple cummerbund and all."

"I think the principal couldn't stand the grumbling any longer. Not that it did us any good."

Stacie gratefully let the conversation return to more normal channels, so the heat in her face could have a chance to die back. Because the problem wasn't whether Adam Fraser was worth a tumble in the hay. She was clear on that point. It was more about all the other stuff. The need-to-take-care-of-you stuff. The happy-you're-around stuff. The flutter-in-the-heart-region stuff. That, she needed to think about.

As the three women were taking their mugs over to the bussing station, Jane said, "So, what's the mystery man up to today?"

"You didn't hear?" Donna let out a guffaw. "Susan's got him for a hike in the Forest. Her all day one. With new hiking boots. Oh man, is he going to suffer!" They exchanged a three-way high five – something they'd become adept at over the years – waved to Doreen, and headed home.

Oh, man, had he suffered.

He was fairly sure he hadn't whimpered. But it had been a near thing.

The clinic had seen to the blisters. The tour company's van had dropped him at the hotel. He'd checked in and somehow made it up the flight of stairs to his room. Just as Stacie had promised, his bags were lined up neatly in front of the luggage rack. He'd ignored them. He'd been soaked through from the downpour, and freezing. He'd peeled out of his wet clothes and left them all in a pile on the floor. He downed a couple of ibuprofen, both for the assorted pains assaulting his body and for a headache that had been niggling for the last hour or so, then decided he had to manage to stay on his feet for another few minutes and ran the hottest shower he could stand.

He'd rummaged in his suitcases on his knees – something he'd never admit to anybody, ever, it was so humiliating – to find his other jeans and a shirt. After struggling back to his feet he took pity on his anorak and hung it up, then found a section of yesterday's Toronto newspaper – disregarding the business section he'd kept the paper for – to put the boots on. They looked sad and worn out and soggy, sitting there.

They'd felt so *good* in the store.

The rest of his hiking wardrobe was heading for the laundry tomorrow, if he could walk that far. At the moment he thought it likely he'd never walk again.

He hobbled to the little fridge and found a beer in the minibar, then sank into the lone chair.

Adam sat in the window of his room at the hotel, looked out across the Harbor, and wondered what he'd actually gotten himself into. Not today, but over the last week. And maybe over the last eighteen years or so.

He sighed and reviewed his day.

In making all those beautiful plans for learning and winning over the tour guide, he'd never considered his fitness level.

*Know thyself.* He laughed shortly.

It had started out well. Stacie had assured him she'd see to transferring his bags over to the hotel. He'd even been downstairs early enough to fuel up on one of her sensational breakfasts. He'd chosen the pancakes with fresh, local sausage and maple syrup.

The tour company van had picked him up at the B&B. He'd been surprised to find that the guide was a young woman in her twenties named Susan, hair back in a saucy ponytail that reminded him of Stacie's – but then altogether too much reminded him of Stacie – which she'd pulled through the little opening at the back of her baseball cap. Very well developed calves under her hiking shorts, he noted, and felt the first little brush of unease. The other two hikers were also in their late twenties, he'd guessed, a couple who both had the reddish, slightly weather-beaten faces of people who spend a lot of time in the outdoors. He couldn't see their calves since they wore those fancy pants that let you zip off the bottom of the legs, but he had an uneasy feeling that theirs were well-developed, too.

The first part of the hike was okay. From the beginning the Douglas firs dwarfed him. They were magnificent and smelled like Christmas in the damp air. Periodically they'd come to an open area with a few leathery leaved trees Susan said were called arbutus. From one of these open spaces they were able to look out toward the north, and he got his first hint of pastures, lakes, and the west coast of Malaspina Island. He liked the view and resolved to get into the interior of the island somehow, before he left.

It was misty, but he had his new anorak with him, and after a while, as they began to ascend, the little bit of precipitation that got through the trees felt good on his face. He felt a bit of a pull in his legs, but the slope wasn't steep and he was keeping up just fine.

An hour later, he'd looked back on this innocent, early-in-the-hike self with pity. Because it hadn't stayed gentle.

The other two bounded joyously up the trail like mountain goats. Susan held back politely. He had trudged, no other word for it. They went up and around and up some more, then down to the beach on the south coast. They'd been on the trail for a couple of hours when Susan called a halt for lunch. He'd halted already about ten times, ostensibly to admire the views, in reality to try to get some air into his lungs.

When the rain started, he'd whipped up his hood – and realized why everyone out here wore baseball caps. The rim of the cap kept the water off your face, didn't it? Only he didn't have one. So the back of his head and his neck were dry, and all the rain ran right down into his eyes. Susan didn't comment.

Lunch was a pleasant affair under a tarp Susan pitched on the beach. The young couple were from Portland and had no interest in talking to him, but he fired questions at Susan and she seemed to enjoy answering them. From her he learned a lot about the forest, the types of trees, even the commercial value of them. She told him how the islands had formed, discussed the earthquake risks, pointed out the other islands you could see from the south coast.

It was after lunch that the boots started hurting. They'd gone up – more pauses – then gone back downhill, and that's when it got to his toes. Later he found blisters on the ends of his toes, as well as on the backs of his heels and one nasty one right on the bottom of his left foot. That was the one they'd lanced at the clinic. But that relief was still hours away. In the meantime, he found himself on the top of something that looked like a vertical cliff that had to be two or three stories high, and he was supposed to get down it somehow.

The mountain goats from Portland balanced on the edges of rocks, slid down sheer slopes, and landed at the bottom in about five minutes.

It took him twenty.

Within the first five minutes his legs were shaking so badly they threatened to simply dump him at the bottom, probably with a broken neck. He'd inched his way, grabbing at trees, once freezing up completely when there wasn't a tree to hold onto. Susan stuck with him, her face in neutral, telling him where to put his feet and hands. The couple waited at the bottom, chatting away and enjoying an afternoon snack.

He'd made it to the bottom of the cliff without anything broken. And he'd longed for that rest and afternoon snack, too, but Susan, who around then took on attributes of a slave driver, said they were running late and had to push on. She handed him an energy bar, the rain came down, and away they went, Susan in the lead, the young couple at her heels. The blisters formed and grew. He gritted his teeth and barely kept up.

If anyone had noticed his discomfort – and he'd lay any odds that they all had – no one commented. Somehow he'd made it back to the van and collapsed in the front seat for the fifteen minute drive back to Windon Harbor. Susan dropped the couple off at their B&B. Not *his* B&B, he thought with relief, he wouldn't want Stacie to get a first-hand account of the out-of-shape laughingstock from back east who thought he could handle a little hike. Then without comment or question Susan drove him straight to the clinic, and waited while they dealt with his feet.

And now here he sat by his window, every muscle screaming, hardly able to walk, wondering if there was any redeeming feature at all about this ghastly day.

He had no doubt at all that word would spread like wildfire about the wonderful adventure he'd had.

Which meant Stacie would know. Any minute now, probably.

He banished the idea of going out in the town with his feet and muscles in this state, and without moving reached for the phone to call the hotel restaurant. Ordered up a club sandwich and fries. Suggested they use a pass key to deliver it, because no way was he getting out of his chair. No way would he ever move again, probably.

A few minutes later his phone rang. It was Susan. To suggest he buy himself a pair of sport sandals. His feet might not be happy campers in shoes for a while.

Glumly he flipped open his laptop. He'd managed to ignore work for a whole day. Maybe that was the redeeming feature?

Equally glumly, he closed the laptop again. Why on earth would he want to make this day worse?

Funny thing was, two hours later, his stomach full of an excellent club sandwich and the surprise bonus of a fat piece of carrot cake, feeling relaxed from a couple of beers, he looked back over the day and thought, *What a fantastic experience.*

# Chapter 8

Adam slept well that night, and woke up feeling sore in every muscle in his body, but otherwise good. For breakfast, he munched the energy bar Susan had given him the day before, washed down with coffee from the drip maker in his room, then set out.

First stop – *surprise, surprise* – the General Store. He was greeted like an old friend. He came out with a baseball cap, a couple of T-shirts, a pair of sport sandals – on his feet, over socks – and a swimming suit. The swimming suit wasn't exactly what he'd had in mind since it came most of the way down his thighs and the clerk explained it was for surfing – *In this climate? Are they kidding?* – but it would get him to the hotel's hot tub, and it was that or a skimpy Speedo style. He wasn't about to appear in public in one of those. He knew what the last few years had done to his waistline.

He dropped the new clothes in his room and scooped up his pile of laundry. He put the whole lot, plus his laptop, into his large rolling suitcase and set out for the Laundromat, which, according to the map in his room, was a couple of blocks away from the center of town.

Once there he got the washing machine going and settled down to work. There was no direct Laundromat-Toronto connection, since there was no WiFi, but he could tackle the report he had to send back east about the island, the mood of the town, the likely strategies for getting the logging done with a minimum of fuss.

He stopped pecking away and leaned back, frowning a little. The problem was, it was becoming increasingly clear to him that he didn't want to write this report. He couldn't see any way to avoid fuss – or all hell breaking loose. He couldn't see any way to avoid hurting and disappointing these people who were so welcoming. He'd only been around for a week, but in that time he'd had coffee at Java on the Square once or twice a day, which always resulted in someone drifting over to chat with him. He'd met the town manager, been to a dance, been on a hike – the less thought about that the better, probably – and even had an invitation to a barbecue.

And then there was Stacie, but that put making contact with the locals into a whole different context. One he wasn't about to put in his report back to Toronto.

Windon Harbor was growing on him, even though, as he'd been assured, it was still a little the worse for wear after the winter. He liked the harbor with its marina and whale watching and ferry dock. He liked sitting still in the Square in the middle of the day and not worrying about whether someone would think he was slacking off. He liked lingering over coffee, chatting. He liked not being in meetings six hours a day.

He liked knowing that Halloran House Bed and Breakfast was only a couple of blocks down the main road, turn left and go up the hill.

He wasn't entirely sure how it had happened, but he knew that he didn't want the logging to happen. And he was damned if he could see how to avoid it.

A lousy context for writing his report, but he did what he could to put his mind back in corporate-think. All the points he made sounded scientific. All the perspectives he emphasized sounded like he was one hundred percent behind Callaway.

*Hell, I could make a full page list about Stacie alone.*

No. He wouldn't think that particular thought.

Sitting still turned out to be not such a good idea. When the washing machine finished and he tried to stand from the molded plastic chair, he realized how quickly muscles could stiffen. He rose like an old man and hobbled over to shift his laundry from the washer to the dryer.

Later, after he'd limped back to the hotel, he put on the new swim shorts, wrapped a towel around his neck, and headed for the hot tub. After half an hour of bliss he felt revived and ready to take on the day.

Adam turned up in Stacie's guest lounge Friday just after 1:00, for all the world as if he hadn't moved out the morning before. "I wasn't sure what the protocol was, if I want to see you but I don't live here. So I just came in." He shrugged. "I sort of hoped I'd catch you."

"Generally, my friends phone or …" She wasn't ready to mention the private entrance to her apartment. *Still,* she thought, *that sweater looks good on him. With eyes like that, this man should not be allowed near the color green.*

"I wanted to ask you about the work bee," he said. "Maybe over a cup of coffee?"

"Don't give me that abandoned puppy look. Coffee service ended an hour ago, but if there's any left, you can have it. No, sit," she added, waving him into a chair. "I'll bring it."

"Someone told you."

She grinned at him. "This is the island. I'm impressed that you made it here from the hotel."

She was back in a couple of minutes with a mug of coffee. She sat down across from him "You hobbled all the way over here to ask about the work bee?"

"Explain how this works. How'd you know I hobbled?"

"Well, let's see. Susan said she took you to the clinic to have them check a blister or two. Jess saw you this morning through the Laundromat window and she said it looked like you might be stiff, since you seemed to be having a little bit of trouble with standing vertical. The hotel dining room told my friend Donna, who told me, that you got room service last night and didn't show up for breakfast. Which I'm not feeding you, in case you had any ideas in that direction. And while the sandals and socks are not considered a fashion statement around here, I concede they're practical at the moment."

He pulled at the coffee like it was manna from heaven, even though it had to be hopelessly stale by then. He settled back in his chair, crossing one ankle over the other knee. "This is something I don't think I could get used to. The obsessive interest in my movements. Did you know the town manager stopped me when I was walking back here Wednesday? She knew exactly where to find me, the more I think about it the more I'm sure of it."

"She probably did. I assume you're going to the barbecue?"

"You know about the barbecue." It was a statement.

Stacie sniggered.

"Of course I'm going. Will you be there?"

She shook her head. "Previous plans. Now, tell me why you're here. And don't ..." she glanced around, but no one was within earshot. "Don't say it's because I'm hot, or we're hot."

"It's not. Damn, woman, you make good coffee."

"Told you before, locally roasted, organic, all that. Anywhere in Windon Harbor would give you the same."

"Not as good as this." He took another sip. "I'm here to pick your brains. I want to take part in this work bee thing. But I wanted to know more about it before I leap blindly into it. Can you fill me in?"

She gave him an 'are you serious?' look. "The work bee."

"The work bee. You know, the thing that happens tomorrow when the whole town turns out to make the place pretty."

*Would the full list warn him off? Should she warn him off? The man was positively wagging his tail with enthusiasm.*

*Tail wagging. Hmm.*

Stacie shook her head – more for her own benefit than for his, but he didn't need to know that.

"Glutton for punishment, aren't you? Okay, here's how it plays. In the morning we fill the hanging baskets over at Phyllis's place – she runs the garden center and raises the plants. There'll also be a crew to unpack the banners where we store them at the Barn and iron them and mend them if they need it and thread them on the poles for hanging. Other crews will be in the Square or along the waterfront cleaning. We'll power wash the Square and the waterfront and anything else that needs doing. We'll also be turning the flower beds and adding compost. There are flower beds all over downtown, wherever there's a little vacant space someone digs a flower bed. That takes up the morning.

"Then at noon there's a barbecue picnic in the park on the waterfront. In the afternoon we hang the banners and the hanging baskets, refresh the soil and plant the planters all over the Square. Finish the flower beds. The floral display by the ferry dock takes a lot of person-power. That's the big one that runs from the ferry to the marina. There are a few other areas that get some touch-ups, but that's the bulk of it."

She could almost see him cringe, but he gamely said, "Sounds like fun. Where do I sign up?"

Stacie snorted a laugh. "Don't you think maybe you should do a reality check? You're not the kind of person to have calluses on his hands. The men usually end up hauling dirt and climbing ladders and hoisting banners and things. It can be seriously physical work. You might have to use your feet, too, and that could be iffy. Plus your muscles may not be ready for it."

"I think I might enjoy it."

*Damn, he looks good in those jeans.*

*Do not think that thought, Stacie.*

"The thing is," he continued, "I'm starting to feel more comfortable around here."

"Oh, yeah? Even with the spies on every corner? Not to mention the blisters."

He shrugged. "We all have to start somewhere. So this thing is happening, and since I'm sort of a long-term visitor now, I thought it'd be good to pitch in."

"If you're sure, they'll be assigning work parties about 9:30 tomorrow morning. That'll be at the Admin Building on the west side of the Square. You'll see everyone there, it's easy to find."

*And you don't have a clue what you're letting yourself in for,* she thought.

When he finished his coffee, she ushered him right out the front door and watched him hobble down the drive. "You might want to see about some work gloves," she called. "Try the General Store." Stacie grinned to herself, then returned to her work.

Adam safely out of the way, without a repeat of the kiss-and-clench of two days ago, Stacie took some time to mull over his visit. Something had changed. He didn't seem quite so stick-up-the-ass. He actually seemed to have some genuine enthusiasm for the work bee, which made no sense whatsoever. He seemed almost ... relaxed. Maybe even a little happy. Damn, he was turning out to be nice to be around. Maybe her mother's plan was already working, and the island was starting to get to him.

*Maybe he was starting to get to her.*

*Starting to?*

Stacie picked up her phone. "Mom? He wants to sign up for the Bee."

"Seriously? What kind of shape is he in today?"

"Shall we say, not comfortable in his skin? I think he's discovered some new muscles. And blistered feet. If he does turn up, maybe we can use him on the assignments desk or something. I'd hate to kill him."

"I'll put out the word. We'll be sure he has an interesting time. We'll love him to death and keep him busy. Record keeping's not a bad idea. It'll put him in touch with a lot of different people."

"You're a rescuer. Maybe you should volunteer at the pound."

"And you've inherited too many of my genes, Stacie. I hear there's something going on. Want to 'fess up?"

"Mom," Stacie shot back, "in what way is it fair that you hear things that even my best friend swore not to talk about?"

She could almost hear her mother's casual shrug. "Don't blame Jess. I have my ways, and I extrapolate. Just be careful. I don't want you hurt, baby."

"I don't want that any more than you do. I have to admit, I'm glad he's out of here. There's a temptation element that I didn't expect. You know, Mom, in a lot of ways he's okay. Sure, that big city vibe gets a little tiresome. But it's like he's trying so hard to fit in, and he hasn't got a clue. It's kinda sweet."

"It's not sweet. It's part of their plan." Abby was stern. "Don't let him draw you in, daughter."

Stacie laughed. "Once a mom, always a mom, eh? Thanks for the warning. I do have thirty-four years of experience. Spotty experience, maybe, but I'm not a babe in the woods."

"You are to me. Love you."

Her conversation with her mother over, she headed outdoors to supervise the re-installation of the pump in the fish pond.

Abby had everything prepared, including the guests. She'd invited the mayor and his wife, one of the town councilors and her husband, the sixty-ish owner/manager of the hotel and his wife, and Gladys, the head of the planning committee for the work bee, who was generally considered ageless. She'd hoped to include Roger McMillan, the island administrator, and his wife, but they'd been busy. She figured she'd rounded up a good cross section of the community, as well as putting Adam in touch with the political hierarchy of the island.

She'd left directions to her house at the hotel for him. She'd marinated the chicken in lemon and rosemary and made potato salad. The wine was breathing, the beer, from a microbrewery on the mainland, was chilled. Knowing her company, she'd put bowls of chips and dip around the patio, with a token plate of raw vegetables, just in case.

While Nathan's Forest didn't fall within her jurisdiction, the forest was crucial to the health of the town economy, and Abby would be involved in every step of the fight to save it. Abby didn't kid herself, and didn't kid the mayor and council, about the odds of stopping the logging of Nathan's Forest. Callaway Forest Products owned the land and had the timber rights.

As well, she wasn't optimistic about convincing the provincial government to step in. The current administration was all about big business. Malaspina's tourist industry kept the island afloat, but compared to a corporation whose annual profit was greater than the whole combined income of her island? Dream on.

So, the only viable plan involved salvaging what they could. Of course they'd try for complete protection for Nathan's, but by whatever calculations she did, that was not going to happen. But maybe they could throw up a few roadblocks … probably not literal ones, although that remained a possibility. And maybe they could preserve some amenities for the island, in the name of good will and corporate citizenship and all that.

Because of this complicated situation, it was important that Adam Fraser have a good time on Malaspina. At the barbecue. In the forest. Kayaking, horseback riding, dancing, socializing, anything else the island might offer up to him. Give him enough enjoyment, enough challenge, to make him realize that although their way of life was different from his, it was still good and valuable.

Abby much preferred to catch her flies with honey. She hadn't been thrilled when she heard about the blisters, although she thought the sore muscles might work in their favor. At least the tour service had been efficient and thoughtful, without making a big deal out of it. Door to door, forest to clinic to hotel. And she knew the hotel restaurant had thrown in a complimentary dessert with his dinner.

She'd left getting to her house up to him. It was only about six blocks from the hotel, so she figured he'd make it. She went out to meet him when he came up her driveway only a few minutes late. "Well timed. Everyone's around back. Come on, I'll introduce you."

Adam was hardly limping by this time, although he still wore the sandals with socks for extra padding. "It's great to be here. I haven't ventured too much into the residential part of the town. This is delightful."

Abby wondered about the sincerity of a man who used the word 'delightful'. Wasn't that more a woman's word? But he was probably nervous, dredging up the manners he'd learned at his mother's knee. She liked that he was a little on edge, this man who dared to have something going on with her daughter, never mind holding her island's fate in his hands.

"Thanks. I prefer older neighborhoods, although there are some nice newer subdivisions, too. This is the perfect time of year, if you ask me, when you get the peonies and lilac blooming. And the rhodos, of course." At his carefully neutral face she added, with gestures, "That's a peony, that's a lilac. The big bush by the front door is a late blooming rhododendron. We're lucky with the weather this year, a lot of rain can destroy the blooms. But so far, so good. Frank, Alice, come meet Adam." To Adam she added, "The Bentleys own the hotel. You may have seen them around." She waved the couple over. "That's Bill, my husband, over at the barbecue. You probably won't dislodge him."

Frank got there first. An older man, Frank clearly had found his niche in the hospitality industry. "Welcome to Malaspina. We certainly hope you're comfortable. We're not quite the same as Stacie's, of course, but we do our best."

Adam grasped the outstretched hand. "Thank you. Very comfortable, and a great view." He turned to Alice, who looked motherly, and offered his hand. "Ma'am."

"Pleased to meet you at last."

"Let me guess. You've heard lots about me." Adam gave Alice a smile and a shrug. "Seems like everyone in town has."

"Let's find you something to drink."

And the party was on. Abby left Adam to the ministrations of Bill and her other guests and headed for the kitchen, knowing that his 'ma'am' was bound to win him a brownie point or two from the motherly Alice.

Adam had fully expected a political component to the barbecue, and he wasn't disappointed. But it wasn't until the group had mingled over drinks and chips and the tantalizing smell of grilling chicken for an hour that everyone finally gathered around a large, round table on the deck and the first exploratory comments came at him.

*Exploratory comments? No one could say the island specialized in subtlety.*

The mayor led off with, "So tell us what your company's planning to do with Nathan's Forest."

Immediate silence around the table. All eyes were on him.

"Please, I want you all to understand that I'm not a forester, I'm in administration, finance. Nothing can be decided until our surveyors get a chance to look the land over. Right now we only have crude estimates of the value of the timber."

"So you didn't get a chance to measure the board feet when you were hiking in there yesterday?" Bill said jovially.

Adam felt himself blush. "I think you know I didn't," he said. "In fact, I think I'm the laughingstock of Windon Harbor." Abby shook her head with a smile – she had a lovely smile, and Adam once again wondered why she looked familiar – and handed him the platter of chicken. He served himself, then passed the platter on to the mayor's wife and continued. "It's a resource for our company, and while no one's been to survey it, the timber should be of harvestable size."

"Magnificent in there," Yvonne Wilkins put in. Yvonne was a town councilor, her husband Richard had a boat in the fishing fleet. "I haven't hiked much of it in a couple of years, but I remember that grove – you know the one, Abby, where that little creek goes down ..."

"Yes, I remember. Cedars that somehow missed being logged the first time around. That was about eighty or ninety years ago," she explained to Adam. "Magnificent now. You can get in there and think you're in an enchanted land. It's lowland, too," she added. "Easy for most of the younger ones to get to, and at least possible for the rest of us."

"It's been a while since I've been up where Susan takes her tours. What did you think?" Frank took a swallow of beer and leaned back, intent on Adam.

"Well, it was a challenge." He let his gaze sweep the table. The entire group of them nodded, the women sympathetically. For the first time he wondered how much of this casual backyard gathering was actually orchestrated. "The good news for me is that it meant I had to stop – frequently enough to be embarrassing, to be honest. In a way I'm glad. The views … I'd never seen anything quite like it. There was an eagle … I've never seen an eagle in the wild before, I don't think. And the ocean from up there, it looked like you could see forever. I can't say I'm over the aches and pains completely, but … well, it was sensational."

He sensed that he had their full attention, and maybe that they'd all been holding their breaths until he finished. There seemed to be a general release, and the dishes of chicken, salads, and rolls made their way around the table again.

"Then you have some idea of why we're not thrilled you're here. Not you personally, but you representing Callaway. We on the island love that forest. We don't want to see it cut down."

"I can understand that. I hadn't really had a sense of it before. I knew it was well outside of Windon Harbor, but it didn't occur to me that you could actually see it from here."

"And what a clearcut does to a view … you're not just messing with the landscape, young man, you're threatening our main industry." That was Bill, pulling age rank.

"Which is tourism," Gladys added.

Adam reached into the center of the table for yet another of Abby and Bill's sensational chicken thighs. Life in a hotel had its drawbacks, one of them being that restaurant food was already getting old. "Here's the best I can tell you. We think it would be a good idea to hold some sort of an open meeting, a forum, so everyone on the island who wants to has a chance to have a say."

"How many weeks do you have?" Abby asked. "That's probably several thousand people."

"Oh." Another bite of chicken. Ambrosia. "Well, maybe something involving written submissions or one person representing a neighborhood or something? We have a meeting scheduled on Monday ..." nodding to Abby, "... with Mr. McMillan." Abby nodded in acknowledgment. "Anyway, I'll give you more detail then about Callaway, and if you agree we can start planning, maybe sort out the protocol. Some of our senior people want to come out and meet you, and we'll get some of our foresters here, too. We have a crew that specializes in west coast timber."

"I'm sure you know Roger and I have already been talking about the best way to handle Callaway, so we'll be ready for you." He took that as a warning. He was sure she had meant it that way. "Dessert, anyone?" Abby was on her feet. She bustled around the table, clearing plates. Alice and Gladys got up to help, and Adam did, too, but was promptly waved back into his seat. "You're still company. This time, you get served. Next time, you help."

He liked the idea of next time. He shouldn't, but he did.

He stayed with the men and Yvonne and listened to talk of the challenges around fishing quotas, how the tourist season was shaping up, whether rezoning to allow a new compost plant on the west side of the island would go through. He listened intently, realizing that while it might be a form of paradise he'd never encountered before, it took work and commitment to keep it that way.

He realized, too, that he was developing a niggling interest in being a part of it.

The doorbell to her private apartment rang about 10:00 Friday evening. Stacie frowned and thought about ignoring it. But on an island it could be anyone at all and maybe something important, so finally she hauled herself up from her sofa, where she'd idly been watching nothing much on TV, and went to the door.

Adam. Looking totally unenthusiastic. Couldn't the guy muster a little, teeny smile?

"Hi," he said.

"Hello. What's wrong?"

"Does something have to be wrong? I felt like walking somewhere and you crossed my mind. May I come in?"

"It's the frown. I see you found my door." She turned and led the way into her little living room.

"Figured you'd have your own entrance. There weren't that many possibilities."

"Weren't you at a barbecue tonight?"

"I suppose the entire island knows it. You probably publish transcripts or something." He sounded as if he totally disapproved, of her, of the island, of himself for turning up at her door. Wouldn't it have been easier for him to go straight back to the hotel and go to sleep like normal people?

*Easier for whom? Give the nice man a welcome, Stacie.*

She sighed. She'd hoped to keep her apartment out of bounds, at least until she could be the one inviting him, instead of having him turn up this way. "Then what are you grouchy about? Smiling isn't big for you, is it?"

That made him stop and think. "I suppose it depends on whether there's something to smile about?"

"Calling on someone, especially at this hour, might qualify, if you think about it."

They stared at each other a moment. "You're right," he said finally. "I apologize." Still no smile.

She gave him an exasperated look. She had options, she knew. The best one, bar none, was to send him packing. At this hour, and given her work schedule, she really didn't need the aggravation that his presence promised. He looked totally annoyed that he was here in her living room. So why the hell *was* he in her living room?

If there were other things she might want to do with him, she decided not to explore them.

She waved at the sofa. "Have a seat. Just channel surfing." She perched.

He sat. Close. "Sounds boring," he said. "Let's try something else." Before she had time to react he had a hand on her shoulder and another one on her midriff and was pulling her back on the sofa, and then his mouth was on hers and she continued her education about his lips and tongue, and his hands weren't staying modestly where they'd started, either, but were on the move. And every molecule of Stacie approved.

When they surfaced for air, some long seconds later, hands had found their way under shirts, and brains – *at least my brain,* she thought – had basically fried. "And to think," she somehow got out. "We don't even like each other."

"Did I say that?"

"You implied. Strongly." She scooted out of his reach. They both flopped, heads resting against the back of the sofa. "I guess it's possible that the barbecue was alcoholic, given how little you want to be here. Despite … this."

"Two or three glasses of wine. Good wine, I might add. I was told it's local to British Columbia."

"Enough to make you feel justified to come over here and feel me up."

"Truth is," he said, "I haven't a clue why I'm here. Or why I keep allowing my control to slip where you're concerned."

"Maybe you could pull out some of your fancy management tools and analyze it."

He looked exasperated but didn't answer.

She pursued the advantage. "Are you freaked?"

"A little." He frowned off into the distance, not looking at her. Not touching her. Not connecting with her. But leaving her with the uneasy feeling that he could pounce again at any moment. And an equally uneasy feeling that she might not mind it if he did.

"Is your mind on anything specific, Mr. Fraser? Something big going on in your life? Ruling out the possibility that it could have anything at all to do with me. Maybe you got the local powers that be to agree that cutting down Nathan's Forest would be the best thing since tampons?" His face positively flamed at that. She grinned. "Bring in business and loggers and all that?"

Whatever his skin was giving away about him, his voice was calm. "No. Something tells me Mrs. Fox is too on top of things for that. What's more, I'm not sure I'd see that as a happy outcome."

Her grin fizzled. Stacie pulled herself upright and looked at him. "Tell more."

"Easier to tell with you down here." He pulled her closer to him, semi-sprawled across the sofa cushions. "I seem to like it here on your island."

"You seem to? No, you don't."

"You're never going to cut me any slack, are you? Yes, I think I do. I'm in a position to be more sure of that than you are, so take my word for it, okay? I like the people I've met. I like the forest. I sort of like the town … it's growing on me. I might like it better if there were more places to shop than the General Store."

"There are one or two others. You just haven't found them yet."

"And incidentally, I'd be grateful if you'd shelve your label for me. I'm not the enemy. Oh, no you don't," he said. "Don't bother denying it. That's your code name for me, isn't it? The Enemy. You're not making my job any easier."

"I still don't know what your job is, exactly."

"You don't? It was discussed at the barbecue, so of course I figured by now you'd have all the details. I'm here to arrange a meeting so that Callaway and the people on the island can talk. Is that so complicated?"

"You think I believe that's all? You could do that from Toronto. You're trying to get into our minds, aren't you? Scheming about how to cut down the forest with the minimum of fuss."

He was silent. She had scored. She wished she hadn't.

"And now you find that you like the forest? Most people don't go into rhapsodies and put their corporate positions at risk over a few trees."

"It's not the trees," he said. "It's the way people talk about the trees. It's personal. So it's forcing me to look at the forest from a different perspective."

The man was a continual source of fascination. Who'd have predicted that Adam might see their side of things?

*Could be all talk. Could be big city moves.*

Didn't seem that way, though.

Not to mention the whole weak-at-the-knees, moist-in-almost-forgotten-places thing going on. Adam's appearing at her back door with kisses and more in his arsenal didn't compute with anything at all, since seducing her could hardly be considered a move in favor of Callaway.

Clearly, logic wasn't working, so what did that leave her with? It sounded so simple, just lead him on, recruit him to the side of the angels, and not lose her heart in the process.

*Oh, yeah, no problem.*

In the meantime, it felt good, leaning back next to him on the sofa, her head resting on his arm. Worse luck.

*Of all the back doors on all the small islands ...*

"I want to be sensible and tell you to go away." Stacie reached for a hand, found it, and twined her fingers into his.

"Hard to believe you just told me we don't like each other." He raised his head from the back of the sofa long enough to stare at her.

"I haven't figured out whether I like you or not. I do know you're not to be trusted, though."

His head flopped back down. "I wasn't treated like the enemy tonight. Everyone was friendly, and everyone listened to what I had to say. I can't determine what Callaway's going to do, Stacie. I wish I could."

"Because ...?"

"Because I'd tell them to go find another forest to cut down. I don't want this one to go. This place is getting to me. It appears that you are, too, although for the life of me I can't explain why."

"Think of something you like about me. It would be a pleasant surprise to hear you say something positive."

"Oh, that's not hard. There's the physical stuff, your hair, your eyes, your ... I shouldn't say it, should I?"

"Manners give you brownie points."

"I like the way you say what you're thinking, even when I can see you trying not to. Not to insult the guest in your B&B. Not to offend the representative of Callaway Forest Products."

"What I like about you," Stacie said slowly, drawing it out while she thought, "is that even though you're constantly looking down on everything, you seem so ... almost helpless, wandering around the island, so totally out of your element. But you're game, you keep coming back. You're willing to try, and learn. Why couldn't you stay the Enemy? It'd be so much easier."

"This is easy." He shifted himself closer to her. "Flirting with danger, but easy."

"I can't sleep with you."

"Technically, you could. But it might be better to keep it from becoming a certainty. That would count as manners, wouldn't it?" He pushed up, off of the sofa. His hands started tucking in his shirt. "Could we maybe eat or go for a walk or something?"

"I can't sleep with you because your company's going to roll in here and destroy something my friends and family love. I can't sleep with you because you're leaving."

Adam sighed and pulled her up off the sofa. "Come on. Let's get out of here."

She clicked off the television. He scooped her keys from their hook. She scuffed her feet into trainers, bent to tie them up. She sensed his eyes on the view.

She locked the door behind them. They circled the B&B and headed down the driveway. "We could go on out of town. It dead ends in about a mile, that's about twenty minutes' walk to you, or we could go into town. It's Friday night so the pub's an option."

"Out." They reached the road and turned right. Adam took her hand. "So if it dead ends, where was the town manager going two days ago when she stopped to talk to me?"

"Probably nowhere. Just casually bumping into you. So to speak." She didn't think it was necessary to mention that her mother's car had ended up behind Halloran House, where she'd called in for a chat. In fact, so far she hadn't seen any reason at all to let him in on the fact of their close relationship.

"You're kidding. I was chased up a dead end road by a good looking older woman, just so she could invite me to a barbecue?"

"Entirely possible. This is Malaspina."

He let a silence hang between them for a minute. Stacie didn't mind it, in fact, it felt comfortable. Then he said, "I don't want to kid you, Stacie. You're right about all the things you've said about me and Callaway. But there are two things I didn't expect. One is how you've gotten under my skin." His voice was serious, but he swung their joined hands between them as if they were kindergarteners. "Sure, there's an attraction between us. But it's more than that. I almost called you, Thursday night after the hike. Probably fortunately, I came to my senses and realized you'd laugh me out of town before you'd baby me."

"I might not have. I've got this sympathetic streak. And I've been on hikes with boots that rub, so I know how miserable it can be. But on the other hand, I wouldn't be caught dead at the hotel right now."

"Oh." He digested that. "I get it. Reputations. If they're watching me, they're watching you."

She shrugged. "I don't want to be collateral damage if I can help it." She looked up at him, although in the dark she doubted he could see her. "And I intend to help it. Something for you to remember."

"I'll try to remember. But then, when I'm not thinking about you, which isn't often these days, there's this place. Smell the air." He pulled her to a stop. "The air here, it's so clean. It smells of sea and trees and I don't know what … peonies and lilacs?"

She grinned. "There's tons in bloom besides those. Hawthorn, for instance."

"And of course I don't know what that is. But I can learn."

"Can you? When you'll be gone in, what, a week?"

"Two, most likely. It'll take that long to get a forum set up and the Callaway people out here."

He tugged at her hand to walk on, but she'd turned aside to lean on a fence. "Look. I love the way you can see lights across the water. Other islands, sometimes a boat. It's magical, I think."

"I see what you mean." They leaned companionably on the fence rail for a minute, then he said, "Tell me about yourself, Stacie Halloran. What you've done, what you want to do. I sometimes think I'm falling for you, and that's so far off my life plan it's frightening, and I don't know a thing about you."

*Falling?*

It didn't sound contrived. He sounded like he meant it. Stacie's heart did a quick soft shoe step before settling back down in her chest where it belonged. Her mind, on the other hand, veered straight toward panic. *Logical mind, Stacie. Logical mind …*

"Adam … we only met a week ago, remember."

"Defies logic, doesn't it? And I think that's the first time you've actually said my name."

Her mother had commented that the aching muscles might work in their favor, but would that have been enough to tenderize the frowning, uptight businessman into an ordinary guy? Not that he was there yet, but this certainly wasn't the conversation she expected to be having with him. Stacie gazed out at the lights in the distance rather than looking at him. The night was altogether too conducive to … *don't go there, Stacie.*

They left the fence and wandered on up the road, which was climbing gently. Stacie figured there was safety in the ordinary, so she served him up a condensed version of her life.

"Not that much to tell. We moved here when I was fourteen, when Mom had had enough of Calgary. Halloran House was my grandmother's, I spent summers with her. My dad disappeared years ago." She shrugged. "I can't miss what I never knew. Masters in English, which turned out to be a dead end, job-wise. So much for 'follow your bliss'. So I got a teaching certificate and tried that for a few years, but it was a means to an end – and not what I wanted, or where I wanted to be. I'd been back on the island for a couple of years when my grandmother died, about four years ago. I'd been working retail, waitressing, whatever I could find. I wiped out my savings to fix her house up as a B&B, and here I am."

"And you never married?"

"Nope. Some people fall in love at the drop of a hat. Some don't seem to fall in love at all. I kidded myself a couple of times that I'd found The One …" she couldn't make quote marks with her hands, since Adam was holding one of them, so she emphasized the words with her voice. "But it was just that, kidding myself. What about you?"

"I never married, either. I joined Callaway's head office in Chicago straight out of Ohio State University, then got transferred to Toronto within the year – and met Katherine. My family lives in Ohio, my mom's Canadian.

"I wasn't strictly honest with you about the big city lifestyle," he went on. "A lot of the time it's takeaway for supper, and what's the point in going to the symphony or something if you don't have anyone to go with? My entanglement with Katherine was a long time ago now. I figure we're all allowed one big mistake and a few little ones, and that was my big one. Mostly I go to work and go home. But I've been advancing up the ladder at Callaway nicely. I have a fair amount of authority now, but I could have serious power if I get the next promotion. That's about it, really. Sounds pathetic, when it's laid out like that."

It did. Stacie pulled him to a stop and got her arms around him for a kiss. Not the passionate sort they'd somehow survived earlier, but the kind of kiss that says, Hey, all is not lost, and look where you are now. And look who you're with.

When she let him go and they continued up the road, he said, "Thanks. I think I needed that."

"In a place like this, you almost can't help but have a life. For one thing, the economy of the island is interdependent, like Yvonne's husband Richard takes tourists out for sport fishing when he's not involved with the commercial fishery, while she's on the Council but she's also a fabulous knitter. Jess sells some of her stuff. And so much of the island's economy is tourism that you're constantly interacting with others, islanders and tourists both. Still, my years teaching in Vancouver weren't much fun. I remember lonely."

"And you knew who the Foxes invited to the barbecue, didn't you?"

"Mmm hmm."

He shook his head. "Does everyone know everything anyone does, or is it just me?"

Stacie laughed. "There aren't many secrets. We might get away with this walk without being seen. But if anyone tries to reach me tonight, and anyone else tries to reach you, then they have coffee tomorrow, they might put two and two together."

"Maybe we should let them reach us. I turned my phone off. Do you have yours?"

"I didn't bring it. I don't want to be bothered by a phone call."

"Really? I thought you thought I was a pest."

"You are. Or were. You may not know it, but you earned serious brownie points yesterday. Susan said you really got into the forest, even if your body wasn't keeping up."

*Stop right there, Stacie. Do not mention his body again. Dangerous.*

She carried on. "Not everyone's island fit. But some people are game, some people are miserable. You did well."

She could just see his smile in the dark. "That makes me happier than you know."

They walked on in companionable silence for a while. "End of the road's ahead," she said. "There's a nice lookout. A couple of parking places. We used to come up here, when we were teenagers."

"Let me guess."

"All things considered, it might be better if you didn't." They arrived at the lookout and sat on one of the benches, twisting to look out over the ocean. "This view is amazing. The ferries go by here, for one thing. I love the feeling of boats going away. It's like a promise, when the island gets claustrophobic – and it does, you know. Sometimes. But once it's caught you, you might take one of those ferries, but you always end up coming back."

"You're so romantic about this place. I like that." Adam traced a finger over Stacie's brow, down past her eye, around cheek and chin. "You're lovely."

"I'm cute. Like my name. Ask anyone."

"They're wrong. I could look at you for a long, long time and not have my fill."

She grabbed his hand before serious damage to her resolve could be done. "We'd better get back. I have an early morning."

"As do I, if I'm going to be ready for this work bee tomorrow." He kissed her, and this time it was different again, more what a first kiss should be, she thought. Gentle, not quite certain, not quite probing.

When it ended she said, "Do you get the feeling that we're doing this backwards?"

He caught her meaning immediately. "Yes. That should have been our first. Which I hope you'll forgive me for, by the way. That first time was presumptuous."

"Maybe. But it gave me a lot to think about."

"Come on, then. Let's take you to your door."

They walked back down the hill to Stacie's apartment. They didn't speak much. Stacie felt odd, the opposite of her usual sassiness.

*Mellow? Could you possibly have gone mellow?*

She wasn't sure. But she knew that she liked walking along with this sandy haired man holding her hand. Corny though it seemed, it felt like courtship. It felt like a beginning.

And he'd even started smiling.

*Pull up the drawbridge, Stacie. And hope the Enemy isn't already inside.*

# Chapter 9

On Saturday morning, Stacie vacuumed the breakfast room and guest lounge while she worked out her strategy for the day. She wanted to get her work done so she could head for the Square. The cleaning and planting for the summer season wasn't always fun, depending of course on how you defined 'fun', not with so many excellent gardeners on the island who all knew *exactly* how it should be done, but it was a community event and good for their overall prosperity.

*Not to mention overall unity against the common enemy.*

The common enemy wasn't exactly underfoot anymore, despite turning up twice – *twice!* – yesterday. Stacie ignored the little twinge of … could that be regret? … that gnawed at her when she thought about Adam's moving to the hotel. She knew what was good for her.

She really needed to check in with her mother, to get the island's eye view of how the barbecue had gone.

There was a new couple in Two, and the couple in Four had left to go camping. That room would be empty until Wednesday, a fact she hadn't mentioned to Adam.

It was a perfect day with a clear sky, unusually warm, bordering on hot, for May. Who wouldn't want to be outdoors in the gardens? She could skip cleaning Four until tomorrow, in a pinch. *It's not slovenly if no one knows.* Breakfast had gone smoothly, so she'd been done early there. She'd easily be in time for the picnic and one of the afternoon work parties.

Stacie put some muscle behind her vacuuming and dusting. She resolutely did not think about the previous evening. *I am a practical woman,* she chanted in time to her movements with the vacuum. And whatever it was Adam was doing to her life, it certainly wasn't practical.

*Plus that quicksand wasn't a big attraction.*

And that's what it felt like, after last night.

She got to the Square just before noon, after allowing her better self to dictate that she should go ahead and clean Four after all. The command post had been set up just inside the Admin Building door, a wise precaution since the wind was blowing across the Square, and water was blasting every which way from the power washers. Adam was at the desk along with Jess. She gave her mother points for getting Jess onto this table, keeping it friendly for the Enemy. He looked good in a light blue T-shirt, she thought. Not an overly muscled hulk, but arms that were … shapely.

She was too late to be a morning participant, so she dodged the spray, pulled up a spare chair, and settled in for a chat – catching Jess's thumbs-up when Adam wasn't looking.

"So, how's it going?"

"I don't know," Adam answered. He turned to Jess. "How's it going?"

"Good. Good turnout this year. I gather the hanging basket teams ran out of moss, so a few of the baskets will have to wait until someone can get some more. Otherwise," she gestured out the door, "the Square is sparkling with all the pollen and winter grot washed off. Haven't had a report from the waterfront." Jess hopped up suddenly. "Maybe I'll go see."

Stacie grabbed her arm and pulled her back down. "Uh-uh. Stay put. We're not far off time for the picnic anyway. Then we'll all check it out."

"Alas, not to be. I've got afternoon shift at the shop, so it's lunch in the storage room. But no, no, don't pity me. I'm strong, I can handle it."

Stacie glanced past Jess at Adam. My goodness, the man was smiling. He said, "I could take a shift at your store, if you want to picnic."

"That's so sweet." Jess patted his arm. "But by the time I got you up to speed on the cash register and the credit card thingy and how to lure the innocents into purchasing, the picnic would be over and we'd both lose. Better you escort Stacie here to the picnic. She doesn't know many people and I'm so, so afraid she'll be lonely."

Stacie rolled her eyes. Adam said, "Nothing I'd like better than to show Stacie the ropes. So to speak."

A pause. Stacie watched Jess's eyebrows ascend to her hairline.

*Safer than an eye lock with the Enemy.*

She shrugged. She could think of a couple of possible messages hidden in Adam's words – as he no doubt knew – but no way was she exploring them.

As promised, Adam stuck close to Stacie at the picnic, a fact she seemed not to mind. He might have wished that she'd had on long pants and a shapeless sweatshirt instead of the shorts and halter top she'd chosen, but he dealt with it, mainly by pointedly not noticing. Barbecues did a brisk business in the park by the waterfront and they both munched hot dogs, chatting about nothing much. But to Adam, the chat seemed to convey volumes about who they both were, what they both wanted.

Combine their chat with the warm day, the crowds of people who all knew each other and seemed to want to know him, and the hot dog – something he'd never dream of eating back home – and Adam felt full and fulfilled when he got back to the Square. He checked the list and he found that he'd been assigned to planting duty, filling the planters on the Square with flats of annuals. It sounded simple enough. He had his new work gloves with him and hoped his sport sandals would be sufficient for the job. He couldn't face putting on his not-to-be-trusted hiking boots.

It was a large and rather intimidating woman who explained what he'd be doing. Removing the old dirt required a scoop sort of tool and a tarp to dump the dirt onto, not difficult but tedious. Next he'd load the now empty planters with topsoil and compost, then gently set a dozen little plants into the soil. She showed him how to free them from their containers, how to set them in and tamp down the soil around them. How to water them in once they were in place. She made it look easy.

Adam shoved his baseball cap onto his head, grasped the scooper, gritted his teeth, tightened his abs – somewhere he'd read you should do that when you had to bend over – and started scooping. It took forever. But it was simple compared to hoisting and pouring soil from a forty pound plastic bag. Forty pounds may not look like a lot, but it weighs, well, forty pounds. And it's limp. So if you're holding it around the middle, it'll sag down at the end furthest from you, and pour dirt where you didn't want it. Adam became very grateful for the tarp holding the old soil. Without it all the power washing would have been a waste of time. In the course of his first planter, Adam became thoroughly acquainted with the fiendish nature of plastic bags of dirt.

The little plants were a challenge, too. He was meant to mix three different kinds of plants. His hands in his work gloves were bulky and awkward. He broke off a plant and felt sad about it, as if the plant might take it personally. As it happened, the woman in charge of planting *did* take it personally, and commanded that he lose the gloves for this delicate operation.

Once one or two plants were in the planter, it seemed that all he had to do was dig a hole for the next one and the others would collapse into the new hole. He'd gently retrieve them and try again. It took him close to an hour to finish his first planter, scoop to plants.

And when he did, straightening up with a groan, wouldn't you know there'd be a round of applause? What was with this town? Adam turned around and bowed to the four or five people who'd watched the end of his struggle with the planter. The *first* planter.

It got easier. In the end he completed five planters. That meant scooping and pouring hundreds of pounds of dirt. Then switching from macho to girlie and gently giving a summer home to sixty little plants. *Getting stupid sentimental about planting flowers?* Adam let himself laugh at himself while he stretched his back.

One of the work crews hauled away his tarps full of old soil. He leant a hand, pulling a tarp over to a dump truck parked on the edge of the Square.

He only had to water his little gardens and wash away the dirt that had spilled onto the Square, and he'd be done.

Stacie came over, looking like dynamite in her shorts and pink halter top. Not that it was the first time he noticed. Adam couldn't help it – his gaze went to her legs. *Well developed calves, no surprise there. Shapely. Touchable ... oh no. Mind on the work. Control.*

"Going well?"

"It got better. The first one was really challenging. After that ..." He shrugged and gestured at his planters, feeling absurdly happy. "I've fallen in love with the idea that all summer long all of you will enjoy the flowers I planted for you. Is that corny?"

"Terminally. But isn't it great?" She was glowing. "I love getting my hands in the dirt. I've been down at the waterfront, working on the display there. It's big. But later in the summer when it's in full bloom ... The other gardens around town, too. All those little islands in the intersections. You do know, I guess, that everyone will be heading to the pub once we get cleaned up?"

"I heard. I hope you'll be there?"

She nodded. "Not for long, though. Just to snag some dinner. I'm tired, and I serve breakfast in the morning."

He perched on the concrete edge of a planter, patted it for her to join him. They sat there for a few minutes, companionably taking a break and watching the last of the banners go up. There was dirt under her nails and she had mud smears on her knees, he noted, and one attractive streak of dirt across her right cheek. He could help her wipe that one off ...

"Right. Just have to water these and clean up."

Stacie didn't say anything, but strode across the Square to pick up a push broom and a running hose. She came back and started washing away the last of the dirt under the planters. "You'll find watering cans over there," she said, gesturing behind her with a hand. "You fill the can from the hose. It's about two and a half cans per planter, before it starts leaking out, if memory serves."

Adam nodded and headed for the watering cans.

The watering went without a hitch, thank God. Adam stayed behind to help load up the pickup trucks that had brought in all the supplies, so he was one of the last to leave the Square. He ambled over to his hotel on the waterfront, feeling overall better than he had in … he didn't know how long.

*Another day to remember.*

Although for the life of him he wasn't sure why. He'd kept track of work crews and supplies all morning, and planted a bunch of annuals all afternoon. He experimented with feeling disdain for the annuals, and couldn't dredge it up. He felt personally invested in every one of his little plants, as if he'd named them or something.

He showered, then in his boxers put up his feet for a few minutes before dressing and heading for the pub, and out of habit he opened his laptop.

Four emails from the office. *On a Saturday. Why the hell did I do that?* He shut down the email program, closed the laptop, and got himself ready for a night out, Malaspina Island style. The evening was turning chilly, so he settled on one of his underutilized dress shirts with rolled up sleeves, his new sweater over his shoulders, the skinny jeans.

The pub was mobbed, but he spotted Stacie with a group of her friends back in a far corner and she waved him over.

They'd been keeping an eye out for him. The sense of belonging that the thought inspired made him feel absurdly happy.

*Absurdly* ... because of course he didn't belong here, it wasn't his place or his chosen way of life, and God willing he'd be gone in two weeks. The pub was an adventure, a way to fill in time, and a way to get to know and learn from the natives.

*Wasn't it? Then why did he have to keep reminding himself?*

He already knew Jess from that morning but the others were new. He got himself installed at Stacie's table. "We're doing drinks and a platter of appetizers to start," she said. "Are you in?"

"Sounds good." Since he'd been eating out for over a week, he already knew that food at the pub leaned toward fish and chips and deep fried zucchini. In Toronto he did his best to eat sensibly, but tonight a stir fry wasn't going to cut it.

There was expected chaos while he got a plate and ordered a beer, then Stacie introduced him to her friends, Donna and Tom, who were drinking what looked like iced tea, and Jane and Spencer, who were into martinis. Handshakes across the table. Stacie had a cider in front of her, but didn't seem too interested in it. She stirred it lazily with her straw but mostly watched what was happening around her.

"Everything okay?"

A little smile. "Fine. I'm really tired. I expect I'll go ahead and get my meal, then clear out."

"I'll join you."

"I've got to hand it to you, Adam," Jess said, raising her beer in his direction. "I heard about that extemporaneous round of applause you got nailed with. You handled it with – aplomb? You get brownie points."

Brownie points seemed to be a big deal on Malaspina. First Stacie, now Jess.

His beer appeared in front of him. He and Stacie snagged the waiter and both ordered chicken quesadillas, then he turned back to Jess with a little shrug. "A new low in my life. The latest in a series of lows, it seems. Makes me wonder what calamity's going to strike next. It was either make a joke of it or die of embarrassment."

"Still, what did you think?" Jane asked. "Our community work party must have been a whole world away from your usual Saturdays.

"I can see it now," Jess rambled, slouching back and doing her best to look starry-eyed. "Mornings spent haunting all these spectacular stores with massive selection, better than the Sears catalogue, even, I bet. Then lunch in a trendy café downtown before retiring to the penthouse to work the crossword in the Globe and Mail over a glass of expensive and oh-so-dry sherry. Then out for the evening, gourmet dinner, theater ..." She gave the word a strongly fake English accent, "... before home to admire the view over cognac and grapes, then to bed, most likely satin sheets. I could so get into that."

"You'd love it for about one weekend, then you'd be begging to come back here," Stacie retorted. To Adam she explained, "She tried it for a while. Got so homesick she couldn't stand it. I didn't know about the cognac and grapes part, though. Wonder who that was shared with?"

Jess joined in the laughter around the table. "Well, when a gal lives in a one bedroom condo in downtown Windon Harbor and buys her wardrobe at the General Store, she's gotta have a dream, doesn't she?"

"You forgot the Sears Catalogue," Jane added darkly.

"Ah, the Catalogue. I've found the selection excellent, the style tasteful. Why, whenever I have a night on the town planned – like right now for instance – I curl up with my trusty computer and hit the Sears website. A bonanza of riches."

"Shut up," Donna said. "You're making us all jealous. I'm going to be shaped like a watermelon again, any day now, and all you can talk about is clothes. Do you have any idea how disheartening it is to drag out the maternity wardrobe for the third time?"

Jane aimed a finger at Donna. "Think of it as giving you something to look forward to. Get online and choose something wonderful. It'll be encouragement to get your figure back."

Donna's husband Tom, a large and well-muscled man, grabbed Donna into a hug.

"Besides," Jess chimed in, "you owe it to Tom to keep on with the maternity thing until you finally produce a male heir."

"Based on my much smaller sample, I have to say that the lead-up to the pregnancy is noticeably more satisfying than the pregnancy itself." Jane and Spencer had one child, a boy.

"Please, ladies, you're in mixed company here." That, surprising himself, was from Adam.

"Makes you wonder what they talk about when we're not around, doesn't it?" Tom gave Donna another squeeze, then wrapped his hands around his iced tea. "It's scary."

Donna covered her face. "Please God, let this one be male."

"Give up," Spencer put in. "You're loving every minute."

"I'm encouraged by your cash flow," Stacie added. "I haven't had a full new outfit in a couple of years. I try to keep the old standbys going. It pays, you know," she added loftily, "to buy only classic lines of good quality. These slacks must have cost $39.99. Plus tax and shipping, of course."

Adam listened to the banter and stored what seemed to be useful. This was one of the things that made him a valuable corporate resource. He had the ability to see the significance, to sort and store data until he had the complete picture. And here was a picture he hadn't contemplated. He didn't know all that much about women's fashion, but he'd bet that the humblest file clerk at Callaway never paid less than a hundred bucks for a pair of slacks. Was this how island life was eked out?

*Do any of these laughing, relaxed people look like they're merely eking?*

Adam flashed back to his youth. His mother probably had never paid more than the equivalent of $39.99 for slacks, either. But he'd had a happy childhood. So what did that say about him? About his custom suits? Ties that cost as much as his weekly food budget?

The quesadillas appeared. The guacamole was in a little paper cup, sour cream in another, a dish of salsa for them to share in front of them. Not gourmet Toronto, for sure. What the hell, he liked it here. He had friends at Callaway, of course, and sometimes they got together for a drink after work. But then they went their separate ways, to different parts of the city. So there was none of this bantering at the pub, no gathering with spouses. Hell, he didn't even know most of the spouses. Compared to this, socially it was a bust.

Exploring, he put his left hand on Stacie's jeans-covered thigh and gave a gentle squeeze. She looked surprised, met his eyes for a minute, but didn't shove him away. Unfortunately, there was no way to eat the quesadilla one-handed, so he reluctantly returned his hand to his cutlery. And caught Jess's eye. Of course she hadn't missed it. No one missed anything on this island. He shrugged and grinned and she grinned back.

*This is okay,* he thought. *I like it here.*

It was a nice night, dry and a little chilly. Stacie had thought she'd have a quiet, thoughtful walk home. The day had held some food for thought, for sure. While her morning had been as expected, and planting the floral bed by the waterfront – the floral bed ran almost a full block, so this was no small job – was satisfying, it was watching Adam, first at his planters and then at the pub, that had her thinking.

*More than thinking, Stacie. You've got an itch happening. Needs scratching.*

*Not going there.*

Well, maybe she wasn't in any particular hurry to be quiet and thoughtful after all. Adam had left with her, and without anything being said, let it be known that he'd be walking her back to Halloran House. As soon as they were clear of the pub's front door he'd taken her hand. Stacie could feel it all the way up her arm, the frisson of energy that flowed between their joined hands, the slight movement of skin against skin from his gentle grip as they walked.

Adam had barely smiled, the whole time he was resident at Halloran House. Even their … encounters … hadn't been enough to bring on a sustained smile. But this afternoon, dealing with the planters, he'd had happiness plastered all over his face. He'd actually had fun. This evening he'd rubbed the back of his neck occasionally – in the pub she'd seen it was sunburned, but not too badly – and his face had color to it, and he looked damn handsome, if she did say so.

She liked the way he fit right in with her friends, too. He didn't come over all corporate and superior with Tom, who worked in his father's hardware store. In fact, he never even asked what kind of work everyone around the table did. He took them for what they were, her friends at a pub on a Saturday night.

But she was still confused, by the mixed views she'd had of this enigmatic man, and the mixed signals her mind and her body were throwing at her. *Run for cover, Stacie. Jump his bones, Stacie.* She frowned and pulled them to a stop. They were coming up to the foot of her road, before it began the gentle climb to her B&B and beyond. She swung around so they were facing each other.

"Explain this to me. You liked it. The work bee, the pub. You really liked it."

"I did. Are you surprised?" Sunset was coming later this time of year, and they'd left early. There was still enough light for her to see that he'd raised his sandy eyebrows at her.

"Are you?"

Standing still, he was making free with her hand. Instead of one on one, now both of his were wrapped around one of hers, and he was rubbing, stroking, very gently, but gently was all it took, it seemed. A charge was building up.

"A little. I'm learning not to make any assumptions where this island of yours is concerned." He raised her hand to his mouth and started nibbling at her fingers. "I taste deep fried."

"Appetizers. Don't do that."

"Give me a good reason why not?"

*Why not, indeed.*

"What happens tomorrow? Back to the shirt and tie? I didn't like you very much in your business clothes. You were so stuffy. Did you figure out you're more likely to scare people off, dressing that way? Or find yourself dismissed as someone who doesn't get it? But the way you've gone a hundred eighty degrees, it's a little scary."

"I'll tell you, if you promise not to tell a soul. I have reason to wonder if anything's sacred among you women. It's puzzling me, too." Now he held both of her hands. "I've done things here I'd never have considered doing before. Never would have wanted to. That I've enjoyed it all, it starts a man thinking." Adam paused, looked at her. He wasn't teasing or flirting, that was for sure. "And you. You weren't real to me at first. Now you are. Does that make sense?"

*Too much sense. Warning flags all over the place.*

*Still, who says you have to pay attention to warning flags? What's the worst that could happen?*

*You go over a cliff?*

*Better order up a safety net, Stacie. Maybe from the Sears Catalogue?*

She nodded. "Yes, it does make sense. I guess you weren't real to me, either. It's just that now I'm not sure which you is the real one. That's what's freaking me out a little."

"That's my point. I don't know, either."

Stacie turned to begin the walk up the hill to her B&B, but he pulled her back. "One more thing. We talked about how we were going about this backwards. Not starting from the beginning. I think I'd like to start from the beginning, kind of like a courtship. Maybe that way we'd be on firmer ground. How about you?"

"You're asking for a major life decision from a woman who's dead on her feet and has to be ready to serve breakfast to a house full of happy couples at 8:00 tomorrow morning, Adam."

"Copping out?" He grinned at her. "Then I'll make the decision for us. We go back. We slow down. We start over. How does that sound?" He pulled her against him and got his hand into her hair, cupping the back of her head, and kissed her the way he last had, gently, no teeth or tongue. But then he shifted from her mouth and ran a line of kisses over her right cheekbone, to the corner of her eye, then over to the other eye, and suddenly he was bending down, under her ear.

Stacie groaned and clung, since her knees were sending funny, chemical-reaction-in-progress signals. "This is slowing down?" she gasped.

"Want me to stop?" he asked from somewhere under her hair.

"Yes. No. I don't know." She hadn't experienced anything like this in … years? Ever? "You're making me go all shaky." Her hands had found their way to his back, where they were trying to dig holes in his sweater. His were everywhere, no point in even trying to track them.

She disentangled, put her hands on either side of his head, and pulled him up. Eyeball to eyeball she said, "I think I'm more comfortable when I can see what you're up to."

"I like you all shaky. But okay." *Big city moves, for sure,* some part of her mind noted. When his mouth settled on hers this time, it was still a kiss that could best be described as neutral, not deep. He didn't explore with his tongue but with his lips, brushing, changing angles, teasing her mouth until she couldn't stand it anymore and gripped his head more firmly to hold him in place.

Well, she couldn't blame him if things got a lot deeper in a hurry, could she? Not after she'd started it. Somewhere in that getting-deeper minute his hands found their way under her sweater. He suddenly jerked back, his eye wide. "No bra."

Stacie was having a challenge with basic functions like inhaling, but she managed, "This is the Island. We go for comfort."

"God, I love the Island." His hand worked its way around her rib cage, and the benefits of no-bra became apparent. After a little bit, during which he must have learned a lot about her nipples, she followed suit, pulling his shirt partially out of his jeans. "Mmm. Love handle."

"I suppose you just had to say that," he muttered into her hair.

"I like it."

"I knew I shouldn't wear these jeans. Not a lot of room for expansion." Adam moved her away from him, at arm's length, and she couldn't help herself. She glanced down. Then back up. "Wow."

"Let's go. Or I'm going to have to throw myself in the ocean."

"Let's go because we're practically undressing each other on the busiest road on Malaspina."

Hand in hand they made their way up her street and into her back yard. He turned her and draped his arms over her shoulders. "Here's the thing. I could stay tonight."

"That's not compatible with starting over. Maybe it is in Toronto? But I'm a small town girl, so no, you couldn't.

Besides, I can't." She wondered what more she should say. *Why* he couldn't stay wasn't clear even to her at this moment.

"Not yet?" He wasn't pushing. So she nodded. Easier than coming up with a coherent reason. Maybe she'd think of one tomorrow.

They reached her back door and stood at the foot of the three steps leading up to her tiny porch, hand to hand, eye to eye. The light was almost gone, but she watched his expression under her back door light. And he got it. "I know. I had to try. Sleep well." A gentle kiss on the cheek and he pulled away from her. And winked. Stacie felt her eyes widening.

"Say goodnight, Stacie."

"Goodnight, Stacie."

"I'm glad you're silly sometimes." He turned an amazing, fireworks-on-Canada-Day smile on her, and then he was gone.

*Imagine. Adam Fraser, mister stick-up-the-ass, approving of silliness.*

*Sometimes things changed so quickly all you could do was take a breath and see where you got blown to.*

That night Stacie dreamed of running fence lines, posts going into post holes. When she woke up she remembered every detail.

*Doesn't take a psychologist to figure this one out.*

She sighed and rolled out of bed. Today was going to be either very long or very short, depending on – on what? Whether Adam made an appearance? Good, bad? If nothing else, Stacie knew she had some thinking to do, even though she kept saying that and so far all that thinking was just getting her more muddled. Might work better if the thinking didn't involve the feel of Adam Fraser, or the taste, or the things his hands could do. She was beginning to doubt that thinking was the answer at all.

# Chapter 10

When Adam came down for breakfast Sunday morning the woman at the desk waved him over. "We've had a package delivered for you." She handed over a white paper bag.

He looked inside. It was a tube of sunscreen with a red bow around the middle.

"Any idea who—"

She shook her head. "None. The pharmacy delivers, so it was just one of their usual."

He rummaged and found a card. Someone had printed, "Use it!"

This place. Would he ever understand it?

Sunday afternoon Stacie's mother came for tea. The weather was changing, and a chilly wind was blowing off the ocean, so instead of using the picnic table Stacie put her prettiest tablecloth on the kitchen table. "Hope you don't mind. I always feel too available when I use the breakfast room, even if it is prettier."

"I've seen the breakfast room before, daughter. I'd rather talk to you. What's new?"

Stacie put a plate of homemade scones on the table, next to the homemade blackberry jam. "Mom, do you think it's dumb in this day and age to make scones when I can buy them at the grocery and they're really good? Or make my own jam? Sometimes I feel like some unsophisticated … I don't know. Earth mother wasn't ever what I thought I'd be. I was going to be a brilliant … something. Only I never figured out what that something was. And now here I am running a bed and breakfast on a little speck of an island and living about a mile from my mother. Have I missed the boat?"

Her mother fixed her with the assessing look she'd dreaded since high school, the one that saw right through her. "Whoa. What's this all about?" After a beat, she added, "Let me guess. Our visitor from Toronto."

"Not entirely. It was more the way the conversation went at the pub last night. Where I didn't see you, incidentally."

"We had a few friends our own age over for burgers. The pub's too busy and noisy for me after a day at the work bee. Those women! Getting the hanging baskets made up was a nightmare. I couldn't even pull rank, I don't have the master gardener type expertise." Abby shook her head. "I wasn't ready to deal with the pub, and Bill agreed. Much better all around. But you … what happened? Why did the conversation upset you?"

Seated, Stacie broke into a scone and absentmindedly started buttering it. "It's not just the pub conversation, I guess. It's having our way of life held up to scrutiny. Put under a microscope and tallied and judged." She dove her knife into the jam, not bothering with the spoon she'd put on the table for that purpose, and scraped a thin layer onto the scone. "We were talking about life in the big city – Jess was, Adam didn't say anything, it was just Jess's over-the-top imagination, not anything like what it's really like. Then we got onto the subject of our own wardrobes and mail-order shopping, and not having any new clothes to speak of, for years sometimes. I don't know, it felt like life was going on, on the other side of the water, and leaving us behind. Like I've missed the boat somehow."

"Whenever you take that boat, you come back," her mother said gently, then reached out and put her hand over Stacie's. "Is it Adam that's the microscope?"

"No. Not really. He hasn't said anything negative in a while now. He's just another source of confusion."

Abby nodded. "Thought so."

Stacie put her piece of scone down with emphasis. "Mom, why can't I meet some really nice islander who gets the way I live and I'm not like some novelty to him, and fall in love and settle down and have kids like Donna? Why do I get sent this guy from back east who doesn't understand and probably thinks we're all either cute or suckers, no matter what he says, and anyway he'll be gone in two weeks. What kind of luck is that?"

"No luck at all. Just decisions. Eat." Abby used the spoon Stacie had ignored and dumped more jam onto Stacie's scone. Significantly more. "Sugar's good for you."

"Not to mention I get a mom who pushes sugar on me," Stacie added ominously. But she ate the scone and it was blissfully peaceful for a few minutes.

"So what do you think of him, Mom? Really."

"Really? I think he's a nice man, but not a happy one."

"I know. He always looks so grim. Or I guess I should say, he used to."

"At the barbecue he was relaxed and charming." Abby stopped to sip her tea. "I think he's fitting in well, and we're not even seriously cutting him any slack. And that has him puzzled, because he came here with all these preconceptions. I think he's teachable. And I think he's our best bet for saving any of the forest. I don't kid myself there, all the cards are stacked against us. We can play the tourism card with the province, but we're small potatoes and Callaway's one great big one. So if we can make him an ally, even a little bit, it's good."

"He was really happy yesterday, planting out those stupid planters. I've never seen him like that."

"They're not stupid planters. You're getting defensive. And actually, defensive isn't a bad idea, so I'm not criticizing," Abby added, catching the mulish look on her daughter's face. "I don't want you hurt in all this. Be careful."

"I'm being so damn careful I'm boring myself. It doesn't seem to make much difference. Maybe I just need – forget it. I can't go there. You're my mother."

Abby grinned. "Then use him for his body."

"Mom!"

"I can't call it for you, you know. Just remember your priorities. You're unlikely to be happy in Toronto, especially living downtown, however you end up feeling about Adam. You value family and simplicity. You've built a thriving business. You're a success on your own terms. If he can fit into those terms, for a week or a lifetime, great. If he can't, well, think long and hard."

"Seems like that's all I ever do nowadays."

"Then maybe you'd better bed him. Get it out of your system."

"If you keep that up I'll have to take away your scone. Mothers aren't meant to talk that way."

"Shock value. Gets through when nothing else does. Wouldn't you agree?" Her mother smiled sweetly at her.

"I have the only mom in paradise who tells me to eat sugar and use a man for his body."

"Think about it. And pass the scones, please. Since today's my day for calories, I might as well have the best. And by the way, daughter, that's why you bake them."

# Chapter 11

Abby was ready when Adam arrived at her office Monday morning. She rose and held out her hand, approving what she saw. He'd worn slacks with a dress shirt, but open neck, no tie. *He called that one well. He's beginning to get the hang of it,* she thought. *Good.*

"How are you? I caught a glimpse of you Saturday afternoon. Those planters can be backbreaking. You could have had someone relieve you."

"I've got a new blister." He held up his right hand. "Just a little one. I consider it an honorable wound. And I didn't want to stop. I haven't messed around in so much dirt since I was a kid. I was having a good time, odd though that seems."

"Glad you survived, and that you wanted to pitch in. It tells me you're getting a feel for island life. Just a minute, please." Earlier she and Roger had discussed this meeting, including venue. They hoped that since Adam already knew Abby, by using her office he would be more at ease, more willing to negotiate. Abby punched a few numbers into her phone. "Roger? Could you come on over? ... Yes, about as expected." She hung up. "As you know by now, this is more Roger's bailiwick than mine, though when it comes to the impact your company could have, we're about equal. Can I offer you water or coffee?"

"Water, I think. I've had too much coffee already. I'm hooked on the local roast."

She poured two glasses from the pitcher on her credenza and handed him one.

"Hi, Abby." An older man came in to join them. He looked lean and wiry, as if he spent the bulk of his time outdoors. "Adam, I assume? I'm Roger McMillan, Island Administrator, for the time being. Abby's counterpart once you're out of Windon Harbor. Retiring end of the year. Welcome to Malaspina. I've seen you around."

The two men shook hands. "Pleased to meet you, sir."

"And so to business." Abby moved over to the little conference table tucked in a corner of her office and sat down. She watched Adam note the view from her window before he joined her. The Malaspina Island Administrative Center occupied the west side of the Square and held all the island's administrative offices except the ones at the Yard, which housed the fire station, all the trucks and buses, and one snowplow. The Admin Building itself was brick, perhaps seventy years old, and distinguished, with two stories, a sweeping staircase leading up from the impressive lobby, and large offices. Abby's office was on the second floor. Two old fashioned windows, with panes and intricate framing, provided a view across the Square toward the waterfront with its harbor, dock, and shops.

"Now, what do you have for us?" She gestured at the folder Adam had brought with him.

He took a breath, then nodded briefly, indicating that he'd picked up her signals. They wouldn't be taken lightly, this was business, she was the town manager and didn't have any intention of letting him waste her time. Roger's signals were more laid back, but she hoped that Adam realized that he wasn't someone to be played with. Roger was a man who had power and wielded it when he needed to.

Abby didn't doubt for a moment that Adam himself was a man used to wielding power, not to mention handling high level corporate negotiations, but nonetheless she detected a layer of nervousness underneath his smooth presentation. *Good.*

"You already know that I'm here representing Callaway Forest Products, the company that owns most of the land that's now known as Nathan's Forest." He passed them copies of a map that Callaway had emailed to him and he'd printed at the office center in the hotel. "We've known the boundaries of the land, of course, but didn't have a clear picture of how the Callaway property and Nathan's Forest overlap. Here it is, aerial photos plus land survey. Nathan's Forest seems to be more a concept than an actual mappable tract of land, but this will give you a picture of what's forested and what's owned by Callaway."

Abby studied the map for a moment, then glanced at Roger. "You're right." Her finger traced an outline. "The kids' area, the nature hut and all, aren't Callaway's. And there's a fair amount of beachfront that's excluded. Over here – George Mason isn't going to be happy about this," she said, indicating a section to the east of the forest. "He's been farming that land, the unforested part. Still, he probably knows it's not his. He's a law unto himself, that man. Go ahead." She turned her gaze back on Adam.

Adam met her eyes. "There isn't any easy way to say this. Callaway has a fair amount invested in the land, and we believe it's time to extract some of the timber. There are numbers involved, return on investment and all, I don't need to tell you that. Of course, until our team's here to do a proper survey we won't know the true value or be able to present a plan to you. But since the land is privately owned and we have the rights for logging and export … well." Adam shrugged, indicating *it is what it is*.

"Well. You liked it up the mountain, didn't you?" Roger asked. "You can see what a recreational resource we have here, not to mention contributing to the general beauty and atmosphere of the island. Have you ever seen a clearcut?"

"No, sir."

"I'll arrange it, maybe this afternoon or tomorrow. I'll check with Malaspina Aviation to see if someone can fly you over. Not on our island, but there are some around."

"I'd be interested, thank you."

"So, Adam, your company wants to log Nathan's Forest. Why specifically are you here in this meeting?" She knew why, but Abby was ready to turn the temperature down a notch, make it more formal. She was pretty sure he picked up on it.

"Because we expect to be here on the island for several years. We want to be good citizens. As I mentioned at your barbecue – which was wonderful, by the way, and thank you again – I'd like to propose that we jointly host an open meeting, a forum. A place where our foresters and executives can meet with the islanders, with all of you, and hear what you have to say. What you would like to see preserved, what matters most. At the same time, Callaway can present our tentative plans. I've spent the last week getting a feel for the way of life here, and I appreciate that your first reaction has to be that you love it all, and would we please go away. We're a publicly owned corporation, so we can't do that."

"I see," Abby said. "So you want to hear what we think. Will you listen?"

"I beg your pardon?"

"To rephrase that, will what we say make any difference? Or is this window dressing to placate the natives?"

Adam looked down, then back up at her. His eyes met hers. She gave him points for courage. "I'll do everything I can to assure that your voice is heard. Beyond that, well, I can hope that when they get here they'll be as impressed by the place as I've been."

Roger said, "And recognize that our economy is as important to us as your bottom line is to you? We've got some agriculture and fishing. Our lamb is famous, as are some of our cheeses. I'm only aware of one or two loggers on the island, and they maintain private woodlots, so the actual logging isn't going to provide jobs, even short-term."

He was pointing at Adam with the eraser end of his pencil, emphasizing his points. "But it's tourism that makes our community possible. Losing Nathan's Forest would be bad. Even having visible clearcuts on the mountain would be bad. Don't kid yourself about that. There's virtually no upside for the island economy. Whatever you propose, it's going to be seen as negative. It's going to *be* negative."

Abby nodded and thought about Stacie. "Take that as a heads-up, Adam. Between us."

He pinched his lips together and looked from her to Roger. "I hear you. And I do feel like the bearer of bad news. The best I can hold out right now is this forum. If you'll support it, if we can arrange it together as a joint effort – well, I hope we can figure something out."

Abby went over to her desk. "I'm pulling up the calendar, Roger. Do you have any last-minute updates?"

"Not that I know of."

She brought her laptop to the table and positioned it so they could both see the calendar. "You're thinking soon?"

He nodded.

"Then this is the date." She stabbed a finger at a box. "You can see that there's not much option, when you consider everything else going on. The miracle is that there's a Friday night when the Barn's free. That gives us not quite two weeks. Can we be ready by then?"

Roger nodded. "This isn't going to be a cozy little discussion, Adam. It's going to be big and probably very loud. And it's going to take hours, no point in kidding ourselves about that."

"We need a master task list and assignments. Then we can all get on with it. I'll get the Barn booked."

Abby opened a new document on the computer and typed in bold letters at the top, "Open Forum – Logging Nathan's Forest" and the date. She waited while they all organized their drinks and their thoughts, then led them in brainstorming the tasks they'd need to see to, in order to arrange this forum he wanted.

"We'll want a website. Don't look so surprised," Roger said with a laugh at the look on Adam's face. "We're one of the most highly computer literate communities in the area. Date and time, a mutually agreeable explanation, and a place for people to submit their comments in writing."

"You'll cover the time and expense of getting that set up, of course," Abby stated, not giving Adam space to debate the point. "And we'll want a full record of all comments you receive. Now, what else?"

The three of them huddled for another half hour, discussing possible ways to stage the forum.

As Adam left, notes in hand, he found himself trying to sort things out in his head. The discussion had given him an overload of information, and a sense that battle lines had been drawn. Politely, but drawn nevertheless. Among other things, he had a much better picture of the administration of the island and who the key players were. He'd noticed, for instance, that the mayor wasn't in this meeting. He knew more or less what the Forum would look like and how it would be managed – and that managing it might prove challenging. Clearly, he wouldn't be popular in town once Callaway got down to business.

But the overload came from other directions. The thought that popped in and out of his mind while he mentally framed his memo to the Callaway team was *Island Administrator. Retiring.* He gave himself another head-clearing shake and reminded himself that whether the island administrator retired was nothing to do with him.

Monday afternoon, Stacie got together with Jessica, Jane, and Donna. It was another gorgeous afternoon, so they met on the waterfront and treated themselves to ice cream cones before settling on one of the bench groupings looking out over the harbor.

"At least this sounds like it might be edible," Donna moaned, waving her cone at the others. "Morning sickness starting up. I thought I might miss it this time, but no such luck."

"Dry crackers," Jane said. Everyone ignored that. "So what's new?"

Donna's pregnancy wasn't new. Jane's work as one of the two island lawyers wasn't new. Jess's store wasn't new. Everyone looked at Stacie.

"Okay. I'm in trouble."

"Ahh," Donna breathed. "Tell more."

"I sensed change in the wind at the pub," Jane added. "He's good looking, that's for sure."

"And high time we got the dirt," Jess added.

Stacie grumbled, "No dirt to speak of, but news for sure. Here's the chronology. Last Friday, Mom had him around for a barbecue."

"So? You didn't go. You were out at chick flick night with us, remember?"

"Home by 9:30 like a good little B&B hostess. Everything prepped for Saturday morning, so I was flopping on the sofa, channel surfing, when who turns up at my door?"

"And you didn't find a way to tell me all this Saturday morning? This is good." Jess took a massive lick of her cone, her eyes dancing.

"So we went for a walk and talked. Well, first we made out a little—"

"Really?" Donna's voice changed from alto to squeak. "Ooh, I remember making out, strange lips and hands all over and not knowing where it's going—"

"Down, girl." Jane swatted at Donna. "They're more or less mature adults. They know exactly where it's going."

"Or where it's not." Stacie put a decided end to that conversational direction. "I don't know what he thinks, but I don't see any reason to get any more involved with the Enemy, who on top of everything else is going to be gone in a couple of weeks, once we get through this forum thing. Oh, he met with Mom and Roger this morning to plan a meeting where we can all speak our minds about logging the forest. So anyway, we broke it off while we still could. Mutual consent. But the walk was nice. Risky, but nice."

"Risky how? Oh, from your place you went up to the lookout, didn't you? Come on, I bet he couldn't keep his hands off of you."

"He could. We talked. That's the risk. I mean I could be in serious lust. Well, okay, maybe I *am* in serious lust. But he's more than window dressing. If I'm not careful I could fall for him."

"Not good," Jane said. "Not good at all."

"It's like he's a kid on his first trip to Disneyland. He can't quite believe us, the way of life here. It makes me wonder how he let himself get so buried in his fancy urban lifestyle. There must be small towns and nature in Ontario."

"I hear he's a regular at the General Store nowadays, upgrading the wardrobe." Jess giggled.

Adam picked that minute to walk by. He saw them and waved but didn't stop. They watched him until he got to the turn for the municipal dock, where he climbed into an old Ford pickup.

"Wonder what that was about," Jane said.

"Whew," Jess said with a mock wipe at her brow. "The long view's good. Guys should wear jeans – nice ass."

"Hands off," Stacie said flatly.

"No worries. That fine ass is all yours."

"I recommend avoidance," Jane said. "He isn't staying at the B&B anymore. It should be possible to just not be around."

"Not if he keeps turning up at my door. I can hardly say, sorry, we're closed."

"Of course you can, if you want to."

"Remember the mantra. Enemy. Enemy. Enemy."

"It could be," Stacie sighed, "that the Enemy's already breached the barricades. Because then there was Saturday."

"Post-pub. Very gallant of him to leave when you did. Any odds you didn't go your separate ways at the corner."

"Not exactly. We talked some more. Just so you don't think this is some shallow fling or anything."

"You could be using him for his body." Donna crunched on the last of her cone, then got up to throw away her napkin.

"Believe it or not, that's what Mom suggested. That's not how it's playing."

"Your mom? Oh God," Jess groaned.

"Well, if nothing else he fits in the desirable category. You could have one heck of a fling."

Stacie grinned. "Donna, tell me this. Are you going to be around to pick up the pieces?"

"Not me. I'm preggers. No moral support at all."

"Got the ultrasound booked yet?"

"Another couple of weeks."

The topic drifted from Donna's pregnancy to Jess's excitement about a new line of jewelry to Jane's current fury at Spencer. *They swore by make-up sex, those two,* Stacie thought. She sat back in the sun and let the conversation roll over her. If need be, Donna would pick up the pieces, just as Jess and Jane would. They'd been there for each other forever. Nothing was going to change that.

That's why she lived here. That's why she would fight for her island way of life.

It wasn't anything like a commercial flight, Adam thought. He held on tight. The little two-seater Cessna dipped and swooped all over the place, even when there wasn't any obvious reason to. The old guy at the controls obviously had been a stunt pilot in a previous life.

Roger had been as good as his word. He'd been in touch not fifteen minutes after Adam got back to the hotel from their meeting, giving him a name and phone number to call if he wanted to see a clearcut. No charge, the island would pick up the expense. But he really thought Adam should have a look.

Well, it would give him some time away and something potentially useful to do with his afternoon. So he'd called, and before he knew it, it was all arranged. They'd left from the little private airport on Malaspina and flown across to a neighboring island, and now Adam got his first look at what his company planned to do to Nathan's Forest. The Cessna dipped low enough that he could see the stumps and jagged ends of trees sticking up, the bare dirt. Once he saw a deer picking its delicate way among the downed logs that no one had bothered to remove.

"Company'll come along sometime and clear away enough of this that the tree planters can get in," the pilot said into his earphones. "Fifty years from now there'll be something resembling a forest down there again. Except it'll be artificial as hell, all the same species, same age." The old guy looked like he'd spit at the clearcut if he could.

It was a wasteland, no doubt about it.

They circled the clearcut, then the little plane did another dip and swoop, and they took what must have been the scenic tour over the Gulf Islands. The pilot went on with his narration, flying over houses, docks, tugboats and a ferry, a few towns. Once Adam thought he saw whales. He said little.

An hour later they were back on Malaspina. Adam said all the right things, hopped out of the pilot's truck at the entrance to his hotel, and went upstairs to think.

His company was going to create a patch of devastation like he'd just seen, on the side of the hill the islanders called a mountain, there on the southern coast of Malaspina Island. The thing would be butt ugly. It would be visible from a lot of the island. Callaway had the right to do it. There was good money in it. He'd been around forestry enough, even in his finance and admin capacity, to know there were other approaches to logging, but nothing that would be as commercially viable, that is, nothing that could be done as cheaply and get the logs out in volume.

What the hell could he do about it?

Short answer, not a damn thing. He'd known before he ever got here that the dice had been cast. They'd take the logs and run, and all the nonsense in the world about being good citizens meant exactly nothing.

There'd be some work for a few of the islanders, he was sure, if anyone had logging skills. It sounded like not many did. And perhaps they'd replant, like the old guy had told him happened when the big corporations came in and cut down the trees. Perhaps college students could handle that. Then they'd be gone.

The optics wouldn't be good. He had no doubt at all that Malaspina Island would use every publicity trick in the book to make them back off. He'd have to put that in his reports back to head office. Callaway had a few tricks, too.

Adam had been on the island exactly eleven days. And for reasons he didn't understand, he had switched sides. And that left him in a hell of a mess. He couldn't afford to slip up now. If he didn't play his cards right, it could cost him almost eighteen years of fighting his way up the corporate ladder.

Scruples be damned. He'd come this far. All the companies did it. Callaway was no better, no worse than any other. It wasn't selling out the island, because he'd never bought in. And he'd never be on Malaspina Island again, so he'd never have to face them ....

Decision made, he went to the hotel dining room for supper. He'd thought about walking around town, maybe getting fish and chips down on the waterfront. But he couldn't quite make himself do it. He felt as if anyone he met would know what he was doing to them. As if they could read his mind.

*Hell. In this crazy place they probably could.*

# Chapter 12

Tuesday morning after breakfast, Adam went to the General Store. When he came out half an hour later he had a new pair of khaki shorts that hit just above the knee, and two more T-shirts, one of them a souvenir of Malaspina Island with a stylized view of the harbor on the front. The weather had been spectacular, unusually warm for May, and half the island had made the switch into shorts and t-shirts.

He hadn't owned a pair of shorts in years, and he liked the way he looked in them. He'd been on the island for less than two weeks, but he'd swear his stomach had flattened a little. And was that a hint of muscle in his calves? Not like Susan's, or even Stacie's, but still, it felt good to be more in shape, even if only a little bit.

He cautiously avoided thinking about Stacie's legs and where they really ought to be, vis-à-vis his improving waistline and everything south of there.

Back in his room he duly recorded the purchases on his spreadsheet, then stripped off labels and changed into the new clothes. Not the Malaspina T-shirt, that would be too embarrassing, but the plain navy one. That morning it gave him unbridled satisfaction to be doing Callaway work in shorts and sport sandals – but he suppressed that thought as unworthy of a future CFO.

Early in the afternoon he left the hotel and ran straight into Jess, who didn't stop but gave him an obvious once-over and stated, "Nice legs," loudly enough that a couple of heads turned. Jess disappeared down the street with a wave. His blush had faded by the time he got to the corner of the road that led to Stacie's.

He hadn't seen her since Saturday night at the pub, other than that glimpse with her friends on the waterfront, and he was wondering where their conversation had left them. Not to mention the obvious buzz between them. More than buzz, in his case. Saturday night it had amounted to pain, before he got things under control again.

Sunday and Monday he hadn't sought her out. Not that he'd made a point of avoiding her, exactly … or maybe he had. Facing facts, he'd probably have to restrain himself from grabbing her and kissing her senseless, should she appear when he wasn't braced for it. Rather, it had been hectic, what with the meeting with the island administration people and a backlog of work from Callaway.

On top of that, somehow by Monday afternoon the island already knew about the Open Forum, and they all wanted a piece of him. Monday he'd been invited to another backyard barbecue, twelve people attending, this time. He was legitimately busy. He didn't need to make excuses, he simply didn't have time to dance attendance on her.

Plus that the Stacie thing was intimidating.

*It made sense to cool things down a little. Especially with the whole island watching.*

*Looking for justification? How about cowardice?*

*Did she miss him? Did he even dare to consider how much he missed her?*

Yeah. He considered it far too frequently, on several different levels. His blush wasn't the only thing that was becoming chronic.

Adam got to Stacie's back yard as she was standing up, pulling off a pair of gardening gloves. Since he'd last been there she'd dug up half the grass in her little private back yard. Her hands and knees and t-shirt were dirty, but tidy rows marked with stakes and string crossed the plot in front of her.

She looked him up and down. "Good legs," she said, deadpan.

He should have expected it. "Glad you approve. Let me guess … vegetables?"

"I like practical." She pointed. "Beans, potatoes, the taller plants are tomatoes. Zucchini, lettuces, Hubbard squash …" She broke off and made a circle the size of a beach ball with her hands. "If that one works I'll have squash all winter, they grow, like, this big."

"That's a lot of work since Saturday."

Stacie shrugged. "Borrowed a tiller."

So far she hadn't moved any closer to him, and he'd stopped a good six feet from her. He waited. Seeing her after not seeing her for a couple of days left him unsure of his balance, like he'd better tread carefully, because he didn't know the terrain.

*She hadn't sought him out, either, remember.*

She bent over, took a swipe at her grubby knees, not that it helped much, and headed for the back door, calling over her shoulder, "I'll put the sprinkler on the whole thing later. Want an iced tea?"

"Yes, thanks," he called after her. She disappeared and came back a couple of minutes later with clean hands – she'd ignored the knees – and a pitcher and glasses on a tray. He stood there by the garden for a moment and looked at her. She looked hot.

*Two meanings there.*

She radiated sun and life and her skin was crying out for —

*Oh, shit. This was cooling things off?*

There was a new dirt steak on her face, she must have done that before she washed her hands, and she obviously hadn't stopped to check in a mirror, redo her makeup – *what makeup?*

*He was marooned in a place where women didn't wear makeup and looked great without it, and didn't worry about dirt on their faces. That, plus the no-bra episode ... was it any wonder he was always off balance? What would Malaspina Island throw at him next?*

*What would Stacie throw at him next?*

He wouldn't mind if some of that radiance was because of him. But most likely it was the vegetables.

She put the tray on the table and nodded toward the little tree at the foot of her garden, about three paces from the picnic table. "Hawthorn," she said.

He went over to the hawthorn, plucked a leaf and tucked it into a pocket. "Thus begins my career as a naturalist. Tell me something. Someone sent me a gift last Sunday. Sunscreen" He watched but she didn't react, just poured tea into the glasses. Did that mean she did send the sunscreen, or she didn't and that's just the kind of thing that happened around here? He wished to God he knew.

And she wasn't telling. "Kind of thing that happens. How's the neck?"

*Better if you'd put your hand on it.*

"Fine. I haven't caught a lot of sun the last couple of days. Work."

She cocked an eyebrow, then slid onto one of the benches. "You don't sound thrilled, Adam. Shouldn't you be doing something you at least like, if it's going to dominate your every waking hour?" She picked up one of the glasses and set it across the table from her. He ignored that and slid in next to her, bumping their arms together.

"I do enjoy it, most of the time. Anyway, it's work. You're paid to do a job, not to enjoy it. This isn't a vacation."

"Isn't it?" She was studying him, up close and personal. He felt the heat rising and felt her eyes tracking it. A little smile danced at the corners of her mouth. Adam was more and more convinced that Stacie liked his blush and didn't mind in the least triggering it.

He became businesslike. "About three quarter time, in terms of traditional work. A lot of what I usually do, I still have to get done. I'm here with you right now and maybe I could justify that as part of getting to know the people on the island. But I'll be working on financial statements and such tonight. It's a job."

*Keep justifying.*

"I'll be prepping all the ingredients for tomorrow's breakfast. Wednesday's a fancy oatmeal, so I'll have all the bits and pieces ready tonight and just cook it up tomorrow."

"So it's a weekly rotation?" She nodded. "Once it's all prepped, then what?" Adam kept his eyes on her face. It changed so much, with the lighting, with her mood. Right now she looked fulfilled – *not by me, though* – with that glow lighting her up. Maybe it was just the way her darker skin took the sun.

"Then? Like you saw on Friday. Usually I'm ready to just read or watch TV or a video. Sometimes there's something happening in the town or with my friends. Tonight?" She shrugged. "Quiet night."

"Sounds familiar. I'll be working until about 8:00, probably, then I'll be doing the same. It seems to me we could sit and watch two TVs, or sit and watch one. Since I can't invite you to my place, could I invite myself to yours?"

A pause. *It's amazing how quiet a garden can be*, he thought. As if the bloody birds that had been carrying on nonstop for the last hour were waiting to see what she'd say. Maybe, if you listened carefully, you could hear the ocean down in the cove. The breeze rustled the hawthorn tree a little, but that was all. No traffic, no sounds from inside the B&B. He reached across the table and picked up his glass of tea about the same time he realized he was holding his breath.

Stacie cleared the iced tea things, then sank into a chair in her living room. What on earth had just happened? Why did he keep doing that? *How* did he keep doing that? No kidding, Adam, on top of her regular work, was depleting her reserves.

*Not to mention her will power.*

And that was accompanied by those little, persistent tightenings in some very personal places. The places that were coming awake and wanting more.

And the real problem, the heart of the problem, was that she liked his company. He was an innocent, at least where island ways were concerned, and irreverent and smart. And conflicted. She believed that about him. They might not be doing him any favors by showing him the island way of life, if it was going to mess up his mind.

*Don't think about it later. Don't think about it at all. Control, Stacie.*

She wanted definitions. She wanted clarity. She liked him, dammit, but friends was only a part of what was going on.

*Friends with privileges?*

That wasn't it, either. It was more than that. It was the connection she felt, just knowing he was on the island somewhere. It was whatever it was that made Adam Fraser more than a friend and more than the object of pent-up and usually not evident female lust.

Big city charm, that's all it was.

*Right, convince yourself.*

Probably back in Toronto women were falling into his bed in droves, so he thought she'd be the same. *Ha!* Especially since he'd be gone in a few days, once they got this blasted Open Forum thing out of the way. He was *so* not going to happen, no matter how much her friends thought he'd be worth it.

And now she'd have to deal with him tonight. What on *earth* had made her agree?

*Mindless TV? You poor, naïve idiot.*

She hauled herself out of the chair, feeling excited and unsettled. Glasses from the iced tea washed and left in the drainer to dry, she headed for the shower.

By the time Adam turned up, a bit after 8:30, in the loose jeans – oh yes, she'd noticed the difference in the two pairs – with a t-shirt and the sweater he'd worn on Saturday, Stacie had a cheese plate and some raw vegetables tucked in the fridge. She was working on the assumption that he probably hadn't eaten any better than she had that evening. She'd also decided that they could drink pop or lemonade. The risk inherent in anything even a little bit intoxicating was all too obvious to her. The television was on, but she hadn't even surfed to see if there was anything worth watching.

He came in her door and gave her an absent-minded hug. He looked as if TV was the most he was going to be up to.

*Callaway Forest Products wearing you out?*

But then her kind angel took over. *He's a tired man, Stacie, that's all. Just tired.*

*No, not all. He's a wreck.*

She settled him on the sofa, then, against her better judgment, circled behind him and began a probing neck and shoulder rub.

He twisted around. "You'd be so nice to come home to," he said, and turned his not-as-rare-as-it-used-to-be smile on her. Then he settled back and let her tend to his muscles, which, she quickly discovered, gave a new meaning to tension.

"How do you get any sleep if you're keyed up like this at almost 9:00 at night?"

"I have my share of restless nights. Who doesn't?"

"Me, for one. I usually sleep really well. If you want, I have some chamomile tea, that's supposed to be –"

He waved a hand, sort of limply, like the hand itself didn't have any more energy in it than the thought. "Thanks, maybe not."

"You don't know until you've tried."

They were quiet for a few minutes. Then he said, "Talk to me, Stacie. Tell me where you're going. What you dream about. This?" He gestured around him at the B&B. "You've built something really good here, but I have to wonder if it's all you want."

*Ah, the old talk-to-me ploy.*

She could do with ballast. She didn't let her thoughts wander down dream paths much, these days. "Family, I suppose. But what's the point in thinking about the husband-and-kids thing when it isn't going to happen? I weigh it in the balance and I know what the odds are. The future?" She shrugged. "It'd take a cataclysm of some sort to change anything, and don't forget, this is Malaspina."

"Where nothing ever changes? Seems to me that it's a prime spot for cataclysms. To me, anyway." His eyes were closed.

"Yeah, but you're coming from a place where you need lots of shaking up, just to figure it out. For me? I'm here. And not likely to leave."

"You're hard working and focused, that much anyone can see. You have good friends. I don't think you're a very wild or spontaneous person. That doesn't mean you can't have a dream out there somewhere."

"Dreams." She gave his shoulders a final pat and circled the sofa to collapse near him, her head against the back of the sofa, her eyes unfocused somewhere across the room. She propped a foot on the battered coffee table. "I can build a romantic fantasy just as well as anyone. I don't take it seriously though. There's no point."

"I'd like the wife-and-kids thing, I think."

She looked over at him. "Your own romantic fantasy?"

"It may be too late. At my age? I scarcely even know where I'd meet a woman to share a dream with. My poor parents," he added with a chuckle. "Pat, my sister, she's in about the same boat. No grandkids in the offing. At least they don't nag us about it."

"It's not the husband-and-kids bit entirely. It's about having someone to build a dream with. That someone hasn't come along."

"We have a problem here, Stacie."

"I know."

She thought about it. The edges of their shared problem seemed fuzzy. His arm went around her shoulders, but without drawing her close. It was more a comfort and a connection than a hint at more to come.

He raised up so he could look at her. "So what do you eat for breakfast?"

"Huh? Where did that come from?"

"Just curious. Something I've wondered about."

"Corn flakes. Toast. Grapefruit. The usual stuff."

"Not your own cooking?"

"Are you kidding? I'd be a blimp."

"Does anyone ever want corn flakes?"

"Mm-hmm. I keep breakfast cereals on hand. Especially when someone's been here for several days, sometimes they just want to get back to basics."

"You do know your business."

"Halloran House might be part of the romantic image, but basically it's a job, Adam. Same as yours. I like it, but it does restrict my freedom and it does mean that I'm on duty six mornings a week. And I do an awful lot of cleaning. But it supports me and lets me pay for Mike – the teenager who helps in the yard – and a garden care service in the summer. And I'm rebuilding my savings. That's important to me. I don't want to be a charity case when I'm old."

The silence hung between them, and neither seemed inclined to break it. *This is good,* Stacie thought. *Quiet. No lust or drama. No desperation to get our hands on each other …*

*And you're kidding whom, exactly?*

*Well, maybe a little lust. Okay, more than a little. Maybe lots?*

Stacie's thoughts came unhitched. She really wanted to experience his skin beneath her hands, his light evening beard, the texture of the sprinkling of reddish hairs on his chest, which she'd noticed through the open collar of that dress shirt, at the pub. She wanted to see his face, see his eyes when passion caught him and reminded him that he was in an earthquake zone. She wanted to push him to his limits and beyond. She wanted to be there when he couldn't hold out any longer. When they had no choice and he took her —

*Whoa! Good thing you're not desperate.*

*Yeah, right.*

Stacie gave up fighting her no-lust thoughts, since it was obviously a losing battle, and let her mind go where it was determined to go anyway.

How he would approach discovering her? How it would be for his hands to explore her more fully than they'd allowed themselves so far? Even sitting quietly, talking, was affecting her, deepening whatever was going on between them.

*How was she supposed to stop thinking like this?*

*Getting harder by the minute, Stacie?*

*No, the getting-harder was his role, not hers.*

Laughing at herself made it easier to apply the screeching brakes. *Save passion-laden thoughts about Adam for some other time.*

*Going nowhere, girl.*

Stacie moved a little closer. "Politics?"

"Tend to the right."

"Left for me. Religion?"

"Not to speak of. Not something I think about, really."

"Raised agnostic. Still agnostic. Dream vacation?"

"Europe, probably. History we can't even conceive of."

"Europe sounds good, but it's a long way from here. I wouldn't argue about Hawaii, though. From this end of the country it's so much closer. Wild parties?"

"Too old."

"Tell me about it," Stacie groaned. "Some things are best wasted on the young, and that's one of them."

"Kids?" he asked.

"What about them?"

"I already know you want them. How many?"

"A couple would be great. I'm not quite old enough that I'm feeling threatened, but I'm aware of that damn ticking clock. But you know, if it doesn't happen, I'm surviving my friends having kids. Jess and I talk about it sometimes, if we'd consider adoption or artificial insemination or something, assuming the right man doesn't come along. But I don't know. You?"

"One or two. It's hard to imagine without having the mother of those kids in the picture."

"Or the father."

"It's hard to imagine growing old single."

"Lots of things are hard to imagine. Even if they're beginning to seem inevitable."

Their conversation meandered through other topics, whatever one of them thought to ask the other. They spoke, fell quiet, spoke again.

Then, out of the blue, he grinned. A relaxed grin. An at-home-and-comfortable grin. "Of course, there's the whole matter of our culture clash. Maybe it's time to try for an armistice."

Then he turned, his mouth was on hers, her body sent highly positive messages of relief to her brain – *at last!* – before her brain discovered totally new neural paths firing off signals to those quivery bits she'd so adamantly ignored earlier. Hands and bodies developed minds of their own, and by the time their eyes next met, 'relaxed' wasn't a word that had any application at all.

"Oh, boy," he groaned. "This can't go on much longer if we want to keep our options open." He pushed himself away from her, panting a little. He stood up and prowled around her living room, giving her a clear view of why he had to back off. He jammed his hands in his pockets, fisted. "Thing is," he said after a minute, his breath more or less restored even if the rest of him wasn't, "I've never been drawn to the caveman thing, and I think I'm beginning to understand it. I was hoping for hours, more or less. Not minutes."

"We're hot?"

He laughed. Adam. Right out loud. "You are so good for me."

Stacie was in the grip of what could be called a hot flash. If this kept up she'd have to go into Victoria and buy herself a fan in Chinatown. Cooling things down seemed like a right, a positive, idea.

*No, it didn't.*

*Necessary, then.*

"I thought I might put out some food. I doubt either of us ate properly earlier."

"Good thought. I don't know about you, but I need some recovery time." Adam flopped back onto her sofa, limp. Mostly.

But when she came back into the living room a few minutes later, after setting the table and putting out the cheese and veggies, he'd fallen asleep, just like that. She wondered what on earth kind of tight wire he was walking, to move from passion – unfulfilled – to exhaustion so quickly.

Whatever else he was – and she was still trying to figure out how impossible and inevitable weren't mutually exclusive – she knew this thing between them wasn't any easier for him than for her, with the added complication of his being the focal point in the upcoming battle for Nathan's Forest. Right now, if she could give him space to relax, well, okay.

As for the other, the not-relaxing part ... *shelve it, Stacie.*

It was a little after 10:00 when Adam woke up. He looked around for a moment, disoriented, before he sorted out that he'd fallen asleep on Stacie's sofa. She looked over at him from her kitchen door. "Come on in. Dinner time."

He stretched and yawned. He'd been covered up with a light, fluffy blanket. Stacie, of course.

He heaved himself off the sofa and settled in a kitchen chair. "Thank you. I hadn't realized how hungry I was. Am." He put some brie onto a cracker and bit into it, then nodded, swallowed, and said, "You're right. This is the best idea I've come across all day. Falling asleep maybe was the worst, given how many other things we could have been doing."

"Not the worst to me. Having you asleep in my living room felt good. And you needed it. Eat."

"You are a ministering angel."

"Just practical."

"Thanks, Stacie."

"You're welcome." She bit into the broccoli floret she was holding.

Adam looked over at her while they ate. While technically he wouldn't consider himself inexperienced, Stacie fell well outside the realm of any woman he'd ever been involved with before. He'd never dozed on a sofa without feeling like a dork, for example. Or wakened to crackers and cheese simply because she knew he wouldn't have had a decent supper. The pattern was meant to be entertainment of some sort, sex, end of episode. Not quite slam, bam, thank you ma'am, but damn close, now that he thought about it.

Not that he wouldn't like to explore the physical some more with her. *Hell, yes.* What he already knew about her compact body provoked a reaction in him that forced him not to think about her whenever he'd be on public display. But somehow all of that was wrapped up in this sense of rightness. *I wonder if this is love,* he mused. *I wonder if I've finally fallen in love.* He suspected he had. And what the Sam Hill was he supposed to do about that?

*Dream? Dreams were costly.*

"Suppose I said you could have your way with me?" he asked her abruptly. "What would you do?"

Stacie let out a delighted laugh. "I was thinking more or less the same thing."

"Answer to you is, I'd say no. I'd say I want it to be shared, not one sided. Sort of having our mutual way with each other. Does that make any sense?"

"Oh." Stacie turned aside, stared out her window at the night. "Adam, that might be the nicest thing anyone's ever said to me." She was quiet for a moment. Then she shook her head. "The time's not right. I want ... no, forget it. You know you're driving me crazy, right?"

He hadn't been completely sure, despite her enthusiastic participation, but what they were talking about went beyond anything that could, in any way, be considered, well, mechanical. He nodded rather than try to put all that into words.

"But ... I'm sorry, Adam. It's too soon. I know that sounds hopelessly old fashioned and prudish, but that's how I feel. I'm not ready."

"Then I'm not, either. Thanks for talking to me tonight, Stacie. And feeding me and, well, everything."

"Heading back to the hotel?"

He nodded and stood. They moved to the door together.

"It doesn't follow that I can't kiss you goodnight, does it?"

He watched her work her way through the double negative. "Definitely not." In fact it was Stacie who put her hand behind his neck and pulled his head down to meet her mouth. This kiss was different again, more promise than passion, but the promise, he was sure, was there.

He wondered, as he walked into town, how many more flavors of kiss they had between them, that they hadn't explored yet.

# Chapter 13

Adam didn't know what he expected for the official announcement of the Open Forum on Wednesday. The town and island administration had undertaken that aspect, and other than agreeing to the wording he hadn't inquired. A mistake, probably, he mused, if only because it would have looked better in his reports. But it was their island, so his executive decision had been to leave it up to them.

He knew, at least, that it didn't involve the newspaper. Published weekly, the next edition wasn't due out until late Thursday.

Still, he'd expected some kind of pomp. A formal procession from the Admin Building. A town crier in red robes, trumpets or something. He was mildly surprised when he saw the photocopied sheet in the middle of the bulletin board on the Square. The same as the Barn Dance notice had been, only the paper was pale green this time. Somehow he'd expected it to get more play.

Roger McMillan turned up at the bulletin board and stopped to look. "Says it all," he commented with a nod. "You have time for a coffee?"

"Sure." There was always work to do back in his room, but he wasn't in the mood to do it. It didn't seem like he was in the mood very often these days.

*Damn place is seducing you.*

He turned toward the coffee shop on the Square, but Roger touched his arm. "Come on. I'll show you how the locals do it. Don't tell your Callaway pals, though."

Adam automatically promised he wouldn't tell, and followed Roger. They ducked between the Admin Building and the building that sat catty-corner to it on its left, then they cut over a street or two, heading out of town, turned left, and Roger said, "There. Mostly we leave the one on the Square for the tourists, unless we're in a real hurry. It's a good division of market share, and no hard feelings." Roger shoved the door open and entered, calling, "Hey, Doreen!"

"Hey yourself. Where've you been? Haven't seen you for days."

"Getting drier by the minute, without your coffee, my dear. This is Adam, the young man from Callaway. Give me two larges, please."

"Will do. And hello, welcome to Malaspina." Doreen stretched her hand over the counter and shook Adam's while they exchanged greetings. Adam had the interesting feeling that she was looking him over and assessing what she saw. "If you want some other variation on coffee or tea, let me know. Roger has this idea that drip, black, is what everyone drinks, or ought to. And choose a pastry – on the house today." She turned back to Roger. "You, too. I wasn't going to leave you out."

"Actually, straight coffee will be fine," Adam said. "And you really don't need –"

"Of course I do," Doreen interrupted his polite refusal. "Guys need pastries. It's a rule around here."

"Yes, ma'am," Roger said. Then to Adam he added, "If you obey Doreen, good things come your way." Adam saw the wink from Roger, the eye roll from Doreen. Roger led the way over to a table in the window.

"You're lucky to be in the hotel," Roger began, "because you're not that easy to reach. They don't usually give out the phone numbers in the rooms. With luck, the most you'll get is an earful on the street. But watch out for the editorial and the letters in tomorrow's newspaper."

"I gather you're not picking up many positive opinions?"

Doreen came over with their coffees, cutlery, and pastries, warmed up and with little paper cups of butter and icing on the side. She and Roger exchanged glances, Adam caught a small nod, and the next thing he knew Doreen had joined their table. "Only for a minute. We're coming up to morning crazy time."

"Thanks for this." Adam unwrapped the napkin around his the knife and fork. "I think I may need the fortification today."

"You do charming and modest very well," she said sweetly. "Skill learned in the boardroom?"

"Way to go," Roger said. "Doreen, you're meant to bring a measure of civilization to conversations between two men. Behave yourself."

"Never mind that. Tell me what's happening."

Roger filled her in on the notice he'd posted that morning, and the reaction – so far minimal, despite his dire predictions – he'd picked up so far. "One thing I can say, this won't tear the island apart. I think you'll find a lot of unanimity here against Callaway."

Doreen nodded. "Everyone's upset. Not with you, dear," she added, placing her hand on his arm for a moment. "We all sympathize with you, caught in the middle and all."

"I can't say that I'm really caught—" But he didn't get a chance to finish.

"Of course you are. You're fitting in here. Anyone can see that. And no, I'm not talking about Stacie, even though we're all waiting to see how that turns out. And of course we're prepared to lynch you if you mess with her."

Adam blushed. It was beginning to feel like a permanent state. "No, ma'am. I mean I understand."

Roger was clearly enjoying this snippet of dialogue. "Good. Now you know where we stand and we know where you stand, right?"

*They do? They can't. I'm aligned with Callaway. That's my career we're bandying about so casually.*

The door opened and about a dozen people came in. "Here comes the rush," Doreen said. "Catch you later. Behave yourself now," she added as a parting shot to Roger, with another press of her hand on Adam's arm.

"Isn't it fun?" Roger lounged back in his chair. "Doreen has the pulse of Malaspina probably better than any other one person, although Abby and I between us give her a run for her money. Makes coffee break interesting."

The new group filtered around the coffee shop, dragging tables together. Almost all of them acknowledged Roger, and a good number of them said hello to Adam, with a wave or sometimes by name. He didn't sense any of the animosity Roger had warned him about, so the tiny knot that had begun to clench in his middle released a little bit. The whole thing might be exaggerated.

That's what he thought, anyway, until a pretty blonde woman leaned over and smiled right in his face and said, "Just so you know, you'll be a high soprano if you get anywhere close to logging Nathan's." Another sweet smile and she straightened and walked over to her group.

"Oh," he said.

Roger choked on his coffee, then laughed out loud. "Thanks, Suzanne," he called to the woman. Turning back to Adam he said, "Now you're really in the picture."

"Tell me this much. Will it be safe for me to go out in the street for the next week? I feel the hairs on the back of my neck prickling."

"We won't need the RCMP until after the Open Forum, I expect. Some of it's anticipation at the idea of a good fight. I think you're safe."

"Could we maybe change the topic? This one's making me nervous." A small, conversational lie. In fact, he felt relaxed, despite the tiny knot in his middle, the potential for confrontation. "Tell me what an administrator for an island does. What's your work?"

"Want my job?"

"With the logging thing coming up? God, no. I was just curious."

Roger gave him a look he couldn't interpret, then launched into an overview of budget preparation, consultation with other government branches, dealing with irate citizens, and simply keeping the physical aspects of island administration running smoothly. Around bites of Danish, Adam listened, taking mental notes.

Grocery shopping was never one of Stacie's favorite occupations. But supplies were running low and tomorrow she'd need flour for the pancakes, fresh mushrooms and goat cheese for the omelets. Plus the other odds and ends that gathered up on her list over the week. One thing she'd learned running the B&B for three years, organization was crucial. Without it, she'd be in big trouble.

With only one supermarket on the island there was no way to avoid crowded aisles or someone who wanted to stop for a chat, unless you went at 9:00 at night. Fine, most of the time, but Stacie was more than a little messed up about some of the things going on in her life. Especially a thing named Adam, who needed to be booted out of her thoughts and stubbornly refused to be. But this was island life, so she graciously, cheerfully accepted nonstop advice about dealing with the Enemy and getting his secrets out of him, not to mention about watching her back …

*He likes my back …*

*No, no, no!*

So she weathered the bustle and the conversations in the aisles, responded politely, got herself checked out, and headed home.

Driving back across the island – the supermarket was out of town to the west, not on the main east-west road but tucked behind a subdivision – she used the time to piece it all together.

The thing about island life was, you had to have the temperament for it. You couldn't hop in your car and drive away. If you needed arugula and the supermarket didn't have any, you were out of luck. Acquiring larger items always took extra time while shipping companies juggled with ferry schedules. Furnishing the B&B had been a nightmare of schedules and logistics. You took all of this into consideration, and learned not to want too much, because it was too much hassle.

If you didn't have the temperament, she supposed it could drive you nuts. Adam hadn't figured all this out yet. He probably thought he'd just have to snap his fingers and a bottle of Moët would appear. Good thing her mom and Roger had set him straight on the computer literacy rate.

She liked the life and she liked the people. Sure, sometimes she'd like to see someone different from the usual assortment, but mostly she rolled with it.

Did her occasional longing for variety make her more vulnerable to Adam? Did her life on this isolated island mean she couldn't recognize big-city moves? What was his game? Was he serious or was he amusing himself? How the hell was she supposed to know?

Then there was that electricity that buzzed between them, right from the first time their eyes met. She wasn't faking that, and she'd bet he wasn't either. He'd been too appalled.

*What was his game? What was hers? Did she stand a chance of winning?*

*Maybe three weeks of Adam was victory enough?*

*No. It wasn't.*

*Oh, boy. Laugh, Stacie.*

Stacie had just made it home when Adam appeared. She passed him her key from a hand that was juggling grocery bags. "I'll say this, sometimes you turn up just in time to be useful."

He unlocked the door and pushed it open for them. "Let me help." He took one of the bags of groceries from her. "I strive to earn my welcome, ma'am."

Stacie rolled her eyes at the 'ma'am', then chuckled. "You have to have a certain mindset to deal with the supermarket. You can put the bag on the table." She moved swiftly, unloading the groceries. "Be warned, it's all very systematic. When you cook for a living, things get that way." Her personal supplies stowed, she unlocked the door that connected her kitchen to the B&B's commercial kitchen. "If you're following me, be sure you're not tracking in mud."

"I'll be safe and not follow you." He shifted groceries from the table to the door, passing them to her. "Is it really necessary to have two kitchens?"

She shrugged. "When I'm bringing dirty vegetables in from the garden, or when I feel like kicking back and making something for myself without having to worry about every little spill … yeah. It lets me relax, having my own space." She looked over her shoulder from the cabinet where she was stowing bags of organic flour. "Any special reason you're here?"

"Long day for me, too. I'm more popular than ever. It was getting crazy before the official announcement, but now people see the notice about the Open Forum and want to buy me a coffee, invite me to lunch. Haranguing in the most pleasant of ways. I don't know what they think I can do about it, but I'm certainly getting a first-hand impression of how the island feels. I thought it'd be nice to see you."

"And mooch supper?"

"I suppose it would ruin your reputation if we were seen in public? Consorting with the Enemy and all?" He grinned at her raised eyebrows. "Never mind, I'm getting used to it."

"It's become kind of a cute nickname, I think."

"I try not to get my feelings hurt. To be honest, though, it's odd, how that's shifted. When I came here I didn't give a damn what anyone thought of me. Now I do care, and I'm the Enemy. And I'd like to take you out somewhere."

"Why not? I could use an evening of someone else's cooking, and believe me, we're not exactly a secret. At the supermarket people were blocking the aisles with their carts to give me advice. Everyone tells me to be careful, and learn all I can about whatever nefarious plan you have for our forest. The place was a minefield."

"Small correction. Not your forest, our forest."

"Mine."

"Mine."

They both laughed. She came back into her private kitchen, locked the door.

"Okay, then, what's your fancy? One thing this place has is plenty of restaurants."

"Advantage of being a tourist destination. Personally, I like Samuel's on the Wharf. They do this thing with breaded grilled scampi and garlic butter that's to die for."

"You're on. Do we need reservations?"

"Not if we go early. Plus tourist season isn't in full swing yet." She glanced at the clock over the table. "Like about now. Are you good with that?"

"Maybe another half an hour? It's only 5:30 and I just wolfed down some pretzels. A lot of pretzels, actually."

"And didn't bring any to share."

"Next time. This was working man's perks. I missed my muffin."

"I did notice you always ordered the sweet dish, not the egg dish."

"Doughnuts are my downfall, but it's starting to creep up on me. It's challenging."

"Depends on the job, I guess. Maybe you'd like to run by here every morning and do the vacuuming for me. Or even better, clean the bathtubs. Lots of stretching."

"For you, anything. Almost." He followed her out the back door and down into her garden, where she leaned against the table. She watched him prowl her little patch of private lawn. "You know, this whole place perplexes me," he said. "It's so completely not what I expected. We were more or less parachuted into here without a lot of time to prep, then the first thing that hit us was the barn dance. I mean just the name gives an impression, you know? But since then … lately I've been going to the coffee shop on the Square. No Coffee Shack, incidentally?"

"Longing for the familiar? Coffee Shack's all over Vancouver, but not here. I guess we're not big enough for the chains to fight to get in here. There's no rush, far as I'm concerned. There are several places to go that are off the tourist beat, so it's not quite as limited as you probably think it is."

He laughed. "Roger took me to the secret coffee shop. But the one on the Square, it's a different scene. I go over for a morning coffee and because it's usually busy I ask someone if I can share a table. Or someone asks me. Sometimes it's a tourist, sometimes not. A couple of days ago I found myself with five other people, they just kept coming over. Everyone knows who

I am, nobody's got the least reluctance to tell me what they think. And believe me, they all think something, about the way of life here or the forest. Needless to say, I'm outnumbered on the subject of the forest."

"Hey, you weren't lynched. That proves how civilized we are, doesn't it?"

"I never thought about mortal peril. But seriously, this place has gotten under my skin. It's like a different universe. A different culture and I don't know the rules. I was just going through the motions here at first, because that's what I was supposed to do. Then to top it all off, last Friday at the Foxes' barbecue, it was really driven home that Abby Fox is an uber-intelligent woman. Did you know she's a lawyer? Practiced contract law for years before she came here? And the way she talked about the things that happen in the town and all over the island … there's a chamber music festival in August."

"Believe it or not, I did know that."

He grinned. "Yeah. Sorry." He stopped pacing and stood in front of her, gesticulating. "And she had some really well thought out points about Callaway and the logging thing. I took some time out yesterday and walked down to the harbor and I just sat and mulled it over for a while."

"Something that would never happen in Toronto, I bet."

He snorted. "And look like you're wasting time? There's a park close to the office, but you wouldn't dare go there and just sit and think, if that's what you mean."

"It doesn't sound very nice." There was a pause. "And?"

"And I'm thinking right now. But it has more to do with hugging you." He pulled her off the table and gathered her up.

And felt her poking at his mid-section. "Any time you want to start the vacuuming and bathrooms."

"I'm ignoring that. So yesterday, I sat there and watched the boats sort of rocking, and sometimes a boat would come in or go out, and people were walking around and eating ice cream, and I had this memory of talking to them all at the barbecue about tax write-offs and municipal finances. I suddenly got it. That despite the laid back appearance, Malaspina isn't the backwater I … uh oh."

Stacie stiffened, and pulled back to glare at him. She already felt threatened enough. She wanted him close and far away, and she wanted him to understand the island and she wanted him completely out of her life. She wanted him to let her go and – heck, she liked resting her head on his chest. For once she liked being short. It all came together in one mixed-up package, tied up in a bow by his words.

*Backwater? How dare he?* So she let rip.

"How nice. We're not all as ignorant as you thought? And now you're in my back yard and you're basically saying that my way of life is uneducated? Who do you think you are? How dare you belittle me like that?" She was quivering. "You don't know anything! You think your stupid corporation in your stupid city is the best way to live, even if it was making you fat and you can't even go sit in a park …" Jagged pause for breath. "… and I have a master's degree in English. I work hard. I'm not dumb."

His mouth on hers, however briefly, wasn't a bad way to end a rant, all things considered. "Are you aware that we still have our arms around each other?" he asked when he broke off the too-short kiss.

"Oh."

"So calm down. Those were pre-Malaspina thoughts. Pre-you thoughts. They're not what I'm thinking anymore."

She calmed, but she wasn't happy about it. Still, it was a good opportunity to lean against him again. The rant had worn her out.

He rested his chin on her head. "Actually, I go check the planters on the Square every day, just to make sure they're fine. Some of them are positively manic, they're growing like weeds."

"The petunias, probably," she mumbled into his chest.

"I thought you'd want to know, what I thought then, what I'm thinking now, being that I'm the Enemy."

She pulled back and looked up at him. "You are. Dammit, Adam, how can you be the Enemy? Unless you're lying through your teeth about all that stuff about starting to get the way of life here. Which, come to think of it, may be the most likely scenario. I've been warned not to be too trusting."

Abruptly she was out of his arms and perched on one of the table's benches. "Just don't think because I'm obviously attracted to you, you can pull the wool over my eyes." Stacie's voice still had an edge of irritation.

"Something tells me I'd have my work cut out for me if I tried. Let's go eat. We'll walk, I'll lose my extra pound or two, and you can get un-angry at me."

She looked up at him, exasperated, then gave it up. "Let's do that. But if you come out with any more stuff about how backwoods and ignorant we are, I get to kick you in the shin."

"Fair enough." He pulled her to her feet and straight into his arms again. "Haven't done enough of this yet." He leaned in and gently bit her lower lip, then morphed that into some interesting effects involving the same lower lip and his tongue, then his mouth was on hers and scampi with garlic butter would be a few minutes later than planned.

Stacie had quickly, if somewhat shakily, changed out of her grocery clothes into a respectable pair of slacks and lightweight sweater. She grabbed a shawl and met Adam back in the yard. Linking hands, they walked into town.

"You saw the notice?" he asked.

A nod. "I was in Windon Harbor this afternoon. A few notes to mail." He glanced at her, and before he could ask she added, "I send notes to all the people who stay at Halloran House. Just thanking them and hoping they enjoyed their visit. One of these this afternoon was to your Katherine, as a matter of fact. You can have yours if you want it. Thought I'd save postage and not mail it."

"She'll love it, I'm sure."

"Don't sound so glum."

"Then don't mention Katherine."

As she predicted, they were seated immediately. The restaurant was busy, perhaps two thirds full, so they didn't get a window seat, but the picture windows were enormous and let everyone in the room have a view out over the harbor. Nothing much was said until they'd ordered and the waitress had poured their wine, then Stacie asked, "So the island's letting you know what it thinks?"

"I'm tempted to hole up in my hotel room. It's intimidating."

"Coward."

"Prudent."

"Adam, you make me laugh. I wish you weren't caught in the middle of this. Believe me, it's going to be bad before it gets good again. I worry about you."

"Thanks." He covered one of her hands with his own. "It's really polarized, isn't it? No neutral. That's going to make it hard to compromise."

She shook her head. "Would Callaway compromise anyway? Would you look for a middle position? Nobody has much faith in that around here. Sending in the advance scouting party – sorry, but that's what you are, isn't it? That wasn't very clever. Everyone's mistrustful. And now we're on high alert."

"I did have coffee this morning with Roger. You know, the Island Administrator?"

"I know Roger."

"You know everyone. This woman came over and got right in my face. I thought I was about to lose some very personal parts of my anatomy."

Stacie grinned. "I love it. As long as she wasn't leggy and gorgeous."

"She was, actually. Roger called her Suzanne. Somehow I failed to get her number, but I'll keep my eyes out for her —" He broke off when she slapped his hand.

"So, change of topic. Did you buy your ticket?" The Malaspina Players were putting on *A Midsummer Night's Dream*. Stacie and her friends had bought tickets a month ago.

"This morning. But I have to tell you, I don't know about this. Shakespeare? Business majors don't have a lot to do with him."

"In that case you'd better go to the lecture tomorrow night. Some guy from the University of Victoria is coming over."

Adam groaned.

"Then Friday, one of us can pick you up if you don't want to walk. The scout hall's a couple of miles out of town."

Their meals arrived. The scampi, the butter … Stacie dug in. The play was forgotten, along with the logging, prepping for tomorrow's breakfast … They'd both be seriously, gloriously garlicky by the time this meal was over.

Walking home, they dropped hands and wrapped their arms around each other. Stacie burrowed into him, as confused as ever.

# Chapter 14

Adam was up early Saturday morning, feeling saturated with *A Midsummer Night's Dream*. To say he'd enjoyed it might be going a little too far, although an evening holding onto Stacie had its merits, as had certain post-theater events. He felt himself warming at the memory. He got a coffee at Java on the Square and wandered toward the bulletin board, enjoying the cool, damp air taming the color on his face. He didn't remember blushing once in the last fifteen years or so, and now it was a daily, sometimes hourly, occurrence.

He was studying the notices on the board when Jess turned up next to him. "Hey, there," she said.

"Hello. You're early."

She shrugged. "It's getting into the season so I open half an hour earlier. I don't pay myself for that extra half hour, so sometimes I even get a little profit out of it. Looking for something to do?"

"Not desperately. Today alone I have two coffee meetings and a lunch, and I'll be listening to arguments against logging Nathan's Forest at all of them. Right now I'm just browsing, and maybe girding my loins. Do you have a few minutes?"

Of Stacie's friends, Jess was the one he was least able to figure out. He thought he understood Jane, who was quieter and professional. Donna made no sense to him whatsoever, but then she was pregnant, so maybe she wasn't supposed to. But

Jess … she seemed so devil-may-care, yet she owned and ran the classiest – in his opinion, and by now he'd seen them all – gift shop on the island. But she was here and it was a chance to chat.

"Let me grab a coffee first."

When she came back and settled on a bench next to him, he said, "Is it hard work, running your store?"

"Depends on your definition, I guess. Would you say your work's hard?"

He hadn't thought about that. He worked hard, but was the work itself hard, or was it just volume? Or dedication? "Interesting question. I put in long hours, and it's painstaking, there's not much room for a mistake, so yes, I'd say so."

"For me the hardest is the length of the days. Tracking down the things I want for the shop, that's fun. Encouraging local artisans is great. Meeting customers, leading them to see the potential in something, that's a high point. Best, of course, if they actually take my recommendations and buy something. The bookkeeping – someone else does it, it's definitely not my strong point."

"It must mean a big up-front outlay, to get stock."

"Are you pumping me for information, Adam?"

"Yes, but not for any nefarious purpose. I don't understand the nature of the island's economy, or the nature of retail. You're sitting here, so I thought you might be a good person to talk to."

"It's not one size fits all. And there was an outlay, sure, but with so much of my stock consignment …." She shrugged. "It keeps my overhead down and supports the economy. Like, Stacie makes soaps. There's a woman who has alpacas and sells yarn and weaves the most incredible shawls. There are a couple of potters, a couple of wonderful knitters, a paper maker, a seamstress, several jewelry makers ... it's not hard to find quality merchandise. All I have to do is round it out with purchased stuff. That's about the only time I get off the island anymore, when I go visit my suppliers on the mainland."

Adam nodded. "You always seem so upbeat. It's obvious you enjoy it."

"I do." She broke off. A large, dark haired man, probably in his early fifties, came up to them. "Hey, Ethan."

"Hi, there, Jess."

"Ethan, meet Adam."

"Good to meet you at last," Ethan said, and stuck out a hand.

They shook. "And you."

"Where are you working these days?" Jess asked.

"Washout south of Elder." To Adam he said, "Elder's the little village over on the west side of the island. Not much there but a pub and a little grocery." Returning his attention to Jess, he added, "We only did a temporary repair last winter. It's time to fix it properly."

"For the ten people a year who actually use that road."

Ethan laughed. "True, but those ten people live out there and they wouldn't be in town buying your pretty baubles if I didn't get that road fixed."

"It would be grim, they'd probably starve and we'd find their shriveled skeletons sometime years in the future."

"You're nuts. And skeletons don't shrivel." Ethan swatted Jess's leg with his folded up newspaper. "I've got to get going. See you at the dance tonight?"

"You bet."

Ethan walked off and Adam saw his opportunity. "Jess, about the dance." The dance that had been puzzling him for a few days now. It was there on the bulletin board, but Stacie hadn't mentioned it. In fact, no one had mentioned it to him. Given the social and welcoming nature of the island, he didn't get it.

"Oh." Jess pinched her lips together. "Damn, Stacie didn't tell you? Adam, I don't quite know how to say this. I think ... we all think maybe you should give this one a miss?"

"But why?" He was bewildered now. And realized, belatedly, how much he'd been looking forward to it.

"Because of what it is. Here's the thing. We have a dance or some kind of party about once a month. Other than the spring and fall Barn dances, they're fundraisers. We have several charities active on the island, so the profit goes to them."

"I like that. It sounds like the kind of thing the people here would do."

"Well, the charity this time – I'm not even sure if it's a registered charity or not, but whatever – it's the Nathan's Forest Defense Fund."

The implications hit him instantly. He'd been about to have another sip of his coffee, but instead lowered his cup. "I see."

"So if you go – I mean it's not that we wouldn't like to have you there and all, I mean nothing personal – but if you go, you're contributing to the fund that's dedicated to fighting you tooth and nail. Not good optics, probably."

"You're talking lawyers. Serious battle."

"Well, of course. Did you think we were rolling over and dying for you?"

"No. I guess not." He hadn't seen this on the horizon. He'd better let Callaway know ... although how much financial backing could this little island raise? And what quality lawyers? It might not be so much of a threat.

As if she could read his mind, Jess grinned at him. "*Pro bono,* a lot of it."

"Well, damn."

"Poor baby. You wanted to dance." Jess patted his hand.

Yes, he'd wanted to dance. He'd wanted a waltz with Stacie that didn't see them at arm's length from each other. Although he wasn't quite ready to admit it yet, he'd wanted to jump up and down to ABBA.

He'd wanted to feel welcome. And for once, he didn't.

"It's for your own good, you know. Not exactly a career advancing move, I'd think, turning up at a fundraiser to fight your company. But we'll miss you. And I have to get to work."

Jess bounced to her feet. Then, to his total amazement, she leaned over and gave him a peck on the cheek. "I hope you figure it out soon," she whispered, then gave him her saucy grin and bounced off toward the waterfront.

*Figure it out? What was she talking about?*

Adam also stood and paced disconsolately around the Square before returning to his room. He suddenly had a lot more to think about than he'd had earlier that morning, and his thoughts weren't happy ones.

First off would be to draft an email to Ralph. That wouldn't take long, since he didn't know the magnitude of this fund or the quality of their lawyers.

But after that he had to work out how he was feeling.

Isolated, yes. Sad, yes. But the bottom line, once he'd run through all the possibilities, was hurt. He felt hurt that they'd obviously made the decision for him. Hurt that they hadn't seen that he could easily justify his attendance to Callaway if he ever had to. Hurt that the bottom line was that they didn't want him there.

Was that too harsh? Maybe. Maybe this was simple self-pity. But whether it was or not, Adam spent that Saturday feeling, well, like he didn't belong.

And that forced him to realize how much he wanted to belong.

And that took him nowhere at all.

# Chapter 15

On Sunday morning Adam woke feeling restless and unfocused. He went down to the hotel dining room for some breakfast, bacon and eggs, because he was actually getting tired of pancakes and waffles. Good, but he'd bet Stacie's were better. He headed back up to his room, wondering how he'd fill his day.

There was work to do. There was always work to do. He only had to look at his laptop and work would materialize. He didn't want to do it.

He'd gathered up brochures from the hotel lobby, so he spread them out on his bed. The one that had caught his eye was for kayaking. But the day was gray, the ocean looked cold, and he'd never kayaked. The beginner's program involved things like learning to roll, and he wasn't up for that much challenge. Maybe the hike into Nathan's Forest had taught him something?

Without a car, he wasn't going far. And suddenly, he wanted to go far. He wanted to get out of Windon Harbor. He knew by now that all he had to do was set foot out of the hotel and people would call to him, wave, corner him to give him an earful, with varying levels of politeness, about the nerve his company had, thinking they could log Nathan's Forest. Adam truly didn't want to be the man to tell them that it was going to happen and there wasn't anything they could do about it. For the same reason he didn't want to run into the mayor, or Abby Fox or Roger McMillan, or just about anyone he'd met.

He didn't like the position he was in. He didn't like carrying around his company's plans like a guilty secret.

And he especially didn't like knowing that they'd all be disappointed and furious in equal measure when they figured it out, and that the disappointment and fury would mostly be focused on him.

Of course he'd be long gone by then. But that didn't make it okay. It had become personal, and he wasn't sure how that had happened.

*What was happening to him?*

Maybe he could take the ferry over to Victoria. *Then catch the evening one back again?* No, the ferry wasn't that much of a thrill, and it was chilly, a breeze blowing right off the water.

He made a pot of coffee and poured himself a cup, then sat glumly at his window.

Sunday morning was quiet along the waterfront. A few tourists were out, he could see cameras and binoculars. A whale watching tour was loading up.

*I don't want to get out of Windon Harbor. I'm lonely, that's all.*

He was likely to stay lonely. Stacie had let him know that she had plans with her mother that afternoon. Where else was he supposed to go? He was uncomfortably aware of how much his world these days revolved around Stacie.

*It's temporary. You'll get out of here and get back to normal.*

At least he'd talked to her yesterday and knew that she hadn't planned to go to the dance, either, so that's why she hadn't mentioned it. He doubted it was out of solidarity. She threw herself heart and soul into her business, and sometimes she got tired, he'd seen it around her eyes.

Well, one way or another he couldn't sit around here all day. He was getting more and more morose.

He eyed his hiking boots with doubt. The man at the sporting goods store had sold him some paste to massage into them, and while they'd never look new again after their soaking in Nathan's Forest, they did look softer. He tried them on. It took a little walking around the room for his feet and the boots to settle into each other, but there didn't seem to be a pitched battle going on in there. He thought he might risk it.

Adam phoned down to the restaurant and ordered a bagged lunch. He stuffed his key and a few odds and ends into the khaki bag – in Toronto it would be called a man bag, here it was a plain rucksack – he'd bought yesterday at the General Store, and headed out the door.

Lunch in his bag, he stood at the entrance to the hotel for a minute, then started off. As if he had no control at all, his steps turned him right, past the right turn to the Square, another couple of blocks down, left onto Stacie's road.

He passed her B&B. He didn't stop. He was still feeling hurt and excluded about the dance, even with the explanation. Maybe he wanted some kind of a life here that wasn't entirely about Stacie.

Now that thought was enough to give him cold shivers.

The road was a little steeper than he remembered, but he was pleased that his legs handled it easily. The lookout at the end of the road consisted of a turning circle with a couple of parking places facing out over the ocean. He could see a few houses along the water, but couldn't see Stacie's, it was blocked by trees. He could see her patch of beach, though. A couple of people were out on it, gesturing at the view.

It was still early, the 10:10 ferry was pulling out. He sat on a bench and watched. The ferry sent a wave of sound across the island. Everyone knew the sound of the ferry horn. Whenever they heard it they all stopped to check their watches, followed by a nod or a sad shake of the head, as if the ferry running late required commiseration.

The lookout wasn't as private as he'd thought, that night he'd walked up here with Stacie. In fact, there were three houses on the turning circle. He'd liked it better when he thought it was more isolated. Not what he wanted this morning. Adam trudged back down, aware of a tug of disappointment.

A few of the stores along the waterfront, the ones that catered to tourists, were open, but they didn't tempt him. He studied his map of the island again, then shoved it into his bag and headed north, hoping to find a trail heading out of town from the north end of the harbor.

As usual, almost everyone he passed as he walked through the town waved or said hello. He waved and smiled back, because it was expected. He seriously wanted to be alone with his gray thoughts this gray morning.

But his thoughts were leading straight to feelings. And he wasn't about to let that happen. The whole falling-in-love business? Some complications he didn't need. He liked her a lot, but feelings? *No. Please God, no.* There were simply far too many reasons why not.

The trail was well marked – of course it would be, since it was on the tourist map. It was paved for the first stretch but he held out hope that further on, when it changed from a solid to a dotted line, he'd find a real trail. And some solitude.

*You had solitude in your hotel room.*

*That was involuntary. This is voluntary.*

Adam walked for over an hour. He ran out of paved trail fairly soon. From then on it was rough and he had to pay attention, but even so he stumbled over roots a couple of times. The trail snaked along a bluff paralleling the coast for the most part, but once it cut inland and uphill and he had a glimpse of what the rest of the island was like. Trees. A plowed field with a little green showing in it. He could see a corner of a lake out there and wondered how big it actually was. There weren't any major lakes on the island map, but he didn't really have a sense of the scale of things. Houses here and there. He was realizing more and more that while the harbor activity was intriguing, he wasn't particularly drawn to the ocean.

Living here would be hell, boxed in by all that water.

*Only if you're expecting it to be.* He hadn't felt trapped at all at the Barn, at Stacie's, in the Square.

*Anyway, who said anything about living here?*

It was past noon when he stopped for lunch. There was a little grass knoll by the trail so he took off his anorak and sat on it. He pulled out his water bottle and drank, then explored his lunch. A sandwich with roast chicken, lettuce, avocado, and what proved to be wasabi spread. Jalapeno chips – they'd remembered from the last time he ordered a lunch, when he'd been more specific. A carton of apple juice and a giant chocolate chip cookie. He couldn't fault the lunch. Adam settled on his anorak and began on the sandwich. He hadn't seen another person for almost an hour. He'd wanted to be alone. He was alone.

Adam did a survey of his body while he sat and ate. His feet were holding up, which was a relief, although he'd been prepared to turn around at the first hint of a sore. He felt energized, and took a deep breath or two. He looked at his hands and thought they'd changed color a little, a little tan? He took the baseball cap off and ran a hand through his hair. He was probably due for a cut. Somehow that wasn't the kind of thing he thought about these days.

He felt good. Physically, better than he'd felt in a long time. Maybe he should get back to the gym.

A couple of joggers came by, heading away from town. They smiled and waved, he smiled and waved.

Adam pulled out the map and made a rough guess at where he was. If he went on along the path for another ten minutes or so, it looked like he could connect to a road that led inland back into town. That appealed to him, even though it would be longer. He really was itching to see the island. But mostly, he wanted distraction, something to keep his mind away from Stacie and the predicament he was in.

That afternoon, back in his hotel room, Adam did something he hadn't done in years. He stretched out on his bed and took a nap. The GPS on his phone told him he'd walked nearly ten miles including the detour by Stacie's place. He'd come home with nothing hurting and a pleasant fatigue. He considered the hot tub, as a precaution against sore muscles, then just peeled out of his clothes, pulled back the covers, and stretched out.

An hour and a half later he woke when the phone rang. It took him a couple of rings to figure out where he was, then he almost dropped the receiver when he tried to answer.

"Adam?" Dear God, it was Stacie.

"Hi. I was just … relaxing."

"I wanted to tell you, a gang of us are planning a movie night. We're canvassing the island to see what's available. We thought we'd set up at the scout hall. Would you like to come along? Jess lives a couple of blocks from you, she'll swing by and pick you up."

"I didn't see a notice. Is this impromptu?"

"Totally. Movie nights happen fairly frequently. It's just that no one can bother to plan them."

"You've got all the equipment?" he asked like the idiot he was.

"Actually we use a bed sheet for the screen, and we have to hand crank the projector."

At least she didn't sound annoyed. He thought he picked up a giggle. "Are you laughing at me?"

"You need it. Think you can sort out the truth from the fiction? Amazing, isn't it, how modern technology seeps its way into life. I hear it won't be long before everyone on the island has electricity. We'll get rid of the latrines next."

"I think I get the message. What time?"

Some talk in the background. "About seven?"

"I'll be downstairs waiting. Should I bring anything?"

"We'll get some snack stuff from the grocery. Don't worry about it."

"Thanks."

"See you later."

Then she was gone. He lay there for a few more minutes, thinking about the effect even a short phone conversation with her had on him. Then he hauled himself off the bed and headed for the shower.

Adam had been smart enough to make no assumptions at all about movie night. Nothing on this crazy island seemed to be what he expected, so by now he figured he was better off simply showing up. There were probably seventy people in the scout hall. All traces of *A Midsummer Night's Dream* were gone. As soon as he and Jess arrived he was recruited to help set up the chairs. From the small kitchen he could smell popcorn, and noted what looked like an assembly line from the microwave out to the serving counter where people put the popcorn in brown paper bags. Popcorn and pop, three dollars.

As he arranged the chairs he watched another crew set up and test the computer/projector arrangement. The movie was *Top Gun,* which he hadn't seen since he was a boy. Well, somehow the actual movie was incidental, based on the obvious enjoyment of the people milling about.

He went to find Stacie. She was down in the basement, pulling out rolls of paper toweling and toilet paper. He helped her carry her things back up to the relevant rooms, then she settled into a couple of seats in the fifth row while he went to get their pop and popcorn. Coming back to her, he reflected that he hadn't felt awkward, or judgmental, once since he'd arrived at the Hall. He'd simply done what they asked of him, along with everybody else.

He'd fit in. The black cloud lifted, a little.

The movie finished about 9:45, and the scout hall was spotless by 10:15. Jess shouted out across the room, "Hey, Stacie, do you want me to drive Adam home?" Stacie shouted back, "I'll get him there," and that was that. If anyone in the room didn't know they were seeing each other, they certainly knew now. Anyone who hadn't already noted them holding hands during the movie, anyway.

He'd liked the holding hands, even if he'd already done it all the way through *A Midsummer Night's Dream* two nights ago. With folding chairs, not to mention being right in the middle of her friends in Windon Harbor, he'd been reluctant to put his arm around her, but by now they'd made holding hands into an art form. He'd just about forgotten how erotic it could be to feel a woman's nails scraping gently over his palm. Or how simply satisfying it was to feel his hand caught in both of her own, not moving at all, simply being there.

At her car she looked over at him and said, "Straight back to the hotel?"

He'd looked right back and said, "Do we have to?"

"I'll pay for this tomorrow." By about 10:30 they were in her living room, on her sofa, and doing a lot more than holding hands. Her hands were in fact otherwise occupied, pulling his shirt out of his waistband before they'd even sat down, and now they were exploring, first along his back, then moving to brush his chest, his nipples, sending shivers down his body. Then she'd wrapped her arms around him and dug in her short fingernails. He hardly knew what she was doing, he was going nuts, the softness of her skin, the taste of her ...

Her hand was inside the waistband of his jeans, reaching for his butt, and his own hands had unbuttoned her slacks, when it hit him. And her, at the same time. They jerked back and stared at each other, eyes dilated, barely registering.

"You, too?" she managed to say.

"This is killing me."

"In one week you're gone."

"I know." he got up and groaned, his jeans shifting against his arousal. "Stacie, I wasn't kidding. This is beyond painful."

"We could go on." Her voice was small and unsure, but she said it.

"No. Dammit, we can't. I've done a lot of things in my life, I guess, but I can't go there. If you were nothing to me … God, Stacie, if you were nothing to me I could have what I'm dying for. Doesn't that sound backwards somehow? But I can't do that. I won't. It implies …."

"It implies what you won't promise. And I won't, either. Adam, please go away. Before I cave in."

He reached out a hand and pulled her up. His hands were shaking, and he didn't bother to try to hide it. "You pack quite a punch."

"So do you."

Then she was in his arms again, her hands down on his butt – but at least outside of his jeans this time – his hands under her shirt. They stayed like that, squashed together, until he literally couldn't stand it anymore. "I need to get out of here," he gasped.

"I need you to. Go." She stepped back and gave him a little push.

Walking home he was in serious discomfort, and reeling, and floating. How on earth had he had the control to stop? Tonight hadn't been about getting to know her. Tonight had been all about wanting her, and maybe it was shallow as hell, but if he'd wondered before, he was sure now. He loved Stacie Halloran.

But that didn't get him any closer solving the basic problem of what to do about it.

# Chapter 16

Monday … Adam privately thought of it as his last day of freedom. He already knew that a lot of Tuesday would be taken up readying things for Ralph and Katherine and the rest of the Callaway crew.

Try as he might, he couldn't get his head wrapped around the expectations his corporate world placed on him.

*You've been having too much fun. Time to snap out of it.*

The car rental company had phoned to say they finally had a car for him. He'd arranged to pick it up at lunchtime.

He flipped open his laptop and pulled up his spreadsheet. And laughed at himself. He'd damn near replaced his whole wardrobe in the last two and a half weeks. Two pairs of jeans, four T-shirts and two long sleeved casual shirts. Sweater and jacket. Hiking boots, socks, sandals, shorts, swim trunks. Baseball hat, rucksack, work gloves. A couple new pairs of boxers, just because he liked the look of them. He'd barely worn any of his original wardrobe since his first days on the island.

He made a mental note to get to the Laundromat tomorrow, before they descended on him.

Next he flipped to another document. This one amounted to a diary. It had begun as a record of contacts made, information gained. It still filled that role, but he realized, as he read it through, that it had changed. It had become a record of his time with Stacie. He'd never actually recorded when he'd kissed her, when her hands had found their way inside his clothing, when things went from lukewarm to molten lava. But he knew, from the rest of the description, exactly what had happened.

The diary also didn't record what had happened, in a more global sense. If movie night had taught him anything, it was that he could learn to live on Malaspina Island. He'd felt as if he'd come alive, helping out with the various work parties, enjoying an old movie on a folding chair, going home early.

And that left him feeling as helpless as if he were facing down a runaway train.

Knowing he was adapting didn't change the basic facts of his existence. He lived in Toronto, he earned his living there, his life was there. Everything he'd worked for, everything he'd built up, was there.

Neither of them could be uprooted. And neither of them was looking for a casual fling. It was hopeless.

At least he had work to throw himself into. After today, the corporate persona had to be back in place. With the reports, the meetings, the estimates, the strategies.

*Think of it,* he thought somewhat grimly, *as a shield. The best defense you've got.*

He spent the morning working, in almost constant touch with the team back at head office. He'd rented a meeting room in the hotel as their command headquarters, and he tested the connections and WiFi.

*This room's going to be my home for the next few days, with Katherine and Ralph and the team. Dark thought.* But it wasn't thought itself that was dark, as much as his attitude toward it. At this point, he didn't see a good way to fix that particular attitude.

They'd turn up Tuesday evening. Wednesday afternoon they'd all meet with Abby and Roger, and Thursday they'd host a dinner for the island's movers and shakers. The Open Forum would be Friday. And that would be the end of it. They'd have a war room session on Saturday, then they were all flying home on Sunday. It was the end of the line.

Emails answered, administrative hassles dealt with, and some financial stuff reviewed, he shut down his laptop and headed out.

He stopped at the restaurant to pick up yet another bagged lunch, then walked to the rental car agency by the ferry dock. The air was soft and heavy, but warm. The television hadn't said anything about rain, but you couldn't tell. He'd been rained on in the forest, while he knew that Windon Harbor had only had showers. *Microclimate*, he thought, a word with only academic meaning before the island.

*I'm already dividing it up. Before the island. Now. And after.*

In his less fitted jeans, the purple plaid shirt he'd bought for the barn dance, and sandals, no socks, he felt good. Loose.

Today he'd get to do what he hadn't been able to do before, explore the island. The road the tour had taken to the forest skirted the east coast, but he hadn't been inland, or over to the west coast. Adam was eager to see what lay beyond the bounds of Windon Harbor. And with Callaway about to descend, this would be his last chance.

He checked out the rental, put his lunch in the trunk, and headed out, his tourist map of the island on the seat next to him.

There was regular but not heavy traffic on the main road across the island. About half way to the coast he stopped in a lay-by and sat in the car, looking at the field across the road. It stretched to a row of trees and hedges in the distance. The field was covered by white dots that resolved themselves into slow moving sheep, with lambs bounding around without a care in the world. They might be on pogo sticks, they were so bouncy. Surely he'd seen lambs in a field before, but for the life of him he couldn't remember when.

This was paradise.

He liked the ocean well enough, he supposed, but he didn't feel a deep draw to it like the islanders seemed to. Maybe because he'd grown up in the middle of the continent. But here …

There was a flowering hedge up ahead. On a whim he pocketed the keys and got out of the car. He could smell them well before he got to the hedge. Little roses, with only five petals. Even he recognized the smell of roses. But these had so few petals, but so much scent. He could pick some and take them to Stacie … no. Not a good idea. They might not live, and he didn't know the local customs around picking flowers in hedges. If there was one thing he'd learned by now, it was never to take his own assumptions for granted.

A truck going the other way pulled up and the man rolled down the window. "Hey there, Adam. Everything all right?"

He returned the man's smile. "Everything's fine, thanks for asking. I just stopped for a minute to admire the view."

The truck drove off and Adam returned to his contemplation. He'd recognized the driver. Two days ago the man had harangued him for fifteen minutes about the forest. Today he stopped to see if he needed help.

*This island*. He shook his head.

Behind the hedge, set well back from the road and on a slight rise, he saw an old house. Old in the sense of stately, not decrepit. The place looked empty and probably was, since there was a For Sale sign at the driveway entrance. Adam walked a little way up the drive and stood there for long minutes.

There was something about the place that caught him. He could see bouquets of roses in the kitchen, roses from the garden out back. He idly wondered if there was a garden out back, but didn't go to check. He could see sitting on the front porch, which ran the width of the house, watching the lambs in the field across the street. He could see throwing open one of the old-fashioned double hung windows before going to bed with the scent of grass or wet dirt or alfalfa or whatever it was they grew around here, wafting over him.

*Wafting over them. Plural. Stop kidding yourself.*

*Most likely it'd be the scent of fertilizer and compost.*

Adam shook himself to break the reverie and returned to the car.

Driving on to the west coast, he mused on his assumptions, and on Stacie. What the heck had happened? Why did he have to meet the first woman in years who interested him in the least, on a little island off the west coast of North America, and on the other side of what was going to become a nasty dispute over logging rights? If he knew one thing for sure – and for the last week he'd questioned if he actually knew *anything* for sure – it was that he'd let himself become completely, probably irrevocably, entangled with Stacie Halloran. Not just for the physical thing, although that left him aching. For the other stuff, too. The stuff he didn't usually let himself think about. Future stuff.

*And then there's her coffee.*

He reached the end of the road, the west coast of the island, a few houses grouped around a pub and a tiny convenience store. He pulled into a parking lot next to the pub, collected his lunch, and walked down to the beach, grinning at nothing in particular.

*And exactly when had he started smiling so much?*

He had the beach to himself, and was grateful for it. This place was giving him a whole new approach to solitude. In Toronto he'd tended to avoid solitary time that wasn't filled with work to do, thinking it either a waste of time or a waste of resources. He'd been having a hard time dealing with the solitary evenings that had started piling up on him at home. Malaspina Island pushed him in another direction. There was so much friendliness, so much sharing, that he found himself seeking out alone-time.

The beach simply called out for him to follow it. He glanced north and south, found himself approximately half way between rocky – what would you call them? Headlands? Anyway, places where rocks seemed to jut out into the sea. With no particular plan he headed south.

Within a couple of minutes he'd worked out that the tide was out, and it was easier to walk on the shiny, wet sand than on the dry. He mentally thanked the staff at the General Store for recommending waterproof sports sandals.

Within another couple of minutes he was carrying the sandals, feeling the sand underfoot. It was cold, yes, but it sort of massaged his feet. Fifteen minutes along, just before the rocks, he sat on a piece of driftwood and dug his toes into the warm, dry sand, and ate his lunch, a roast beef and tomato sandwich, on a crusty bun with sesame seeds this time. The gulls arrived with infallible timing. He idly tossed crusts, enjoying their company.

And then, lunch finished and rubbish stowed neatly back in the carryout bag, he just sat there. The sun was fighting with the clouds, and occasionally shot through, but the air was all misty and soft. There was almost no wind. *You're becoming a poet,* he grumbled in his mind, but at the same time he could feel the last of the usual knots unkink.

*A man could breathe this air forever.*

He thought about Katherine and the hostility in their relationship. He'd thought it was natural competition, with a hint of bitterness at the way their long-ago liaison had ended. Now he wasn't so sure there was anything natural about it. It was nasty, plain and simple. And he could be just as vicious as she could. He didn't like to see that about himself. It was as if the island forced him to hold up a mirror and really look, and the image reflected back was ugly. He wondered if it had to be that way.

He thought about Callaway, the dog-eat-dog culture that paved the way to the top. He thought about what the promotion would mean – and suddenly wondered why he'd want it.

*I've got to get back to Toronto. I'm losing my grip on reality. This damn place is affecting my brain.*

A couple with a dog passed him on the beach. They were holding hands and occasionally launching a ball from a plastic sling kind of thing. The dog was in ecstasies, chasing the ball, going into and out of the surf, shaking himself and soaking the laughing couple.

On vacation? He'd bet not. He'd bet they lived here.

He thought about Stacie. Her determination to run the best B&B on the continent, on her island, on her terms. Her calmness in the face of Katherine's rudeness. The way she got in his face and challenged him. The way she felt and ... well.

*You won't even be on the island in a few days' time.*

But that walk, after the barbecue. All the walks, talks, holding hands. Talking like they had a lifetime of talk to do. Lazy, not pushing the relationship, but they both knew. Even if it wasn't their time, they knew.

And then last night, after movie night. But he didn't dare think about last night. It had been too close.

Sighing, he stood and retraced his steps. The sun was winning the battle, for the moment, and the wet beach reflected the clouds. Funny, he'd never noticed reflections of clouds before.

Back at the pub, he contemplated going in for a beer, but decided against it. Perhaps he'd use the weight room at the hotel – good use for the beach bum swim shorts – and work off some energy.

Driving back across the island, he corrected himself. It wasn't energy. It was trepidation. He definitely, absolutely did not want Katherine here. He didn't want any of the team from Callaway here, but mostly, he didn't want Katherine.

"Share a pizza tonight?"

"Okay."

*That smile. Like there was nothing better than him and pizza.* Adam could laugh at himself, the way he was drawn to Stacie's door.

*Don't forget what happens to moths.*

*Sizzling in the flame.*

He shoved the moths out of his mind and turned to the business at hand. "Tell me what kind you want. Personally, I go for all dressed. Except anchovies. And pineapple. Two things that don't belong on any self-respecting pizza."

"On this one point we agree completely. Although I could skip the ground beef, too."

"But pepperoni. You're good with pepperoni."

"Oh, yes. Double."

"Look for me about six? I'll have the pizza delivered here. It'll be cold if I walk it over."

Stacie nodded. "Good. But go away now, please. I have things I need to do."

Adam stood up. "I'll be here. And if I die in the flame, so be it."

She gave him her wrinkled-nose frown, the one that meant she was puzzled by him. "Does that mean anything?"

"Yeah, Moths. Nature. Never mind. This is a placeholder." He bent over her where she was sitting at her picnic table in shorts and a skinny little top, recording entries in a program on her laptop, and kissed her. A throwaway kiss, but something to think about. He straightened. "See you later," he said.

He'd dropped in on a whim, on his way back to the hotel from his drive across the island. He wanted to tell her about his afternoon. He wished he could tell her about some of the musings he'd had, there on the driftwood log. But no, that would imply things he wasn't able to imply. Like a future, for instance.

On Friday he'd gone to the play with her. On Saturday he'd sat in his hotel room and mourned – yes, that was the word for it – mourned his absence from the dance.

On Sunday, yesterday, they'd had that movie night, and what had happened afterwards left him frustrated for the rest of the night. Stacie too, probably. It had been that close, and he now knew what most of her felt like. But they'd both come to a screeching halt. He wasn't sure of her reasons, but he had no doubt about his own. To himself he called it honor. He'd thought about how much more hurt she'd be when he left, if they'd finished what they started.

All true, but he also knew that he'd been scared. He was scared. If he let himself get any closer to Stacie he'd be forced to examine things about his life, and his assumptions about his direction in life, that he didn't want to examine.

Because this had gone so far beyond anything he could ever have predicted, he wasn't sure anymore what he was dealing with.

*In two and a half weeks? Impossible.*

*Unfortunately, not impossible.*

He knew that she'd gotten into his mind and heart and he wanted desperately to know that he'd gotten into her mind and heart, and almost as desperately hoped he hadn't. Because he couldn't bear the thought of hurting Stacie Halloran.

Of course, he'd like to get into more than just her mind and heart. And since it wasn't a three-week flirtation anymore, he couldn't go there.

And then today he'd driven across to the west coast. And seen the house.

And now here he was, finding her in her garden, offering to bring pizza.

Then taking himself off to do Callaway's bidding for the rest of the afternoon. At least Toronto would be shut down by now, so he could work in peace without too much risk of emails or phone calls interrupting him. Then he'd order the pizza, which would let another whole segment of the town's population know what was happening between them, if anyone was left who didn't know yet, but that wasn't anything he felt the need to dodge any longer.

*It's for real. Too real.*

Contemplation be damned. He was trapped in a situation that didn't have a tidy resolution, and he knew it. But somehow he couldn't resist making it worse.

When Adam got back to Stacie's that evening he found everything set up out in the garden, on her little picnic table, including a full roll of paper towels. Flowers he couldn't name were in bloom and the plants in her vegetable garden looked healthy, and the table looked like spring with a pretty pastel floral tablecloth and napkins. Stacie came out carrying a couple of square blue plates. She set them down on the table at their places and said, "There. Pizza came a few minutes ago, it's in the oven."

He'd brought a bottle of shiraz. "It's Australian. I haven't tried this one, so I hope it's okay. Do you have an opener?"

"Sure do." She took the bottle from him and gave a good twist to the top, then set the bottle on the table. "I'll get glasses."

*First blood to her,* he thought glumly. Why hadn't he noticed it was a twist top bottle?

*Something about being besotted?*

She brought glasses and the pizza box, and they helped themselves. It was loaded, and juicy. It took Stacie about two minutes to have pizza sauce all over her face and fingers. He ripped off a couple of towels, handed them to her.

And got a shrug for his efforts. "Thanks. When The Pizza Pan says loaded, they mean it. I'm constitutionally incapable of eating one and not ending up a mess."

"Okay by me. I'm used to seeing you with dirt or sauce or something on your face." She laughed at that.

He finished a slice of the pizza before he said, "Something I want to tell you. There's a reason I wanted to see you tonight. Besides wanting to eat with you and kiss you and get my hands all over you. I was out driving around today. I passed a house. It's for sale, and I thought of you."

"Why? Why would I want a house? I have a house."

"Listen." He held up a hand to show her that this was important. She grabbed the hand, lessening the effect. "Because you told me once that you'd thought of expanding, but couldn't figure out a way without wrecking the architecture here. This might be the way. Not one bigger B&B, but two." Adam could feel himself getting animated, thinking again about the old house near the center of the island. "Of course I haven't seen inside, I don't know anything about it, but the location's dynamite and the house itself looks gorgeous. With some fixing up—"

Now it was Stacie's turn. She waved her hand to stop him. "Adam, you don't know what you're talking about. I think I know what house you mean, the old Thompson place. But it's miles away. The cost of buying it, and the rezoning, and all the renos, and then it would mean having a staff, and that means finding people I'd trust to do it the right way ... it would be too much. I'd never be able to find the time to handle it. And anyway, I can't afford it."

"I can."

The two words hung over the table, seemingly with a life of their own. A rather unpleasant, threatening life. She let go of his hand.

"I'm not working for an absentee landlord. I've proved I can be my own boss."

Their eyes locked. The food was forgotten. Adam sighed and said, "I've put my foot in it again, haven't I? I think we'd better put the rest of this pizza inside, or it'll be stone cold." He scooped up the pizza box and carried it indoors. When she caught up he was punching buttons on her stove. She elbowed him aside and did the buttons herself, while he slid the pizza into the oven.

"Come on," he said, and took her hand to encourage her back outdoors. "Wine is needed." When they got to the picnic table he handed her glass to her, then clicked his own to it and said, "I'd never, ever think of hiring you. God, Stacie, you'd drive me crazy. First with doing everything your own way, then with this." He took the glass from her and put it down next to his own, and they were kissing again, with an edge of desperation that alarmed him.

He ended it, and stood gasping with her arms locked around his waist. "Time out. What I was trying to say in my bumbling way is that you could be a sort of consultant. To fix the place up the way it ought to be. Then maybe consider a long-term lease. Where I'd be strictly hands-off."

"Adam, do you have any idea what my profit margin looks like?"

"No, but …"

She shook her head and twisted away from him. Her gaze traveled down across the garden toward the little cove and beach. "The only reason I could afford this place is that the house was an inheritance. If I'd had to deal with even a small mortgage, I couldn't have done it. I used up just about all my savings converting to the B&B, upgrading. I couldn't afford a lease, especially since I'd also have to hire a manager. Even assuming she lived in, there isn't enough potential profit. Plus, most people would prefer to be closer to town, so the place is location challenged as well."

"Oh. For me, I love the location. Something about the farmland and the hedges. Corny, maybe, but it really drew me in. But I suppose from a tourist perspective … I guess you know your business a lot better than I do, huh?"

"I guess I do."

"Well, it was just a thought."

"A nice one. I like that you drive around the island thinking about me."

"Like I think about anything else? It's a great house, Stacie. It's old, it has character. It might be the novelty, I guess. I grew up in the suburbs, everything the same. Now I live in a condo, all very concrete and modern. There's just something about it."

"You constantly surprise me. Are you a romantic, Adam?" She looked up at him.

"Might be. It's something worth exploring, don't you think? Help me to know myself? I recognize that this is dangerous, especially being the second in ten minutes, but I'm willing to take the risk." He reeled her in for long and thorough kiss, one that somehow involved a sufficient degree of melting that he could feel the length of her … and knew exactly what she was feeling along the length of him. When by mutual consent they broke apart he said, "I'm looking forward to doing that again in a little bit, when you taste more of pepperoni."

She grinned. "Me, too."

"And the house?"

She shook her head. "Let some nice family buy it. It'll be best."

Between them they got the pizza back out on the table and ate, keeping hands modestly to themselves. Adam could have stayed on that bench all night, for the pleasure of talking to Stacie, watching Stacie.

# Chapter 17

Callaway had descended like a black buzzard Tuesday evening. Now, Wednesday morning, they were having their first strategy meeting. Taking refuge behind his laptop, Adam tamped down the unsettled feeling in his gut and stared at the comments posted on the website. Not for the first time, of course. He'd been tracking them since the day the notice went up about the Open Forum.

*He had to admit, the island was consistent. The comments hadn't started out positive and they sure as hell hadn't improved.*

The comments ranged from rude suggestions about what Callaway could do with itself – there was one that made Adam shake his head, given the physical impossibility, but he liked the visual – to well thought out position statements. From individual notes, some anonymous, to neighborhoods and the Windon Harbor Business Association. But one way or the other, they all opposed logging Nathan's Forest. Every single one of them.

"None of this is unexpected," he observed to the men, and Katherine, sitting around the table with him. "I don't think it's personal, I'm confident I've made a positive impression here. But that's not going to counteract the islanders' impression of the potential economic impacts and loss of enjoyment. As I've reported, they've been making use of the forest, even running tours. They've lost sight of the fact that they don't own it. And this means, as I'm sure you're aware, that the Open Forum will have to be handled with kid gloves."

"This guy hosting it, Roger ..." Ralph consulted his notes, "... McMillan. Is he going to be able to keep control?"

"I'm not wildly confident about that. Or perhaps I should say that 'control' has a different meaning here." Adam stood to walk over to a side table where there was a coffee station set up, relieved to shake his legs out. Clearly the weeks of no dress shirts or slacks or ties had altered his comfort levels. Like the other men in the room he'd loosened his tie and popped the top button on his shirt. This was brainstorming, after all, and even the usual formality of Callaway's executives allowed for that level of relaxation. Not as good as jeans and a t-shirt, though.

Katherine, he noticed, had on a power suit, a deep plum colored thing, and three inch heels that could impale you if they stepped on you the wrong way. But there wasn't anything new there. She looked tired. Jet lag, probably. Adam failed to sympathize.

He returned to the table and went on. "I'm on a first-name basis with all the senior people in both the island and the town administrations." *Let them know he'd been on the job and knew where the influence lay. No need to tell them that everyone was on a first name basis with everyone else on Malaspina.* "I haven't found anyone who has any particular forcefulness in his approach. That seems to be the preferred way to run things – laid back. You get the feeling that major decisions are made over backyard barbecues."

"What are they going to fight us with, Adam?" Katherine asked.

"I'd say the same facts and figures we already know about. The tourism angle – I've been able to compile some figures there." He passed out the pages. "There's also the difficulty of logging the upper slopes, which has come up more than once."

"We're talking helicopters?" That was from one of the guys in Operations.

"I don't know. You'll have to see for yourselves. They do say the timber isn't highest quality up there. It's rocky. As for what else they're thinking ... you have to appreciate that they haven't exactly been confiding in me. I'm going to guess they'll go for an appeal to good will, leaving amenities behind. Probably publicity. Possibly lawyers. I don't know enough about our possible impact on environmental regulations to be more specific."

"And your proposed strategy?" Ralph asked. "How do we calm things down and make them accept our plans?"

"We just do it," Katherine put in. "These people aren't going to accept what we propose, period. They think they're entitled to the forest. They aren't going to be willing to see that they're not. Facts be damned, as far as they're concerned. They're insular here and they don't expect things to change."

"I don't agree with you," Adam said. "They aren't in the least insular, for one thing. I've been astonished by the conversations I've had, people stopping me on the street or sitting down over coffee. Their arguments are cogent and well expressed. Some of this stuff on the web, well, it's the typical drivel you get when people think they're anonymous. I haven't heard anything like the violent opinions those jackasses throw out."

"True enough," one of the men from Operations said, nodding.

"Second, it's a well educated population who happen to have chosen an island lifestyle – and believe me, it is a distinct lifestyle. There's a lot of community involvement. In fact, I've never encountered anything like the participation they get when something's happening. I think it's likely that the Barn – you remember the Barn, Katherine – will be full to overflowing Friday. That lifestyle includes valuing the forest, so it makes sense they'd fight for it. I'd expect them to be well organized, and I don't think we can discount their ability to match our arguments."

He looked around the table. Ralph, Katherine, the two men from Operations, and himself, each with a laptop open on the conference table. No one looking in the least bothered about what he was telling them.

"How about we don't say anything much?" Ralph asked. "We listen and nod and take notes. You've arranged for recording the whole thing, I assume?"

Adam nodded. Abby had assured him it was all in hand, and he trusted Abby. More than he trusted the Callaway team, in fact. "We'll have the recording along with a transcript, and they will, too, of course. The thing is, I've been told, and I've told you, that they want an outline of what we plan. Extent, timelines, extraction methods. They know that a lot of that isn't determined yet, but they want the broad strokes. You can expect that to come up when we meet with Roger and Abby this afternoon. They're astute. We're not going to fool them with platitudes. And I think they really want us to stand up in front of them and deliver the news. Face to face, so to speak. It's the island way, or something."

The one who really wanted them to stand up and deliver the news was Adam. He thought maybe it would make him feel a little less like scum.

They went on, reviewing the format for the Open Forum, the strategies to handle anger, the responses to probable questions. Adam's gaze lifted and he let himself look out the window toward the harbor for a moment. People were walking out there in the sunshine, taking a coffee break, getting ready for a whale watching tour or waiting for the next ferry. For the next three and a half days, until they all left Sunday morning, his world was this meeting room and these colleagues. Planning – *plotting might be a better word for it,* he thought grimly – the best way to insinuate Callaway into the island and destroy their forest.

*Our forest, not theirs,* he reminded himself. And returned his attention to the meeting.

"No getting away from you, is there?" Stacie stepped aside to allow Adam into her small mud room, then on through into her living room.

"Hey, it's a small island. Not cooking tonight?" He grabbed a kiss as he went by her. It was as if they'd been doing it forever. He looked like a corporate vampire had drained the energy right out of his body. He looked a little troubled.

"Is that why you're here? Looking for food? Shouldn't you be dining in style with your colleagues?"

"I breakfasted with them. I lunched with them. I found myself needing some air."

"I have leftovers. There was extra oatmeal this morning, so I figured I'd pair it with some fruit salad. Not exactly a guy kind of meal." She headed to the kitchen, with him trailing in her wake.

"I guess I'm not a usual kind of guy. As long as there's enough."

"Not lavish, but adequate. There's beer, cider, wine. If you like."

"Thanks. Something for you?"

"Wine, please. There's an open bottle of pinot grigio in there somewhere."

Adam fixed their drinks, then stood to one side and watched her while she worked in her kitchen. She put the leftover oatmeal and some milk into a pan on the stove and started chopping an apple for the fruit salad. He swirled wine in his glass, held it up to the light. Nodded and took a sip. He put his wine down on the kitchen table and slumped himself into a chair.

And blurted out, "What the hell are we going to do, Stacie?"

"Well, that's blunt." She turned from her sink and frowned at him. Then sighed. "Okay, I guess we really have to have this conversation." She went to the fridge and pulled out some raspberries and an orange, then grabbed a banana from the bowl on the table before she returned to her work station. At least making a salad meant she didn't have to look at him. "You're dangerous, Adam. You threaten my peace of mind. You've been here long enough to see how that's important to me. We don't live on the edge here. I don't want to live on the edge." She added quietly. "I don't want to be hurt."

"I don't either. And I don't want to cause hurt. I'm not blind to the risk."

"I don't like playing with fire."

"Is it fire? Where you and I are concerned, I guess it is. For me, it's all part of the same big whole. You, the island, the logging. I feel like I'm dealing with a personal relationship that's unfolding in an alien culture, with business thrown in for good measure. It's so different here. I don't know, it's like I've forgotten the rules of a game I've known forever. Now with them here ...." He gestured with his hand, a gesture that said, *This is too much,* then again picked up his wine and drank.

"Not to mention that your business is threatening my way of life. I can't get around that easily." She cut the orange in half and squeezed it over the other fruit. She washed her hands and sat down at the table, keeping her distance.

"But at least we're talking. I wish we had years, because I don't think we'd run out of things to say. Still, I have a reasonably good idea of what you want out of life. I wish I could say the same for myself."

He took her hand. Bumped their two hands gently on the table. "Your life is completely entwined with the island, isn't it? Whatever dreams you realize, they'll be here. But for me ... everything I've built up in my life is based on a different set of beliefs and assumptions. What I understand is playing the game, getting ahead. But these days, after a while I just want to get out and go for a walk, see what's happening in the harbor, say hello. There's always someone to say hello to – I guess it helps that I seem to be notorious. As if someone had posted a picture of me somewhere that says, 'Be nice to this man'."

Stacie studied him, bemused. "Did it ever occur to you that people here might actually like you?"

"I'm not sure it's ever really mattered before."

"Adam, that's pathetic. Of course it matters."

"Plus I'm being hit with culture shock right now. I was in meetings all day, reviewing what feels like the same stuff over and over, talking for the sake of hearing our voices. I got them all out this morning for a coffee and a walk around the

Square. I can't say it was a hit, at least not for Ralph and Katherine. The operations guys liked it okay, I guess."

"It wasn't a hit with you, your first days here. Maybe it takes more time."

"More than they have. More than I have to make them feel it."

"How'd the meeting go?" Stacie knew from several sources about the meeting that afternoon with the Callaway team, Abby, Roger, and the mayor of Windon Harbor.

He drank another mouthful of wine before fielding her question. "As expected," he said finally. "The Malaspina team was gracious and determined to get answers to their questions. Ralph and Katherine were smooth and stonewalled as much as they could. It was the best I could hope for, I guess."

"And you're stuck in the middle. Trouble with Katherine, Adam?" Stacie looked concerned.

"That's a given." He shrugged. "Look at me. Do I look anything like the man who first turned up at your B&B?"

She studied him. It had been so subtle she'd hardly noticed, but ... "No. You don't. Your hair's not in that spiky urban thing that looks like it has half a tube of gel in it. You're a little sunburned. When your eyes go red-rimmed it looks more like being in the wind than lack of sleep. I think you've lost weight, despite all the restaurant meals. And almost anyone looks more comfortable in jeans. I don't think you'd voluntarily have worn jeans three weeks ago."

"I hope you can understand this ... for me, it's not only about you. Mostly, but not only. You're part of a package, and I've got this thing going on in my head that says your life's here and my life's at the other end of the Air Canada flight from Vancouver to Toronto. I can't see where the win is for me anymore."

"Then …." But Stacie wasn't up to saying what she was thinking.

*Then you'd better go. We'd better not risk this any further.*

The timer on her stove rang. She met his eyes.

"Saved by the bell?"

"You knew what I was going to say?"

He nodded. "I didn't have the courage."

She got up and pulled out two of her square, blue plates. She arranged a pile of the fancy oatmeal and a spoon of fruit salad on each one, scooped up cutlery and napkins, and served him his dinner.

Before he got his first bite in his mouth he looked at her and said, "Any idea what we're going to do?"

"None."

They ate in silence. Later, they sat in her living room. For the longest time he didn't even kiss her, just ran his hand over her hair and held her against his chest. She was grateful for his arms wrapped around her.

# Chapter 18

Stacie didn't have a ringside seat for the Open Forum. She hadn't wanted one. She was about ten rows back, over to one side. From relative obscurity she could watch – Roger at the podium, the mayor and her mom on one side of the raised platform. On the other side were the people from Callaway. Katherine, whom she remembered better than she wanted to. An older man she assumed must be Ralph. Two younger guys looking ill at ease on stage, who had to be the foresters, the guys from his Operations Division.

And Adam, of course, back in his corporate persona. He'd been the last of the Callaway team to arrive. He wore a light gray suit and he'd had a haircut. She'd watched him working his way through the Barn, stopping at least a dozen times to talk, shake hands, share a comment. Malaspina Island liked Adam Fraser. Stacie hoped he could see that.

Her mother looked formal and composed, Roger casual and comfortable. Katherine looked bored and authoritative, Ralph looked impatient. Adam was doing everything he could to keep his face blank. Too bad she knew him as well as she did. This wouldn't be an easy evening for Adam.

The Barn was full a good thirty minutes before the Open Forum was scheduled to begin. The noise – well, what could you expect? It was the usual combination of social hour and business, in this case a business that had the whole island on edge.

Jess perched on the edge of the seat next to her, craning her neck. "Do you reckon things will get out of hand?"

"We'll see." Stacie was a woman of few words that evening.

The wait to the start of the Open Forum was interminable. She'd picked up on Adam's tension, or maybe she was manufacturing it for herself. One way or another, this meeting had her freaked.

At least until her mother caught her eye and gave her a thumbs-up.

It began. The format was simple. The man named Ralph made a presentation that must have been written by a committee. He spoke about how much they valued the west coast and island lifestyle. He told them how important tourism was to their economy. He praised the openness and friendliness of everyone he'd met. Stacie sighed. At least Adam had never been so blatantly full of bullshit.

Next he spoke about the economic interest Callaway had in the timber in Nathan's Forest. He mentioned investments and stockholders. Referenced back to them, how he was sure they were glad there were men like him safeguarding their investments. Next to her, Jess grimaced. "Stuffed shirt," she whispered.

"Full of himself," Stacie agreed.

He mentioned the able administrations – both of them – on the island. He managed to forget her mother's name. *Fox? That's so difficult?*

Ralph stressed that there were no firm plans yet, that they didn't actually know what they had in the forested land on Malaspina. "We know," someone called out, echoed by another voice shouting, "Keep it that way."

"Now it begins," Jess said. No need to whisper, there was a clamor in the audience.

Finally the open part of the Open Forum began. Person after person spoke at one of the two microphones set up part way down the two aisles. The lines to speak reached the back of the room and never got smaller. As soon as someone sat down, someone else stood up.

The islanders had it well orchestrated, Stacie thought. No one spoke too long. The presentations weren't repetitive, although they did cycle through a few general themes. Occasionally either Roger or Abby would be called on to speak to a point. Their comments were short and on target. They both had plenty of facts and figures of their own, including a rough estimate of the board feet in the forest – *which is more than Callaway seemed to have,* Stacie thought – the dollar value of tourism to the island economy, the island and municipal bylaws that would have to be considered. Both made it clear that Callaway had some serious hoops to jump through.

With a subtext that the island would be there to make sure they jumped through them. It was the politest no-holds-barred battle Stacie had ever seen.

By 10:30, three and a half hours after the meeting began, the lines showed no signs of thinning out, and Roger called a halt. A short discussion was held about resuming the next night, but that was voted down by almost everyone. Most people seemed to feel that the salient points had been raised, and the salient questions had not been answered.

Then the man named Ralph told them all that the two men from Operations would be staying on Malaspina for a few more days to get into the forest and look around. He hoped the island would make them welcome. And Roger looked him dead in the eye and said, "That could be difficult."

"Why? We have hotel reservations. We have to have the information, and this has been our plan all along. We can't tell you good people …" Stacie winced. "… anything more until we get in there."

"Oh, they're welcome to stay," Roger said, at his smoothest and mildest. "The problem is access. It seems that all the land surrounding yours is in private hands. No public right-of-way. Something about a lapsed lien that no one renewed. And this morning the usual access was closed off."

The Barn went quiet. Everyone, including Stacie, had been going to the forest for years. No one had ever had any problem with access.

Roger looked out over the hall. "It's a private road. I received notice today that it's been closed. Go out there now and you'll find a gate and a padlock, which I trust you all to respect. So, no access. I've already notified the tour companies. Sorry, folks." Then he pounded his gavel and closed the meeting.

Stacie couldn't hear herself think. She and Jess looked at each other and did the only thing they could do – they burst out laughing. As they inched their way to the door, she spared Adam one look, a longish one, but he was surrounded by Callaway people and didn't see her.

Outside, she longed to know how long this bombshell had been waiting in the wings, but she knew there was no chance she'd see her mother that night. And she had guests to serve tomorrow. Thanking God that everything was prepped, she hugged Jess and headed for home.

The Callaway staff had wanted him present for a post mortem. He should have stayed, because fingers would probably be pointed his direction. He'd point them right back, of course. To the Callaway staff who'd compiled the map, for instance. To whoever didn't renew the lien allowing access to their land. How did they miss that there was no right of way? And given that it didn't turn up on the map, why should he have thought to pursue it? He was well aware that leaving could be a career threatening move, especially with Katherine in the meeting to draw attention to his absence, but somehow he couldn't bring himself to care.

So he'd bowed out, pleading contacts to soothe, some final goodbyes to say, and he'd run for it. Adam turned up at Stacie's private door about half an hour after the Barn had cleared out, his jacket and tie left behind in his room. He sort of thought she might be at a post mortem herself, he understood by now how intertwined she was in the life of the island. Or if not a post mortem, she might simply not want to see him. *The gauntlet had been thrown, that's for sure.* But he had to try.

But she surprised him by being right there. She let him in without a comment, slotting herself into his arms as soon as the door was closed.

When breathing became a normal habit again he said, "What did you think?"

"That despite that clever move at the end, things aren't looking so good for the side of the angels. There's no stopping it, is there? It was so obvious. They weren't really listening. I bet they haven't even read the web postings."

"Oh, they have. I made sure of that."

"And when that man was so condescending to Mom, I wanted to sock someone."

He pulled back from her, eyebrows raised. "Whoa. Back up. Mom?"

She gave him her biggest smile. "You haven't worked it out yet?" She watched his face while he sorted through the Forum, finally made the connection.

"Abby," he said with a rueful chuckle.

"Gotcha!" She dug him in the ribs, then giggled when he returned the favor.

"That's why I always thought she looked familiar somehow. I like your mother, Stacie." Safely in each other's arms again, he said, "But you're still speaking to me anyway?"

He felt her shrug. "You're not really one of them, are you? You stopped being the Enemy a week or so ago. I don't mean because of this …" and here she ran her hand into his hair and quickly kissed him, "… but because you get it. I've watched it, we all have. You've already pointed out that you're not the same person who sat in my breakfast room three weeks ago."

"And ordered pancakes. And never told you how good they were. I was a jerk."

She pulled away and settled on the sofa, turning to face him when he joined her. "You didn't have any choice tonight. We all accept that. And you were quiet. You weren't in our faces about Callaway."

"I think it's fair to say it went about as planned, with a few glitches. We expected the force of public opinion. Ralph's speech was ghastly, I couldn't believe it came out so badly. No one expected the right of way issue."

"Are you going to get into trouble for not being there for your post-meeting meeting? Don't look at me like that. Of course they're all meeting right now, your side and mine. Figuring out the next moves or something."

"Nothing I can't smooth over. I let it be known that I was keeping fences mended and communication lines open tonight. Isn't that what they sent me here for?" His hands started to explore, but she swatted him away.

"It's really late, and I'm keyed up. I'm making hot milk. Want some?" She stood.

"Stacie ..."

"Hmm?"

He took her hands, looking up at her from the sofa. "To be really honest ... what I want tonight is to make love to you. Not just sex, okay? I know you'll probably say no, and I know that's the best, but ... well, I wanted to tell you that."

She freed her hands and buried her face in them. "You make it hard to think."

"So do you."

She dropped her hands and shook her head. "No, Adam. I'm in too deep already. If that happened, when you leave it would kill me. Please don't ask me."

Stacie turned and was heading for the kitchen when the front doorbell rang. She froze, then shrugged and said, "I have to. It could be a guest who forgot a key ...."

He stood in the door of her apartment and watched Stacie open the main front door.

*Holy crap.*

Katherine swept in, there was no other way to describe it. "Hello, my dear," she said. "I was looking for Adam ... and look, I found him." Somehow she created a draft behind her that sucked them both in her wake into Stacie's private living room. Once the door was closed, she draped her arms over his shoulders and said, "Here I thought we'd see each other tonight. But – oh, of course. I understand."

This was Katherine at her worst, he thought. The whole act was fake and he thought he detected scotch on her breath, but for the life of him he didn't know what she was up to.

"Katherine, go on back to the hotel. Please. This is a private residence, and I'm here on private business. I'll see you in the morning."

"But it's not private business, is it, darling?" She dragged a finger across his cheek. He could feel her nail. "It's my business, too. And just look at you and your little waitress. So flushed. Looks like I lost, doesn't it?"

*Lost?*

She turned to Stacie. "Of course, if he offered to split the winnings with you, that might invalidate your victory, don't you think? Is that what he did, dear?"

Stacie stood rock still, looking bewildered. Her eyes went to him.

That's when it hit him. The damn wager. He'd forgotten all about it. He froze.

She was still talking to Stacie. "I mean, five hundred dollars is a lot of money. Of course, I don't know what your price is, but I expect that struggling to keep a place like this afloat, you could use some extra cash. But that's really not playing fair, Adam."

He forced himself back to life. "Get out of here, Katherine."

"I'm going. I know where I'm not wanted. But I'm a businesswoman, darling. I need confirmation before I fork over that much money. I hope you enjoyed him, dear," she said to Stacie. "Something we have in common."

Stacie shifted to stand in front of the door. "A bet?" she said to Adam.

Katherine was in there before he could answer. "She doesn't know? How sweet. Then since it's obvious what you two have been up to, I concede defeat. I'll write a check first thing in the morning. Good night, you lovebirds." Katherine pushed her way past Stacie and out into the guest lobby.

Stacie stood in her doorway until Katherine was out of the building. Then she closed the door to her apartment and turned to him.

"A bet."

Adam sank down onto the sofa and covered his face with his hands.

"I think you'd better talk, Adam. Now."

He couldn't. He shook his head.

But she'd figured it out. "You had a bet with her." At the contempt in her voice his insides went to ice. "If I have this worked out right, you bet her five hundred dollars that you'd have sex with me. Was there a time limit? Until you leave the island? Or until the Forum? How were you going to prove it? Steal my panties?"

She stared at his bent head for a minute, then said, "Come with me." She grabbed his arm to pull him up, and dragged him into the mud room. "This is a door," she said. Her voice could have frozen the sun. "You came in it. I expect you're clever enough to find a way to get yourself back out of it. I certainly suggest you try. Because if you don't, I'm throwing you down the outside stairs. Clear?"

"Stacie ...." He was sure she could hear the pain in his voice, but she didn't respond.

"Get out. Now." The menace was unmistakable.

Without knowing what he was doing, how he would get back to the hotel, how he would live through the night, Adam found himself at the bottom of her back steps, watching the door close. Quietly, firmly. As if it would never open again.

Which, of course, it never would.

# Chapter 19

Saturday was hell. Adam never left the hotel. He had a headache that wouldn't go away, maybe from the drink or several he'd had after he finally made it back to his room Friday night. But that wasn't until very late. So late that at one point a police cruiser stopped to ask if he was okay.

"Yes, just walking the waterfront, thinking."

"It's great that you appreciate it. We'll miss you around here, young man." The cruiser drove away.

*No, you won't. Not when you know.*

Abby Fox tried to phone him, but he let it go to voice mail. He spent all the time they wanted him to in their war room, reviewing the Forum, discussing the personalities. Going over strategies, influential contacts, the powerful use of money if need be. Katherine was the personification of cooperation.

He assumed he'd eaten something of the lunch they ordered in. When they proposed going to Roscoe's for dinner he declined, saying, falsely, that there were some people he had to say goodbye to. He didn't remember eating anything Saturday night. At least he knew he hadn't drunk anything, either. Alcohol couldn't float him up from the depth of this misery. Not that he deserved an escape, anyway.

They all caught the 10:10 ferry the next morning. Adam stood at the stern of the boat and watched the crew cast off, then went indoors to sit with Ralph.

"Good job, Adam. The meetings and the Forum went well. The information you sent was invaluable."

Adam thought it had all been a disaster. Showed how much his perspective had changed in the last three weeks. "I'll miss it here." He figured he had to give Ralph that much, since anyone could see he was in rough shape.

"Been a little bit of a vacation, has it? You needed one. You don't take enough time off. You're sunburned."

"Not surprising. It seems like everything that happens on the island happens outdoors."

"Not enough time on the ferry to get any work done. Maybe on the plane we could go over the figures for …." Adam let Ralph talk, half following. On the plane, with any luck, he'd sleep. They'd just have to understand.

He glanced out the window, but it faced the wrong way. Malaspina Island was gone. It might never have existed.

# Chapter 20

Adam had been home for three weeks. Nothing had changed at Callaway. The work, the people, the pace and pressure, all exactly as he had left them. He expected to feel right at home, and went about his work as if nothing had happened.

One might say, as if he hadn't proved himself to be beneath contempt and not deserving to live.

One might say, as if he hadn't finally found the woman he could spend his life with, and thrown her away on a stupid wager with Katherine.

She'd actually come through with a check for five hundred dollars. He'd stuck it on the wall above his desk at home. So he wouldn't forget. Rather like a death by a thousand cuts.

Katherine's look when she threw the wager in Stacie's face made him want to slap her across the room. He knew he could be vicious where Katherine was concerned, but he'd never involved anyone else in their competitions. Not like that.

He'd still like to slap her across the room. It was a frustration he'd have to live with. If it had been just him, and if he could have managed to get her alone outside of Callaway, he might have risked it. But he had someone else's standards to live up to now.

If nothing else, Stacie Halloran would make a better man out of him. Even though she'd probably never know it.

Still, it had been a good day. A fabulous, day, actually, by any normal standards. The highlight came mid-afternoon, when the president himself came into Adam's office to inform him that the sought-after promotion to CFO was his. He'd had his hand shaken by half a dozen men, walked to his new office, told his new salary. Later there'd been drinks in the conference room to celebrate – too many drinks.

The look on Katherine's face was priceless. But no, he was trying not to think like that. The new version of Adam was above that, or was trying to be.

Before all the celebration, it had been work as usual. A morning meeting, presentation of facts and figures related to a proposed takeover of a small logging operation in northern British Columbia. One that might be useful to Malaspina, once that was all straightened out. It had all summarized nicely and the way the higher-ups had wanted it to, so he'd looked good. Again. He was so good at looking good.

It was after seven before he got back to his condo. Fourteenth floor, just like he'd told Stacie. View that reached out over Lake Ontario, if you stretched to the left to see around and through the other high rises. This was it, his home base for the years he'd spent clawing his way up at Callaway.

Now he'd made it. To the top.

He pulled a bottle of scotch down from a shelf and poured. But after all the celebration earlier he couldn't stomach any more alcohol. He was certain to have a hangover tomorrow as it was. He couldn't hold the liquor like he used to. *Age,* he thought. *Almost forty. And this is what I have to show for it.* He dumped the scotch and poured a glass of water, drank it in one go.

He prowled his condo. It was nice enough, but impersonal. Some years before, he'd hired a decorator to give him something contemporary and masculine, and that's what he had. Black leather, red and black modern art on the walls, beige carpet and side chair in a beige and black pattern. Chrome in the dining area. He'd considered adding one or two small touches of himself, but nothing he tried seemed to fit, so in the end he'd left it alone.

It looked so damned lonely. Like no one was home.

He should eat something. He pulled out a stack of take-out menus, but nothing appealed. In the end he rode the elevator down to the lobby and called in at the deli on the ground floor, just as it was closing. They made him a pastrami on rye, and he rode back up with it.

*I wonder if Stacie likes pastrami.*

*Hell,* he thought. *They probably don't even have pastrami on her stupid little island.* But he knew that a) they almost certainly did, b) the island wasn't stupid, and c) he was trying to build distance. Between himself and the look on Stacie's face. Between himself and Malaspina Island, where he'd never be again. Itemizing the extent of the damage was one way to control it, at least in his mind.

As if the situation with Stacie weren't bad enough, one thing that especially troubled him was what her mother would think of him now. He'd found it so easy to work with Abby Fox, and was truly impressed by her competence. She'd been kind, provided introductions and a touch of social life, and he'd betrayed her daughter in a way he could still hardly believe himself capable of. No, she wouldn't have any use for him, not anymore.

To say he didn't sleep well that night would be an understatement. It was the alcohol, of course. And the excitement of the promotion. Tomorrow he'd be at work in his new office, doing his new job, and basically nothing had changed. He'd have the ear of the inner circle now, he'd have more money to play with, he'd have a title after his name.

He'd have everything he'd worked for, for the last eighteen years. He'd done it.

*Maybe tomorrow night he'd sleep. Sure he would. No doubt about it.*

# Chapter 21

Dear Stacie,

    I'm sorry.

Adam

Dear Stacie,

    You might like to know I got the promotion. Or more likely you won't give a damn. But I wanted you to know. I couldn't think of anyone else who'd celebrate for me. I guess you won't, either. But you're the one I'd want to.

Adam

Dear Stacie,

    I bet your vegetable garden is getting ripe. How are the flower boxes in the Square? I think about them. I think about the people on the Square seeing them and thinking of me.

    Actually, I'm not entirely sure I want them to think of me.

Adam

Dear Stacie,

I wish I knew what to say to you. It isn't getting any easier. I look back and I wonder how I could have done what I did to you. See? I can't even name it. Wager. There it is. I used you as a pawn in a wager.

Thank God we never made love. I don't think I could have lived, if we had, and you believed it was because of that.

Adam

Dear Stacie,

I avoid the word 'love'. I think I said I was falling for you, or other weasel words. I see now that I was falling – in love – with you. But I couldn't commit to it. It's too big a word, and I was scared. And while Malaspina Island grew on me, I wasn't willing to see myself there, long term. I was too wedded to my work, my life in the city. My loss, I know. I'm not only a jerk, I'm also afraid to face the truth.

Adam

Dear Stacie,

Rate-Your-B-and-B.com continues to love you. It sounds like you've had a good summer season. I hope that's true. I could second all they say, by the way. You've created a great place, and you run it so well.

Adam

Dear Stacie,

I've made some big decisions in my life. And I'm terrified of them. But excited about them, too. Maybe I'm finally growing up. I'll tell you when I see you. I hope I'll see you. I want to see you. You can tell me you'll hate me forever or punch me out or whatever you think is appropriate. I can't live with this. I have to try to see you.

Adam

# Chapter 22

Adam didn't send any of the notes he wrote to Stacie over the summer, of course – and cursed himself for a coward. But what if she wrote back? What if she told him categorically never to come near Malaspina Island again? No, actually contacting her was too terrifying.

So when Adam knocked on Stacie's back door on an October afternoon, he was arriving empty handed and with no idea at all what she was thinking, although he assumed it wasn't anything good, if she was thinking about him at all. Maybe she wasn't. Maybe she been able to get over the whole thing and never look back. Mentally he crossed his fingers that she'd be home. But there was no answer, so he turned around and looked at her back yard.

Most of the vegetables in her garden were gone now, but a couple of the tomato plants hadn't been pulled up yet, and the squash vine was still there, entangled with some other, unnamed vines and sporting one massive squash, almost as big as she'd shown him with her arms, that day.

He hadn't even checked into the hotel. He'd worry about that after. Or not. There was always the evening ferry.

The lawn was littered with leaves. He was grateful that he had both a warm sweater and his anorak with him, because the air was chilly. But the day was clear and it certainly felt like autumn.

He had sent her one card, a week or so before. Nothing complicated, a scene of a beach on the front, and inside he'd written, "I'm coming. I hope you'll let me see you." Nothing else. There wasn't anything else he could say in a card. This was face to face, or nothing. He hoped it wouldn't be nothing, but knew better than to hope too hard. She had every reason not to see him, or forgive him.

Behind him the door opened. He turned and there she was, in jeans and an oversize sweater, exactly as he remembered her. Their eyes met. She said nothing, and all his speeches went right out of his head. *Read me,* he thought, or maybe prayed. *Please.*

She moved aside, holding open the screen door. He stepped around her into the little mud room. The screen door slammed, and they stood there, awkwardly. She wouldn't look up at him.

"Come with me," he said, aware that he seemed to have lost full control of his voice. "I want to show you something. Will you come with me?"

Still silent, she picked up her keys from the hook by the door and led the way outside. She locked up and they walked to his car, which he'd pulled into her private driveway.

Once they were moving, heading for the cross-island road, she finally said, "What is it?"

"A house. I told you about it once."

"Oh. The old Thompson place."

"The owners aren't named Thompson, though."

"No, the Thompsons moved out years ago."

"That happens a lot around here, doesn't it? Someone leaves, but leaves the name behind. Nathan's Forest, the

Thompson place." He hadn't wanted to mention Nathan's Forest, but the risk of it becoming an invisible elephant between them was too great. Even if he was destined to be torn apart because of his work with Callaway, better to get it out of the way.

"A couple of sisters lived there next, but after one of them had to go into a nursing home the other didn't want to stay. It's been on the market all summer."

"I know. I've been watching the listing on the web. I went out this morning to see if it lived up to my memory of it."

The house was about eight minutes out of town, one of the longest eight minutes he'd ever endured. He pulled in the driveway, parked the car, and got out. He started around the car to assist her, but she'd scrambled out on her own and stood looking around.

"So different from where you live." If Stacie's place was all about gardens and ocean vistas, this house on its gentle rise had a wonderful vantage point for the rolling fields and patches of forest around them.

"I think the sisters had goats at one time."

"I love this. The fields … there were lambs last time I was here."

"They'll be off for slaughter soon, if they aren't already."

And there went his romantic view of agricultural life. But Stacie lived in the real world of Malaspina Island, and lamb was an important revenue generator. He knew this, but he didn't want to think about it right now. "Come on. Let's go in."

Walking up the path, it felt like the most natural thing in the world to take her hand. She didn't resist, but kept her eyes on the house. "I haven't been in this place for close to twenty years. Mom brought me to visit once or twice. I was a teenager, I don't think I was very impressed."

They climbed the steps. "I like this," he said. He let go of her hand to fish the key out of his pocket, then gestured to either side of him. "A big front porch. In a community as fixated on lemonade as this one, it seems perfect."

"Don't start."

"I wasn't. I meant it. With this view … it all seems to fit. And I do like lemonade, for the record." He propped the screen open while he worked the key in the lock, then pushed the door open for her. "Whatever comes next, I'd like it if you could recognize that I do have a few normal, human traits."

She half smiled at that. Then they were standing in the wide entry, the elegant old oak staircase rising to their right, the living room double doors to their left, and Adam figured that his grace period was over.

He turned to face her. On some unimportant level he was aware of the pain in his right palm where he clenched the key. He shoved the key into his pocket, leaving his hands undefended. "I had so many speeches written in my head. They wouldn't do any good, would they?"

She wandered around the entry, almost aimlessly, then turned and sat down on the second step. "Probably not."

He nodded, pinched his lips together for a moment. "Then tell me what to do. Nothing I've done in my life has made me so miserable. Or made me question myself so much. Or cost me so much."

She quirked an eyebrow at him. Her voice was uninflected, a challenge. "Pretty speech?"

He shook his head. "Pretty speeches are easy to say. Right now I can hardly get the words out." To himself his voice sounded strangled. He wheeled around and strode into the empty living room. He was staring out the front window, across the fields, when he sensed she'd come in.

He turned to her. "Tell me how to fix this, Stacie."

She exploded. "Do you know how you left me feeling? Besides a raving idiot for believing in you? Like cheap trash. Like – like a *thing*. Something you might play with for a few weeks, then throw into the garbage. Like I was never even human to you. I still can't figure out how you did it. You felt so *real* to me. I thought I was a good judge of people. Now I even have to question that."

He heard the bitterness. How could he miss it? Her words piled up in him like a tsunami trapped behind a wall. "Let me tell you this. That wager – I'd forgotten all about it. It was one of the stupid things Katherine and I sometimes did, goading each other. Once I started seeing you, I mean really seeing you, not just as someone to serve my breakfast ... after that morning in your breakfast room, nothing was fake. I swear it. After that day, I couldn't get you out of my head.

"On top of that, the more I lived on your island, the more I got to know some of the people and the way of things here, the more I wanted to be a part of it. Hell, the more I wanted you. And how was that for a pretty speech?" he concluded, and wondered if she heard his own bitterness. "I can't even tell you how I feel without it seeming like some kind of lie. But it's not. I had to come here. I had to try. I had to show you this house."

Adam hadn't moved his eyes from her face while he spoke, and she watched him like a hawk, expressionless, but listening. So she undoubtedly had seen when his eyes filled. Angry with himself, he dragged his palms across his face.

"Okay," she said quietly. "Let's see the house."

They went through the dining room and kitchen, the little room off the kitchen that looked so much like a home office. Upstairs they explored the four bedrooms, the single bath. They commented on the antiquated plumbing, tested lighting fixtures. It felt almost normal, as if they did this kind of thing every day together. They studied the view from every single window. They discovered a back staircase. Side by side they studied the trap door into the attic. "We'd need a ladder," he said.

"Maybe next time." He felt his breath catch, and pinched his eyes closed for a moment before he followed her back down the stairs. *Next time.*

At the bottom they once again faced each other. "What do you think?" he asked her.

"Practically speaking?" She ticked off her points on fingers. "New plumbing, probably new electrical. A couple more bathrooms minimum. Full new kitchen, including flooring. Probably needs a new roof. Stripping wallpaper, painting. Sanding and refinishing the floors – but they might come up nicely. Replace all the windows with double glazing. A laundry room, for heaven's sake. I wonder how they did their laundry? And I'm starting to run out of fingers here."

He caught the fingers on her left hand. "But what do you think?"

"Oh, I love it."

"So do I. Have a seat." She sat on the step and he paced. "Now that you've seen it, what would you do with it? Bed and Breakfast? Theoretically. I know you don't want to deal with two, and especially so far apart."

"It could be. The front two bedrooms have a decent separation from the back, and the back stair could be for family. But to generate a reasonable profit, you'd need to use all the rooms, so you'd have to do like I did and convert some of it to an apartment. The layout's not great for that, I don't think, but maybe."

"And if not a B&B?"

"A home?"

"Could be. Is it too far out of town?"

"Depends on what you want."

"What do you want?"

She shook her head. "I can't go there. I have a business that requires me to be on the premises, remember. This'll never be my home."

"Are you okay with that?" He thought he'd picked up an unvoiced sigh under her words.

She stood. "We should get going."

"I guess they all know."

She shook her head. "Only that we fought. And you left."

"Stacie."

Again they stared at each other. This time, it was as if neither of them was quite in control, as if they were both fighting to keep their footing in the middle of an earthquake. Adam caught her hand, touched her fist to his forehead. Then let her go.

The moment held for perhaps five seconds, if he'd been timing it. Then somehow she was in his arms and his head was resting on hers where it nestled against his chest, and he thought she was crying and knew damn well he was. And neither of them moved or spoke for an eternity.

She broke away first, angrily swiping at her eyes. "What are you doing, Adam? Why did you come back?" She turned away from him.

He followed her out onto the front porch, stopping to lock the door. "I would have come, no matter what. I couldn't leave what happened just hanging there. I owed it to you. It's harder to explain why I had to do it for me. I always thought you could just live things down, go away and get out of the line of fire, make it like it never happened. I know you think I'm a callous big city executive with an eye on the bottom line and nothing else, right?"

"No. I don't think that."

"Thanks for that. I had to tell you. Grovel, give you a chance at revenge if that's what you want. Even if it meant watching you walk out of my life forever, all over again."

"I see."

"Beyond that, it's up to you. What you don't know is that I've resigned from Callaway and my condo's on the market. As of this moment I'm unemployed, homeless, and renting a car."

That got her attention. She didn't say a word, just looked at him, her eyes wide.

He nodded shortly. "I spent the summer looking at what I had, and it amounted to nothing. Nothing at all," he repeated, letting her hear the amazement he'd felt. "I had everything I'd fought for, and there wasn't anything in it. So I ... well, I couldn't go on like that. So I ..." He shrugged. "I cut myself adrift, I guess. Until I get it figured out."

"And you're here because ...?"

"Of you, of course. And to see Malaspina Island in the autumn, see if I can figure out if I was living in a dream world or a fool's paradise or what." He took her hand and they worked their way back to the car. "What I believe I want to do is try to make a life here."

He let it hang for a beat. He was pretty sure she'd think he was being ridiculous. "I don't underestimate the challenges. I'm still freaked out by small town life and the way everyone's in everyone's pocket. But I want to try. I could find something useful to do, I hope. People's tax returns, maybe get some bookkeeping jobs, I don't know. Maybe apply for the Island Administrator's job if it hasn't been filled. I haven't checked in a while, in case I got my hopes pinned on it. Maybe I could do some accounting work long distance, telecommuting to Vancouver or something.

"But – and this is a big but ...." He paused, pulling her to a stop. "This all depends on you. If you want me to go, I go. No questions, no need to explain. I can't be here if it's bad for you. If you're prepared to let me try again, I'll stay. And maybe buy this house."

Again she turned away from him. "Take me home now, please."

He opened the car door for her. "Just so you know, it wasn't contempt for you. It was never about you at all. It was contempt for the island, for your way of life. It wasn't you." She looked at him, her face unreadable, then slid into the car. Their drive back into Windon Harbor was silent.

As she got out of his car he said, "Wait." He popped the trunk and pulled out a sheaf of envelopes in a rubber band. "Here," he said, and thrust them into her hands. "From this summer. I couldn't mail them."

She accepted them silently.

She paused on the first step leading up to the door to her apartment and looked at him. It took everything in him not to grab her to him, hold on to her like he hadn't been able to do for almost half a year. But this had to come from her now, not him. So instead he brushed a finger across her cheek and whispered, "I love you, Stacie Halloran. May I call you?"

Her mouth quirked, not quite making it to a smile. She nodded, then slipped into her door and was gone.

Adam stood still for a moment, then went back to the car and drove into town.

# Epilogue

*I didn't know what to expect from Adam, or even if I'd let him see me again. But then, what can you do with a guy who flies across the continent to show you the old Thompson place?*

*What can you do with a man who breaks your heart, then cries in your arms?*

She'd been working on the books when he turned up at her back door. Stacie was proud of those accounts, showing as they did a steady profit. There wasn't much room to grow, given that she was already running at near capacity throughout the tourist season, but she'd been toying with ideas to bring in more traffic over the winter, winter retreats perhaps, or romantic getaways. She had immersed herself in her own independence and accomplishment and was feeling damn good, when bam! There he was.

After he dropped her off she spent the rest of the afternoon reading and rereading his notes to her, and thinking about the old Thompson place. The notes – it was like being there, in his head, hearing his voice. Tracing his summer as best as she could, and wondering who the real Adam was. Trust him? That might still be a step too far. But God, was she glad to have those notes.

Two days after applying for the island administrator's job, Adam had a call from Roger, asking if they could meet the next morning at Roger's office. "There's a lot about this job you don't know, and it isn't going to be my decision. So let's start getting you ready." They spent the next three mornings going over the details, everything from the truck maintenance schedule to tenders for things like snow clearing to – well, to dealing with Callaway.

At least dealing with Callaway didn't mean dealing with Katherine. A few days after his promotion, Adam had run into Katherine in the corridor. And had suggested – politely, given their usual ways of interacting – that she might be more comfortable working elsewhere. They both could see that she had nowhere to go at Callaway. Her leaving party had been an all-afternoon blowout, complete with presentation of what he knew was a whopping big bonus. Adam didn't mind. For all their hostility Katherine was a hard worker and he wished her well. Or tried to.

On his way up to Roger's office that first morning, Adam ran into Abby. Stacie's mom. His face reddened. But if he was going to make a home on the island, he had no choice but to get through it.

Without preamble she said, "Stacie tells me you're working things out."

"I hope so." His heart was pounding so hard he expected internal bruising. "Mrs. Fox, I want you to know how bad I feel about what happened –"

She held up her hand, effectively shutting him up. "If you get this position, you and I will be working hand in glove. So you need to understand how that plays. When Roger's through with you, grab a sandwich and come to my office. There's a lot to learn."

And she walked away. But she spent two hours with him that afternoon, and more time in the next few days, prepping him for the interviews.

And Roger – after their second morning together Adam gathered up his courage and asked straight out, "Why are you doing this?"

Roger shrugged. "Isn't it obvious? The other candidate's from off island. We'd rather have one of our own in the position. Someone who gets it."

Adam turned away abruptly. Roger didn't need to see what flashed across his face.

Stacie had been holed up with Jess at the gift shop – well, to be honest she'd been telling Jess about the last time she'd seen Adam and how they'd been rediscovering the fine art of making out – when the man himself charged in.

"Can we talk?" He was seriously agitated and trying not to show it.

"Sure." It was pouring but they huddled under the awning outside Jess's shop. "There's an offer on the house." His eyes met hers. "I have until 5:00 this evening to get in a counter offer."

They let it hang there for a beat. "Should I?"

She knew exactly what he was asking her. She knew that the job interviews had gone well, and that he had strong backing from both Roger and her mother. She knew what he wanted.

But what did she want?

He was trying so hard not to let his agitation show. *It's the island,* she thought, *or maybe it's me. He's putting himself out there. And he's nervous as hell.*

There really wasn't a question, when you got right down to it. "Yes. You should."

"Thank you." He grabbed her and kissed her, fast and hard. It made her think of that first kiss, before either of them knew what was about to hit them. "Gotta run. I'll let you know."

Then he was gone, off to the agent to make an offer on a rambling old house looking out across a meadow full of sheep. Her dreamy, idealistic man.

Adam clearly remembered standing in the ruins of what had once been his new home. He'd even lived there for a month or so, but the work needed to be done, and he'd decided there was no point waiting, other than the weather, perhaps. February might not the ideal time to begin home renovations in the Pacific Northwest, all things considered. But there you are.

He got in touch with Tom, Donna's husband, to discuss contractors. And found that Tom did this type of work on the side, branching out from the family hardware business. So Tom came over and they discussed things over a beer, and the next thing he knew, the walls were coming out. The whole place needed to be rewired, and since he was adding all those bathrooms and a laundry room, they redid the plumbing, too. And that had left him with a wreck, not a home. Adam had sighed and moved back into a little furnished rental for a few months while chaos took over the house.

In a way he hadn't expected, it had been fun, though. Weekdays he was at work, but they spent hours on weekends pounding out walls and wrapping up the day over a beer. After the first Saturday, he hadn't been able to move his arms, they were so sore. But it got better. And in the course of the work he was getting to know some of the other guys on the island. That was a new experience, to hang out at the pub with other men. Laborers, fishermen, accountants, shop owners, there was no snobbery based on something as external as what you did to put bread on the table. Mercifully, he'd also found electricians and plumbers. The house started to come back together.

They started dreaming, he and Stacie. Daring to dream.

Stacie had never considered selling Halloran House. When Adele, one of the agents at the local real estate company, came over to talk to her, she was caught flatfooted. Her grandmother's house, and all the work …. But the kind of numbers Adele bandied about …. The best she could do at that point was say she'd think about it.

Her world had been full of old houses that winter. She spent a lot of time at the Thompson place. Once the walls were back up there was so much to do. They'd sanded and painted and varnished. They'd chosen new flooring and appliances, new fixtures for the kitchen and bathrooms. As the days moved into spring they'd curled up with garden catalogues and talked about restoring the old kitchen garden and flower beds. They even discussed cleaning out and fixing up the goat shed. They sat on the sofa they'd trekked all the way into Vancouver to choose. Furnishings were still minimal, but it was a start.

A year since they'd met. She could get sentimental, if she chose to.

Adam had lost the love handles by then. It was kind of sad. But damn, he looked good.

The first time they actually made love ... well, sure, it was mainly symbolic. By that time they knew each other, physically speaking, really well. It was the last step, in a sense, in his courtship of her. Proof that the bad times were behind them. He remembered nerves. Maybe he'd given it way more significance than it deserved. But he didn't think so.

She'd noticed the tremor and held his hands for a few seconds, giving his fingers a squeeze. She hadn't been shaking at all. He'd undressed her – to be honest, they'd been a good way along that path already. Yes, he'd known the feel of her, but to see her standing there ... he could have fallen to his knees to worship her, bury his face in her, but she wouldn't let him, she was pushing his shirt over his arms when he choked out something like, "Freeing things up lower down would be better." That was certainly the last coherent thing either of them said for a long time.

Lying beside her, miraculously still deeply joined to her, her hand stroking the length of him, knowing what her eyes saw when they looked at him, the whole mess, strengths and failings. Knowing that some major step had been taken ... Symbolic. Of what they couldn't have had before, not until they'd traveled this painful, beautiful path together.

And later, waking up beside her, playing with her hair, kissing, tasting, gently teasing. Watching her watching his face, letting her take him to a place where defenses were no longer needed, because there weren't any secrets left.

Knowing Stacie. Knowing that Stacie knew him. And knowing him, with no masks or pretense, she'd accepted him. He never wanted it to end.

Stacie's arm was draped across his chest, her head settled on his shoulder. They were on the living room floor of the old Thompson place, lying on the new rug that looked so good against the refinished flooring. From the Sears Catalogue, improbably enough. She asked, "What do you see?"

"With my eyes closed?"

"Mmm. What do you see?"

He'd put his hand on her arm, keeping the contact. "You. Me. A garden with those giant squash things. Kids with dark hair and eyes, on this rug with snow coming down outside. It does snow here, doesn't it?"

"Not often. Sometimes. You manage a snowplow, remember? I see soups and stews on rainy days. Knitting you a sweater … and you'd better wear it." She'd freed her arm long enough to punch him gently.

"Taking you to Europe. And to Hawaii."

"And Ohio. See the grandparents."

"Barbecues. With Abby and Bill, speaking of grandparents."

"Rocking chairs on the porch?"

"Watching the sheep. We could hike across the fields – there's a little stream and some trees, if you go through the sheep field and angle right. I found it a couple of weeks ago."

"Fireplace on cold days. Cookies and tea – okay, maybe coffee for you."

"I can learn to like tea. Feeding the goats?"

"Really?" She'd raised up to look at him, but he'd refused to open his eyes. "You really want to renovate the goat shed?"

"One step too far?"

"Maybe one step at a time."

She walked into the kitchen of the old Thompson place, and stopped dead. He'd arranged six rosebushes on the old wooden kitchen table they'd found in the want ads, the one they'd refinish one day. Old fashioned ones, the kind that were scented. They were still in their pots, labels attached.

He said, "A man likes to give a woman flowers when he asks her to marry him."

She looked from him to the roses, back to him.

"Marry me, Stacie?"

She read the labels on every one of the roses before she answered. Why was it that everything that happened where Adam was concerned set her heart to knocking at her ribs? Would she ever get over that?

Then she smiled. And walked straight into his arms. In her memory she said yes, but maybe she didn't say anything at all. At any rate, he got the message.

Nathan's Forest. He remembered his reaction when Stacie had first told him the name of their forest, how prepared he was to scoff. Our forest. And now, his job to save it.

And this house would always be the old Thompson place, he supposed. Until one day maybe it would become the old Fraser place. When their grandchildren came to visit.

This sense of history and roots was still new to him, but he no longer laughed at it. He loved the idea that their house held memories he didn't even know about, that other families had lived and dreamed, laughed and cried here. They would, too.

The sale of Halloran House went through in May, in time for the new owners to benefit from the upcoming tourist season. The amount Stacie got for it staggered her. The house alone was worth a bundle, of course, but a lot was for her client base and reputation, as well.

She was proud, she'd done it and done it alone. She could do it, even if she didn't have to anymore.

Still, there were tears when the papers were signed and it was done. Adam was with her, quietly. He'd held her for hours that evening.

She'd kept some things, of course. Some furniture, some knickknacks, the memories she valued most from her grandmother. They were in the Thompson Place now, her new home.

Her breakfast recipes hadn't been a part of the deal, but she'd thrown them in anyway. She was glad she'd done that, believing that in a small way it contributed to the island. She admitted she was sad about selling, of course. But it wasn't going to work for her anymore, not with the way everything was changing.

Abby appeared at the top of the stairs. "Adam."

He was propped against the wall in the entry, daydreaming, waiting for them to come down and the whole thing to start. So he didn't hear her at first.

"Adam!" He jolted awake and looked up. "Come up, please, quickly."

Up? Nothing could be wrong, could it? He felt the blood squeeze out of his heart as he bolted up the stairs, past Abby and into their bedroom.

Stacie was standing in the middle of the floor in her gown. The one he wasn't supposed to see yet. It was sleeveless and modest with an old fashioned Empire waist – not that he noticed. She was smiling. No, beaming. "Come here," she said, then took his hand and placed it on her belly. "Be still. Wait."

They stood there, suspended. And then he felt it. The slightest ripple under his hand, so faint he might have imagined it. Except he didn't.

"I know it isn't exactly the best time, but it was too important. The first time, Adam."

They stared at each other. He clutched her hand.

Abby put her head around the door. "People are waiting. I'm going down."

Adam shot a look at Abby, then another at Stacie. "Your mother's supposed to escort you."

"Change of plans," Abby said.

Adam smiled at Abby. He was coming to really love this woman. "Tell them we're coming. Tell them to start."

Abby's footsteps disappeared down the stairs. His eyes locked on Stacie's. A minute later the music started.

"Shall we?" he whispered. "The three of us have a wedding to go to."

He placed her hand on his arm. Together they went down the stairs of the old Thompson place, the new Fraser place, into their future.

# To My Readers

Hello, and thank you for choosing *Seducing Adam*. I hope you've enjoyed your read. (And, it goes without saying, I'd be beyond grateful for a good review!)

About the setting: Off the coast of Vancouver Island, more or less sandwiched between Victoria and Vancouver, British Columbia's Gulf Islands are indeed magical, to visit or to live. If you ever have a chance, give one of them a try. You might like to visit http://pinterest.com/lizanncarson and check out the *Seducing Adam* board for a look at typical Gulf Islands scenery (although not all the photos are actually from the Gulf Islands) and a few images that reflect how I see Windon Harbor.

That said, the administration of the Gulf Islands is nothing at all like the one I've pictured in *Seducing Adam*. I hope I can be forgiven for giving the fictitious Malaspina Island an equally fictitious governance structure.

The scene divider used in the text is the silhouette of a hawthorn leaf. This one is probably an English hawthorn, not the black hawthorn native to the Pacific Northwest. English hawthorn is a common garden variety. In the wild it may be considered an invasive species.

To keep up with upcoming romances, visit my website, http://lizanncarson.com. There you'll find notices about book events and my musings about life as both a writer and an inhabitant of the real world.

Happy reading,

LizAnn

# About LizAnn Carson

It's interesting, trying to condense who you are into a paragraph or two. For openers, there are the basics: husband, three kids, and three kids-in-law, with a shifting grandkid count. I live in Victoria, British Columbia, a smallish city that's large enough to have all modern conveniences, but not so large as to have hours-long traffic jams or heavy duty pollution. I can follow a trail to my local supermarket, or I can be downtown in twenty minutes.

I'm a woman with a lot of interests, although there's usually one on top of all the others. At the moment, and for the foreseeable future, that interest is in writing romances – books that will leave a happy feeling behind. But beyond that, I enjoy a variety of crafts. I like weight training and yoga – and don't do enough of them. Once, a long time ago, I owned a yarn shop. My career, on the other hand, was in the world of computer systems development.

Life is such a gift, and there's always something new to learn, some new path to explore. You can follow some of those explorations with me on my website/blog, http://lizanncarson.com.